No Talking after Lights

No Talking after Lights

Angela Lambert

HAMISH HAMILTON · LONDON

HAMISH HAMILTON LTD

Published by the Penguin Group
27 Wrights Lane, London W8 5TZ, England
Viking Penguin Inc., 40 West 23rd Street, New York, New York 10010, USA
Penguin Books Australia Ltd, Ringwood, Victoria, Australia
Penguin Books Canada Ltd, 2801 John Street, Markham, Ontario, Canada L3R 1B4
Penguin Books (NZ) Ltd, 182–190 Wairau Road, Auckland 10, New Zealand

Penguin Books Ltd, Registered Offices: Harmondsworth, Middlesex, England

First published 1990

Copyright © Angela Lambert, 1990

Filmset in Monophoto Garamond
Printed in Great Britain by Butler & Tanner Ltd, Frome and London
A CIP catalogue record for this book is available from the British Library
ISBN 0–241–13004–2

Author's Note

The school in this book is based on the girls' boarding-school which I attended in the 1950s, for after spending seven years there I would find it hard to imagine any other; and the Headmistress described has the actual appearance of the Headmistress who presided over us, in affectionate tribute to her lifelong influence. Other than this, all the characters, staff and girls, their history and families, are wholly fictional, as are the events.

I am grateful to Jack and Libby Clough for their hospitality in Gower, and for their knowledge of the peninsula, which they generously shared with me.

I would also like to thank my editor, Clare Alexander, for her patience and skill.

To Dee Bryan-Brown
my best friend for thirty years

Prologue

Raeburn was, as Constance's mother said the first time she saw it, and would say again every time it was mentioned, a beautiful school in the heart of the country. Yet for the girls who boarded there the school was embodied above all in the massive Easter Island presence of the Headmistress, the Hon. Mrs Henrietta Birmingham. In the minds of parents the school, like a group photograph, evoked the 120 girls who attended it, and in particular their own tidily uniformed daughter. For its dozen teachers the school represented pupils at desks in class-rooms, lessons to be prepared, books to be marked, and staff-room rivalries; for the matrons the school existed in terms of creased counterpanes and feverish girls; to the domestic staff it was little more than a steamy, clanging kitchen; while to the gardener and his boy it was acres of grass to be rolled and mowed.

The main school building was a long, three-storeyed, mock-Tudor country house with sixteen bedrooms and a servants' attic. It had been built in the 1890s, for one of that extinct tribe of hostesses whose lives revolved around the rituals of weekend house-parties at which they manipulated their powerful, pleasure-loving men. The outward appearance of the house had hardly changed in six decades.

In later years when girls – now grown women – thought of their old school, they saw it more vividly than the distant childhood world of home. Their dreams continued to be set in its undulating landscape long after their schooldays were over, while in nightmares they would find themselves still hemmed in by the school rules, *walking* – not running – in stiff-legged panic along narrow corridors, and would wake up relieved to find they were adults after all. Whether or not they had been

1

happy at Raeburn, they usually remembered it in high summer. They would hear the bell's insistent double beat and see the building with its many chimneys riding high over the serene Sussex countryside, its sloping green lawns dotted with girls in summer frocks.

But all this was obscured in February. It was bitterly cold, the great bulk of the school ploughing like an ocean liner through sheets of freezing rain. Rain lashed the bare trees beside the drive into dripping, creaking life as Constance King and her parents bumped along its uneven surface on the way to their first meeting with the Headmistress.

Constance peered through the car's steamed-up windows at girls in ankle-length hooded cloaks buffeted by the wind as they stumbled with bent heads between class-rooms. They looked sinister and faceless.

'Which are those monks who wear the long brown cloaks?' she asked.

'I'm not sure, darling . . .' her mother began, but her father interrupted.

'Don't be such a twerp, Constance,' he said irritably. 'And comb your hair. Try to make a good impression.'

The rotten old school's not making a very good impression on me, she thought mutinously. I'd much rather go to Wimbledon High. She doubted if she'd be given the choice. There were seven weeks left until the end of term, but as her parents were being posted to Kenya in May, it was a matter of urgency to find her a suitable boarding-school.

Her father parked the car carefully and reached down for his Colonial Office briefcase. Mrs King patted her hair, took out a gold compact and pursed her mouth while she dotted lipstick on to it. Then she smiled encouragingly at Constance.

'Isn't this *exciting*?' she said.

Her father cracked open a black umbrella and the three of them dashed into the shelter of the porch.

As they sat waiting in the hall, a girl of enchanting loveliness emerged from the Head's study and came towards them, smiling. She was as light-footed as a flower fairy in one of Constance's old storybooks. Shining tendrils of hair escaped from her pony-tail and floated round her small, pointed face. Constance's mother nudged her conspiratorially as her father half rose to his feet.

'Are you Mr and Mrs King?' the girl asked.

'Yes, indeed. Yes, we are. Not too early, I hope?' he replied, and Constance winced at his eagerness to please somebody who couldn't be more than sixteen.

'Not a bit. My name is Hermione, and the Head says, would you like to come in? It's that door, there...' She led the way and held it open for them.

'*What* a pretty girl!' whispered Mrs King, but Constance disdained to answer.

Mrs Birmingham received them in a drawing-room furnished with aristocratic randomness. Everything was old and comfortable and good, but nothing matched and nothing was artistically arranged. The curtains were chintz, the sofas and armchairs were covered in a different chintz, and the furniture was shabby, sagging at the corners. The mantelpiece displayed a few school cups, some studio portraits in silver frames of Mrs Birmingham's family (including one of her father in full court dress, wearing breeches and glossy, thigh-length boots), a silver pheasant and a small gilt carriage clock. There was also a rabbit modelled in clay by one of the girls and another even more formless clay lump whose glaze had dripped and blurred as though still wet. On a circular mahogany table just inside the door stood a cut-glass vase of early daffodils whose granular scent tickled Constance's nostrils. A selection of recent books and magazines was fanned around it: John Betjeman, *The Silent Traveller*, H. V. Morton on Sussex, and *Country Life*. The log fire burning in the wide stone fireplace added a warmth and cosiness that the room might otherwise have lacked. It was a pleasant, welcoming room whose lack of any attempt to impress successfully implied that Mrs Birmingham came from a good family.

Plain, flat-chested and be-spectacled, Constance King (what an unfortunate name, thought the Head: the girls were bound to call her King Kong) was not an engaging sight. But she seemed clever, and the school certainly had vacancies. Due to the austerity of the last years, it had not grown as rapidly as she had planned. In 1946 she had accepted the fact that her husband's health would never improve, nor would he earn enough to maintain them in comfort and send their brilliant son James to Oxford. But country-house prices were lower than before the war, so she had invested her father's legacy in this house, which she had seen offered for sale in *The Times*. It had been requisitioned for use as a hospital during the war and was scruffy and neglected. Few people had money to spare at that time; she had bought it cheaply at auction, and sold off some of the land and several cottages on the estate. Leaving only the drawing-room and study untouched, she had had it converted as quickly and cheaply as possible, and honoured her father's memory by naming the newly founded school after their family home in Scotland. She had counted on the Raeburn School for Girls having nearly 150 pupils by now, and the missing thirty made a difference. Some staff even had to double up and teach two subjects.

Mrs Birmingham had already glanced at Constance's general-knowledge test (they called it an entrance exam, but in practice she didn't reject any girl, no matter how stupid) and had been impressed by its clear, accurate answers. The child was only twelve, but she'd soar above the dimmish Upper Third. Best to try her in the Lower Fourth.

The Head moved smoothly through her practised recital of the school's advantages. Experience had taught her when to pause for questions, and she could usually anticipate what parents would ask. The Kings were not the sort to inquire about opportunities for riding or ballet, though Mrs King might ask to be shown a dormitory; nor did they seem academic, so she could avoid the under-stocked library.

'The school was recommended by a colleague in the Colonial Office,' Mr King ventured. 'I wonder if by any chance Constance would be in the same class as his daughters – ?'

Before he could finish, Mrs Birmingham said, 'That would be the Simpson twins, I dare say?'

'Michaela and Felicity,' Mrs King concurred, her face brightening at this evidence that the Head did indeed know every girl personally. 'Would Connie be in their class? It *would* be so nice for her. They could be chums.'

'Well, they're a bit older, of course. Constance is only just twelve, I believe' – affirmatory smiles – 'And the Simpson girls are over thirteen. But I'll see what could be arranged. And now, perhaps you'd like to see one of the dormitories?'

These dormitories were not inspiring, being the former housemaids' sleeping quarters in the attic and guest bedrooms on the second floor that had been crudely sliced in half with plasterboard partitions, but she sensed that the Kings were won over already. She opened the door of the drawing-room and looked out into the front hall.

'Ah, Madeleine,' she said, catching sight of a passing girl, 'would you show Constance King the Lower Fourth for me, and perhaps the studio, and bring her back here in ten minutes? Thank you, dear.'

Madeleine smiled winningly at Constance, but as soon as the Head turned away her expression changed.

'Are you going to be a new girl?' she asked indifferently as they walked along a dark corridor. 'That's the staff-room ... You'll hate it here.'

'Yes, I know,' said Constance unexpectedly.

'Everyone has nicknames. Mine's Madine. They'll probably call you Con, if you're lucky. Otherwise...' her voice trailed away. She couldn't remember Constance's surname, and was unable to come up with an instant, cruel invention.

'At my school now I'm called Goggles,' confided Constance unwisely, in a bid for friendship. Madeleine was slight, dark, intense; she had liked her on sight.

Madeleine opened a door on to bedlam. 'Shut up everyone!' she shouted, and as they turned towards her she pushed Constance ahead of her into the room. 'This is Goggles. She's starting next term. Her people have got an Austin Seven.'

Constance looked numbly at the half-dozen strange faces that turned towards her.

'It's only hired,' she muttered to Madeleine.

'But they've had to *hire* it,' added Madeleine, and to Constance, 'My people have got a Humber Hawk. It's the same car as Old Ma B.'

'Who's Old Ma B?' asked Constance.

'You've just been to see her, stupid. Mrs Birmingham. Who d'you think?'

How was I supposed to know? thought Constance. I hate this place. I hate them all. How shall I ever learn their names? I don't want to come here. I wish Mummy and Daddy didn't have to go away again. I wish I could go with them. Why can't I go to school in Kenya like Stella? Why do I have to stay behind? Oh, God, let them not send me here. But she said out loud, ''Course I knew that. Mick and Flick told me.'

'Do you know Mick and Flick?'

'Well, I don't exactly know them. Their father works with my father.'

Madeleine swung round. 'Is it true, Flick? Do you know each other?'

'Shut up Madeleine, don't be such a bully. What are your people called?' Felicity asked Constance.

'King. Mr and Mrs King. I mean, mm' – her parents' Christian names sounded funny when she said them – 'George and Paula King.'

'Yes, we do know them,' Flick said to the room at large, and then, 'It's not as bad as all that here. You'll have a godmother for your first term.'

Constance's heart leapt. Was that really possible? Would cosy, snuggly Auntie Meg be allowed to stay with her for the first term? That would be wonderful. She smiled gratefully at Flick as Madeleine led her out.

Back in the drawing-room she found her parents waiting. The fat, squashy sofas somehow diminished them and made them look almost like children, sitting much lower than the Headmistress, who, from a high-backed wing-chair, motioned Constance to sit beside her mother. 'Every new girl has a godmother for her first term,' the Head was saying, and Constance smiled in relief. 'That is, an older girl is assigned to look after her, show her round, and help her till she finds her feet.'

6

Mrs King put her hand on Constance's. 'There, darling, won't that be nice?'

Constance shook her head, bit her lip and stared at the pale-blue carpet.

Just then there was an urgent knock on the interconnecting door to the study. A tall woman with her hair drawn back severely entered and said, 'Mrs Birmingham, excuse me for interrupting but I wonder if I might have a word?'

'Miss Roberts, my Deputy,' said the Head smoothly, to cover her surprise. 'Yes, of course.' Then she turned to the Kings. 'Will you forgive me for a moment?' She rose to her feet and swept through to the adjoining room.

'Darling, we love it!' said Constance's mother in a low voice as the door closed behind Mrs Birmingham. 'It's a beautiful school in the heart of the country, and the girls seem charming. *Such* nice manners.'

'Yes, I must say I'm impressed,' her father agreed.

And what about me? thought Constance silently. I'm the one who's supposed to be coming here. Doesn't anybody care what I think? But she knew better than to argue here, in this intimidatingly grand, strange room.

Mrs Birmingham returned, her face a solemn mask.

'Tragic news ... tragic news,' she said. 'I am afraid it has just been announced on the wireless that his Majesty the King died last night in his sleep.'

Mrs King's face crumpled with shock, and her husband instinctively straightened his back and sat rigidly as though to attention. Before they could detain her with conventional expressions of grief, the Head went on, 'I am afraid I shall have to call an immediate assembly and break the news to the school. I don't know if there was anything more you wanted to ask?'

'No, no. We quite understand. Forgive us for intruding at such a sad moment,' said Mr King, and the three of them were quietly ushered out.

The Lower Fourth were sitting in a geography lesson, silent and unresponsive. The old-fashioned radiators made the classroom stuffy and they stared out of the blurred windows at the rain that swept across in slanting sheets and obliterated the view.

Geography was taught by Ginny Valentine, their form mistress. Small and pretty, with curly black hair, blue eyes and a brilliant smile, Miss Valentine was popular. Unlike most members of staff, she wore make-up every day and not just for Parents' Weekends. Her nose was always matt with powder, her mouth a bright fuchsia pink, and her ear-rings sparkled as she gesticulated and swung round from the blackboard. This third period on Wednesday morning was usually enjoyable, for Ginny was a good teacher, enthusiastic and spontaneous. But today even her cheerful personality was subdued by the February gloom. She looked up at the sound of a knock on the door of Austen, their form-room.

'Come in!' she fluted, and Miss Roberts entered.

The girls automatically rose to their feet until she said tersely, 'Sit down everyone!' She walked past the rows of desks to where Miss Valentine stood beside the blackboard. Everyone perked up. A visit from the Deputy Head meant something important must have happened. The Lower Fourth sat unusually still and strained to hear as the two women spoke in low voices for a few moments. Then Miss Roberts hurried out of the room.

Ginny Valentine waited for the class to compose themselves and give her their full attention. Then she said, 'There will be a special assembly at 11.15, after a shortened break. The Head will address the whole school. I can tell you nothing more at present. And now' – she smiled briefly, and the attentive faces lightened – 'as there are only five minutes left of the lesson, I want you to open your geography books at page 114. Michaela, will you distribute the prep books, please?'

Michaela, the elder by twenty minutes of the Simpson twins, walked self-importantly to the front of the class and collected a pile of exercise books. Those that were almost finished were dog-eared and crumpled; the new ones were still crisp, with shiny covers and fresh white edges. On the cover, inside a rectangular box with dotted lines, each girl wrote her name and form number. Plain pages alternated with lined ones in geography and biology books (for drawing maps and diagrams); there was squared paper for maths, algebra and geometry, lined paper with red margins for all the other subjects. Geography exercise books were always green, maths ones brown, history blue, biology red, and so on. Brown was for boredom – nearly everyone was hopeless at maths – red, for blood. They hadn't yet reached the bloody bits in 'bilge', for they tackled the reproductive system just before GCE, when they were sixteen and old enough to handle the facts of life. The Lower Fourth were only doing amoeba and spirogyra. Green signified maps and hills and jolly Miss Valentine. Her brisk voice pattered on about rain-shadow areas and ox-bow rivers. She wrote on the board, the chalk making a precise, crunchy sound, saying as she went along: 'Read Chapter Fourteen and answer questions one, three and five at the end. Use diagrams or maps where necessary to illustrate your answers. Prep to be handed in before supper on Thursday ... that's tomorrow, Sheila, isn't it?'

While the twenty-three girls were copying this into their rough books, Charmian – small and blonde with attractive, foxy features – nudged her best friend. 'Stop dreaming, soppy date. She means you!'

Sheila frowned, ruled a line under Miss Valentine's last comment in her book ('4/10 Sheila: you can do better than this, and why no map?') and underlined the words 'geography prep' twice.

The Covered Way during break hummed with the sound of 120 voices as the girls speculated on the possible reasons for an unprecedented second assembly. They queued up for milk in squat bottles, pulling a tab to remove the cardboard disc on top and drinking through a straw. The seniors were allowed tea, which a prefect poured out of a huge, dented teapot into thick-rimmed cups. Some girls crowded round the board hoping to see their names on the parcels list. The bell tolled early for the end of break and they lined up automatically in forms to file along the passage and downstairs into hall.

The Hon. Henrietta Birmingham was a devout woman. She had fallen to her knees beside her chair in the study to pray as soon as she had despatched Miss Roberts to give the staff news of the king's death. *Lord, now lettest Thou Thy servant depart in peace*, she had intoned mentally. *Comfort the widows and orphans*, and *God save the King . . . God save our new Queen Elizabeth.* Elizabeth the Second, she thought to herself, trying out the sound. And now I suppose our present Queen Elizabeth will become the Queen Dowager. She felt an affinity with the newly widowed queen, having been born in the same year, 1900, into the same sort of Scottish family – though her own was not quite as aristocratic as the Bowes-Lyons. She often reflected that she too had married a man whose character was less formidable than her own. She did not dwell on that thought, which was disloyal, and besides she didn't care to think too much about her ailing husband, who spent his days at the Lodge peevishly confined to bed.

During break she wondered what to say to the girls. The King had not been well for some time. He had looked terribly frail in recent newspaper photographs of him waving goodbye to Princess Elizabeth and the Duke of Edinburgh on their departure for Kenya. She had heard a rumour that he had had a lung removed, but there was no need to mention that.

When the bell rang for the end of break she composed herself, patted her snow-white hair neatly back into its accustomed waves and waited until the shuffle of feet towards the common-room had subsided. Then she and Miss Roberts began their stately progress down the stairs and on to the dais. The school awaited them in silence.

'Girls,' said Mrs Birmingham in a low, modulated voice, 'I'm afraid I have tragic news for you. It has been announced this morning on the BBC that our beloved king, His Majesty King George VI, has died.'

The uplifted faces took on shocked, grave expressions as the girls searched for an appropriate response to the news. The king's death was a historic event, and they wanted to look suitably patriotic. Everyone except the juniors, who were too little to be devious, covertly checked the staff and seniors. Many people glanced towards Hermione Malling-Smith, the most popular girl in the school, who looked touchingly fragile and dewy-eyed. None of them felt genuinely, personally bereaved – how could they? – but everyone was anxious that they should seem to be. Charmian Reynolds burst into tears. Sheila leant across and patted Charmian's shuddering back.

'Oh, Charmie,' she muttered, 'isn't it ghastly? Never mind . . .'

Before any girl had time to become overwrought – if one did, they'd all start, the Head thought to herself; emotions ran like wildfire through adolescent girls – she continued in a firm voice: 'And now, it would, I think, be appropriate if the school were to sing the National Anthem: God Save the *Queen*.'

She glanced at Miss Valentine, who left the row of teachers and seated herself at the piano. The school rose to its feet. As the first, sombre notes gave their cue, several more girls began to sob. Strong young voices rose tremulously in acknowledgement of their new sovereign. When they had ended with a rousing 'Go-od save the Queen!' the Head said, 'Let us pray.'

Heads bowed, the staff and girls of Raeburn School prayed fervently for the soul of the late King George VI, for the consolation of his widow, and for the reign of his daughter.

'And now, girls, will you all return to your form-rooms quietly and in single file for your next lesson.'

Mrs Birmingham and Miss Roberts departed in an august diminuendo of powder and the cloying scent of Yardley's lavender brilliantine, which Miss Roberts used to keep her hair under control.

Constance King and her parents were driving back through dank Sussex lanes, under colonnades of dripping branches, past the occasional driveway flanked by heavy gates, through nodding villages with one butcher and two pubs. Constance sat in the back seat of the car and listened to her parents talking about the school fees. When she thought she could speak in a steady voice she leaned forward so that her head was between their shoulders.

'Please not, Mummy. Please don't make me go there.'

'Buck up, darling, don't be such a silly billy. Why ever not?

It's a beautiful school in the heart of the country. The Simpson girls are getting on very well there. And it's *most* generous of Daddy.

'Mummy, honestly, please, not there. They call the Headmistress Old Ma B and they'll call me Goggles and the girls are awful.'

'Constance, control yourself and stop being ridiculous,' her father said. 'And don't let me ever hear *you* using that impertinent, unkind nickname for your new Headmistress. Now listen to me. I'm sick and tired of your grizzling. You're a thoroughly ungrateful little girl. After all the trouble we've been to.' Trying to see her face in the rear view mirror, he went on firmly, 'I shall have to sit down when we get home and work out whether Mummy and I can afford it. It's going to mean a great many sacrifices. But if we do decide to send you there, I don't want any nonsense.'

'Daddy,' said Constance evenly. 'I beg of you, I really and truly beg of you in the name of – everything – don't send me there. I'll go anywhere else. Let me go on to Wimbledon High like everyone else. If not that, I'd much rather come to Kenya with you and save you the sacrifices anyway. Please, please, please, *please* don't make me go to Raeburn.'

Her mother turned and looked into Constance's desperate face. Her National Health glasses were askew and beginning to mist up.

'Darling, Daddy and I will talk it over this evening between ourselves and I promise we'll bear your wishes in mind. All right? In return, will you trust us, and abide by our decision like a good girl?'

Constance nodded.

'Is that a promise?'

Another nod.

'There's a sensible girl. Now, don't get car-sick, we're going to stop for lunch as soon as we see somewhere nice.'

'I wish I had my black tie with me,' said her father.

'You couldn't have known, darling,' her mother said. 'No one will mind.'

*

Although it was nearly eleven o'clock and her usual bedtime was 7.30, Constance's curtains were drawn back and she was still awake. She had been sitting at the top of the stairs, listening through the banisters as her parents talked about the school. They hadn't taken her wishes into account at all. Daddy had said that the Colonial Office would contribute £150 a year towards the fees, and if he cashed some shares and they sold the piano – they couldn't have taken it to Kenya in any case, and it would cost a fortune to store...

Constance heard, understood, and knew herself to be doomed.

One

Everyone said summer was the best term. There was swimming and tennis instead of hockey, and long, light evenings when all the girls were allowed to stay up half an hour later than in the other two darker terms. Even after lights out, those who were lucky and had a bed under the window could read till almost nine o'clock. They woke soon after sunrise, as soon as it was light, to the sound of wood-pigeons cooing in the high surrounding trees. Everyone wore striped cotton frocks, not the stiff, scratchy, Harris-tweed uniform of the rest of the year; they wore straw hats for Sunday and soft, shapeless, felt hats on ordinary days – the more shapeless the better because it showed they had been there a long time.

Waterloo Station at the beginning of term was crowded with schoolgirls in brand-new or freshly washed frocks, newly name-taped socks and shiny new shoes. Fathers supervised the buying of train and platform tickets while mothers hovered round with last-minute advice, reassurance, or expressions of love.

'Remember, darling,' Paula King said to Constance, 'when your Parker 51 needs filling, don't you try and do it. Take it to Mrs Birmingham and ask her politely if she would mind filling it for you.'

Constance knew that it was out of the question to go to the Head and ask her to fill a fountain-pen, but she nodded and didn't argue.

'It cost 31s. 6d.,' said her mother. 'It's a very good one and you must make it last right through your time at school. You look like a little Princess. Everything new. Remember to thank Daddy.'

Constance, who had thanked her father for each handkerchief

and games sock, as new items were added to the pile of school uniform, nodded again. She couldn't speak and she would not cry. Around her dozens of unfamiliar schoolgirls, who all looked the same except for the very pretty ones, were greeting each other with rapturous or scornful cries.

'Did you have t'riffic hols? *I* saw *Call Me Madam.*'

'So what? I saw *South Pacific.* It was wizard.'

'Well, who cares? My brother took me to see *The World in His Arms* and *The Snows of Kilimanjaro* 'cos he knows I'm batty about Gregory Peck.'

'Isn't he smashing? You can't have him, though – he's mine. I've bagged him!' and, turning round, 'Oh, hello, Feeny. Picking up fag-ends as per usual!'

Constance wouldn't have been allowed to see any of the films they were talking about. She had spent the Easter holidays in a state of numb acquiescence, being measured at Kinch & Lack for dreadfully expensive clothes that looked hideous on her since they were all a size too big to make them do for next year.

Her mother had ticked off the items on the clothes list one by one. Sweet tin, they had finally got down to; 2 face flannels (must be marked); hairbrush and comb ('Look, darling, Mason-Pearson brush and Addis beauty comb. Mind you make them last. They're the most expensive'); toothbrush with one term's supply of toothpaste; shampoo. Boots was the last shop they visited.

'What does it mean, "STs (if needed)"?' Connie asked her mother.

'Shush, darling, not so loud. I'll tell you some other time.'

She hadn't, though; and Constance wondered if she would need STs, and what for.

All around them on Platform Nine at Waterloo parents were left to smile stiffly at other half-recognized parents while their daughters found friends and formed their familiar cliques, abandoning home life for school loyalties. Constance recognized Madeleine, who had shown her round the school, but Madeleine avoided her eye. She didn't know anyone else, so she stood looking into the middle distance, longing for her father to arrive and tell her it wasn't true, longing for her mother to stay, longing to be home in her own comfortable hand-knitted jumper and outgrown kilt.

'Can you see the Simpson twins?' asked her mother. 'Their parents don't seem to be here. Perhaps Universal Aunts had to see them off, poor little things.'

Constance wouldn't ask who the universal aunts were, knowing by now that it would be just another grown-up trick, like the godmother at school, which had turned out to mean another girl. She saw her father hurrying towards them and could tell he felt guilty about leaving his office in the middle of the afternoon. He kissed her moistly, formally, in the middle of the forehead.

'There was a little girl and she had a little curl/Right in the middle of her forehead,' Constance's brain chanted idiotically.

'Now, Constance,' he said, 'I want you to remember all the things we talked about last night, to work hard and be a good girl and make us both proud of you. It's a wonderful opportunity. You're a very privileged little girl and you mustn't forget that. We're not asking for gratitude; but we do expect you to work hard and play hard.'

Constance felt the wet kiss fading from her skin and thought, 'And when she was good she was very, very good/But when she was bad she was horrid.'

'I'll have to be off now,' he said, after a long, awkward silence. 'What about you, dear? Are you going to wait till the train goes?'

'I think I will,' said her mother. 'I want to wave till the very last minute.'

'Right-ho, then. Back to the grindstone.'

'Your father works very hard, Connie,' said her mother, adding in a whisper, 'Thank him again, darling.'

Settling his hat back on his head and swinging his tidily furled umbrella, her father strode away down the platform. Constance saw her mother's face begin to loosen. Any moment now she would be in tears. The shame of having her mother cry in front of everyone was more than she could bear.

'Mummy, don't!' she hissed. 'Please don't cry. I couldn't stand it.'

Touched by this evidence of emotion and concern from her undemonstrative child, Paula King pulled herself together and enveloped her stiff little body, smelling of freshly washed hair and new cotton, in a loving hug. Constance patted her mother's shoulder feebly and let herself be kissed.

'Might as well go and find a seat then,' she said. She picked up her overnight case (the trunk had been sent ahead) and climbed the two high steps on to the train.

She walked into the compartment and sat down. Looking through the window she saw with horror that her mother was indeed starting to cry. 'Turn round,' she mouthed through the glass. 'Turn *round*!' Her mother failed to understand, so Constance twirled her index finger until, obediently, her mother turned away. Constance's last image as the train finally drew out was of her crumpled face peering furtively over her shoulder to catch a last glimpse of her daughter.

'You're new, aren't you? What form are you in? You can't sit here. Who's your godmother?'

'I didn't know,' said Constance. 'Where am I supposed to sit?'

'Anywhere except here. This is reserved for the seniors and you're a squit.'

I'm not a squit, am I? thought Constance. What's a squit? Is it anything to do with STs?

'Are the squits the ones who need STs?' she asked, and a tide of giggles convulsed the girls sitting close enough to hear what she had said. They hunched their backs and spluttered into their chests, then looked slyly at one another and began to titter again.

Constance left the seat and made her way through the rocking compartment as laughter exploded behind her. Head bowed and burning with humiliation, she almost bumped into a woman coming the other way.

'Hold on, hold on a minute, where are you going?' asked the woman. 'You're a new girl, aren't you? You shouldn't be here. Do you know which form you're in?'

'Lower Fourth, I think,' said Constance.

The woman smiled quite kindly at her. 'Come along, let's see if we can find your godmother.'

'Excuse me, but am I a squit?' asked Constance.

'Those wretched girls!' The woman sighed. 'No, if you're in the Lower Fourth you're not a squit. I'm afraid that's what they call the little ones, in the third form. It's a horrid word. What's your name?'

'Constance King,' said Constance King.

In the dormitory just before lights out, Constance's godmother, a fifth-former called Sarah, came across to her bed (she'd had to take the worst one, just inside the door) and asked dutifully, 'Are you all right? Are you sure you're all right? You're supposed to tell me if you're not. If you want to cry or anything, come and find me. I'm in Blackbirds. Have you got a teddy?'

'No.'

'We're allowed teddies. It says on the clothes list: "one teddy bear or other soft toy".'

'Must be marked,' guessed Constance. 'I haven't got a teddy,' she said. 'I don't like dolls.'

'Oh. Well. Do you want me to kiss you good-night or anything?'

'No, thank you very much all the same.'

'Don't anyone be foul to Constance, OK?' said Sarah firmly as she shut the door of Starlings.

On the bed opposite Constance's, fat, sloppy Rachel and square-jawed Jennifer, who were best friends because no one else would have them, were poring over Rachel's precious album of Royal Family postcards. These were soft-focus black-and-white photographs by Marcus Adams, Cecil Beaton or Dorothy Wilding. Rachel's mother and aunts and godmothers had sent some to build up her collection and Rachel had bought the rest herself out of her pocket-money. The two of them glanced across at Constance, but not in a friendly way, as though challenging her to show interest. I don't care, thought Constance; I don't want to see their silly old pictures. But she wished her mother had packed a book into her overnight case.

The matron, Miss Peachey, came in a few moments later and

said, 'Lights out,' although the summer evening was still pale and airy and the light wasn't switched on. 'Good-night, everyone. Welcome back.'

'I don't think,' somebody muttered.

Matron twinkled. 'And *no talking*, do you hear? No talking after lights. Try and be a bit better behaved than last term's Starlings.'

When her crêpe-soled shoes had squeaked away down the corridor the girls started to whisper, then to giggle, and one or two sat up in bed and pulled out secret packages from under their pillows and began to distribute presents: bags of sweets or glass animals. Each girl had her own bedside locker on which stood a collection of treasures: a pair of capering Chinese horses or a model of a Scottie dog or a fluffy cat. These animals were often named after a pet left at home. Two girls, Anne and Fiona, were whinnying as they pretended to put their ponies to bed for the night. Glass animals – fish with elaborate tails or upright feathery cats with bulging eyes – were favourite ornaments.

On top of each locker lay the modest beige booklet of the Bible Reading Fellowship: a biblical extract for each day, annotated for private meditation. In pride of place was a photograph of the girl's parents. These ranged from home-made passe-partout frames enclosing jolly family snapshots to elaborate silver frames containing a studio portrait by Lenare or Vivienne or Dorothy Wilding, their signatures scrawled diagonally above an embossed Bond Street address. They provided the best indication of each girl's status. Anyone coming into the dormitory – Matron, prefects, other girls – could see at a glance if someone's people were young, glamorous and rich, and deduce whether they lived in town or in the country, whether family pets were low-status ones like cats, rabbits, guinea-pigs, or high-status ones like a large dog or two, a horse or pony. Sometimes the pictures showed a house in the background. Being rich mattered very much indeed, but boasting about being rich was the worst kind of swanking. The locker arrangements allowed a girl to indicate her social standing without seeming to show off.

Constance lay and looked at the double-sided, leather-framed photograph of her parents that stood on top of her locker like an open book: her father was stern yet young in his tropical uniform; her mother was soft-focused into ethereal, unlined prettiness. They looked nothing like the two people who'd seen her off from Waterloo Station. She hadn't got a picture of Felix, her black cat, to tuck into a corner, nor any glass animals. She lay rigidly in bed, trapped within the narrow iron frame, ignoring the murmurs around her. I will be a tree, she thought, summoning up the old trick. I will feel my roots growing up into my toes, feel my body stiffen and swell and become eternal, immobile – solid, reassuring, tree-like. I am a tree. As the sap ran along her limbs making her fingers and tongue thicken and grow numb, Constance fell into tree-ness and deafness and dumbness and sleep.

Every evening Peggy Roberts and Henrietta Birmingham would sit in the drawing-room together for an hour or two. Nobody knew anything about Miss Roberts's family. She was not impoverished, for she had put £5,000 into the school in return for the job of Deputy Head. She too was a stately and imposing woman, as tall as Mrs Birmingham, though it was obvious at first glance that she had never been pretty. Her great shyness manifested itself in a formality that kept everyone – girls and parents – at a distance. She seldom smiled; she had never been given a nickname. Yet she conveyed an underlying kindness and sensitivity which made Old Girls single her out at reunions, feeling that somehow they should try and make amends. On these occasions they would find conversation as difficult as ever.

For both women, the school was the hub and purpose of their lives. Despite this, and the fact that they had been born only a few months apart, their intimacy was mostly silent. Each was content to spend time in the other's company, but they did not gossip and rarely discussed the school. They watched *What's My Line?* and nature programmes on a flickering black-and-white television; they read; Miss Roberts embroidered tapestry cushions or kneelers and read travel books, especially about Italy. After the news ended at quarter past nine, Miss Roberts would usually go up to her bedroom above the drawing-room, and shortly afterwards Mrs Birmingham would take the car up the long school drive, back to her querulous husband.

That first evening of the summer term Henrietta Birmingham had sat on the window-seat beside the bay windows that overlooked the lawns and the rhododendrons. From this vantage point she could watch the girls who strolled under the cedars, gossiping about their holidays. Under one tree stood the heavy iron roller with wooden handles which the gardener and his lad would drag over the freshly mown grass. Nearby, curving amply like a duck's breast, was the bin into which the grass mowings flew in a twinkling green spray. The Head had watched the sunset streaks against the deep slate-blue of the sky glowing purple as they gradually intensified into darkness like the last embers of a fire, and listened to the seniors chattering and laughing on the bank below the bay window, unaware that their voices drifted up to her in the still evening.

How untrammelled they were by the restrictions that had hedged about her girlhood – the strait-jacket of class and gender, the imminence of war – she thought. Their world was carefree as they picked their self-absorbed way through adolescence, listening only to the beat of their own hearts, careless of death. Even at fourteen she had not been carefree. Her two older brothers, trained in the Eton Officers' Training Corps, had volunteered as soon as war was declared. Her nearest brother, seventeen-year-old Jamie, chafed to be allowed to join them at the front. 'Don't you see, Hetta,' he'd said to her, almost crying with the urgency of it, 'the war'll be over by Christmas and if they don't let me go now, I'll miss it. If they make me wait till I'm eighteen, it's going to be too late. And then how shall I ever face Alistair and Hugo?' The war hadn't been over by Christmas, nor yet by his birthday, but Jamie had worried away at his parents, sworn he wouldn't take up his place at Oxford, until in the end they'd given way.

The afternoon before he left the two of them had walked

over the moors and hills. They hadn't talked much. They were very close; each had always known what the other was thinking. As the heather scratched her feet and fronds of bracken snapped off against her skirt, she had thought, All the joy is fading from my life, all the happy hours have passed, and now I shall never be anything but wretched. Poor Henrietta! she reflected now, as though that girl had been some other person, not herself. How she had longed to do her bit. To be allowed to nurse, or even – imagination strained to devise what might be needed – even just to gather up blood-stained bandages and dressings and throw them in the incinerator. But at her age she was not allowed to do anything except pray. She had prayed with a passion that surely God must hear: *O Lord of these hills and horizons, fasten Thy gaze from beyond on to this my brother and keep him salf.* But in case God should take no notice of the prayers of a selfish child, she had broadened her request to include all soldiers and all officers, yes, and the Germans as well, all those in danger and pain.

The late afternoon had turned a sullen bronze and grey as they walked. The snow was receding from the tops of the hills. Jamie had stared at the crags and clouds with an intensity that transferred itself to her, driving the chilly landscape into her memory for ever.

That night, after praying again on her knees on the cold floor of the nursery – *Let him come back home and I will be a blessed soul and sing Thy praises eternally* – she had climbed into bed exhausted by emotion. When she slept, she dreamed of Jamie's death, saw his fire-encircled figure sprint through a nightmare landscape of broken trees and desolation. She had woken in terror, and been unable to speak of it to anyone. It was her first experience of utter loneliness.

The servants gathered in the hall the next day to see Jamie leave. He was bright-eyed, impatient and proud, his thoughts leaping ahead to the comradeship of the trenches. She felt as though she were hallucinating, entering into his mind, seeing what he saw, knowing what she knew. 'We have already said our farewells, Jamie,' she told him calmly when he stepped forward for a parting embrace. Her mother had been shocked and thought her cold. Jamie had climbed into the back of the motor-carriage and settled himself between his parents to be driven to the local railway station. As they all clustered on the sweep of gravel to watch him go, she had been the only one not to wave or smile bravely (half the housemaids were sobbing), or shout, 'Good Luck!' or, 'Give the Boche one for me!' The shiny, square car made its way along the drive towards the stone gateposts by the lodge, and her keen young eyes could just make out the figure of the lodge-keeper as he swung open the heavy gates to let it pass. She remembered their protesting creak and, as though the moment had been photographed, saw her lanky, fifteen-year-old self in a dress that reached to her calves, with black stockings and shoulder-length hair held by a tartan ribbon: rigid, apart, charged with her premonitory secret.

These girls knew nothing of death. Even those whose fathers had been killed in the Second World War had been too small to remember them. One or two widowed mothers, struggling to find the school fees on a service pension, came alone to Parents' Weekends or Speech Day – plucky little women coping without a man. Their daughters had pictures of both parents on their lockers, but the father was just a young man in uniform: an image, an absence, not a subject for grief.

Divorce, however, was different. When the school had opened there had been no divorced parents. Already, six years later, there were at least half-a-dozen, the product of hasty wartime marriages that could not survive the years apart. Fluffy Mrs Reynolds had turned up at one Parents' Weekend last term with a man who was not her husband and not an uncle either, and had simpered archly as she introduced him, proud of her unsuitable friend. Roly or Ricky or Dicky, she'd called him. No, not Roly; Roly was someone else. They had whisked Charmian off to lunch at the Three Feathers and Charmian, presumably, had noticed nothing. Perhaps she should have a word with Charmian's best friend, Sheila, who was a kind, conscientious child.

Fathers were seldom close to their daughters. It was the mother's responsibility to provide a safe haven for children.

Lord knows, thought Henrietta Birmingham with sudden irritation, they did little enough else. Hair-dos and manicures were the mileposts which measured out their lives. Their finger-nails were burnished to a soft glow by hours of buffing with chamois leather and curved into perfectly matching ivory crescents; their hair was eternally patted into place in order to display their pretty, boneless hands. Most mothers were empty-headed appendages to their husbands, only too glad of the social freedom gained by entrusting their daughters to the care of other women. *Forgive me, Lord, my intolerance to my own sex. I could have been one of them.*

Until a girl leaves home for good to start her own household (it is different for boys; but, then everything is different for boys), her parents' marriage is the proscenium arch within which her life is enacted. Unthinkable that it might collapse, or the curtain come down. A father or mother cannot have an understudy. And that is how it should be, thought Mrs Birmingham; marriage is a sacrament, an indissoluble union for the procreation of children, in sickness and in health.

As a good Christian, she had never questioned her marriage vows, and suffered pangs of guilt for not spending more time with her husband. Had he taken any interest in the school, she would have been happy to tell him about the girls and her daily life, perhaps even to ask his advice. As it was, Lionel Birmingham, a lifelong hypochondriac with a few genuine illnesses – enough to get him classified as Medical Group III during the First World War, so that he had spent it safely behind a desk – had little interest in anything beyond his own bodily functions. But now, at sixty-five, his health was genuinely deteriorating. The doctor had warned her that lung cancer was a possibility, but she dared not pass this information on to Lionel, who continued to smoke heavily, as he had done all his life.

It is time I went up the drive, she thought.

The housekeeper greeted her at the door of the Lodge.

'Not too bad today, Mrs Birmingham,' she said. 'He ate a bit of fish for his supper, and I made him a nice pudding, and now he's listening to the play on the wireless.'

24

'Very good, Ridley. I can take care of everything else. You may go.'

Mrs Birmingham's childhood stood her in good stead with parents and servants, who were awed by her commanding air and old-fashioned voice. Mrs Birmingham said 'orf' and ''otel' and never softened her tone with the mock-deferential requests that some considered necessary nowadays, with servants becoming so choosy. She would not have dreamed of suggesting an extra evening off to her housekeeper, and Ridley, who valued her autonomy at the Lodge and had learned to turn a deaf ear to Mr Birmingham's occasional croaking summons, never dreamed of asking for one.

Mrs Birmingham walked into her own drawing-room, where she knew a tray with Nice biscuits and two cups of cocoa would be waiting. She would have preferred to sit down and drink hers alone and reflect, or perhaps write to her son James in Hong Kong, but all that would have to wait. She lifted the tray and carried it slowly, heavily up the stairs.

'Is that you, dear?' Lionel called shakily.

Of course it's me. I weigh fourteen stone and Ridley's half that. Can't you tell the difference in our tread? Look at the bedside clock. You know it's me at this hour.

'Coming, darling,' she called.

She walked into their bedroom trying not to inhale too deeply, for the stale smell of cigarettes and decrepitude permeated the air.

'Let me open the window – perhaps the night air will make you feel better. Hasn't it been a lovely spring day?'

But, pointing fastidiously at the skin on his cocoa and complaining about the petrol fumes from the drive, Lionel wanted the window left shut.

Dear Lord who has suffered many adversities and always had compassion for the sick, grant me Thy patience, prayed Mrs Birmingham. *Forgive me my intolerance, help me not to show irritation towards my husband, who is sick, sicker than he knows . . .*

Sitting together behind drawn curtains in their cottage, Diana Monk (who taught maths and Latin) and Sylvia Parry (biology) lingered over a sherry. Timetables had been drawn up and roneoed ready to be pinned on the board and they had, by common consent, abandoned coffee and the gossip of the staff-room.

'Why are you smiling like that, Monks?'

'You know why. I'm actually quite glad to be back.'

'Did you have a good time in the Easter hols? Did you miss me?' Sylvia mocked.

'Why should I?'

'No reason.'

A long pause. Finally Sylvia said, 'Pour me another sherry. Please.'

'I'm not used to this. It makes me all red in the face. Do I sound all right?'

'Don't be absurd. Three glasses of sherry can't do you any harm.'

'But I'm not used to it.'

As the sherry swirled through her head Diana began to feel relaxed and rosy with emotion. She had spent dull and dutiful holidays at home in Tulse Hill with her mother and uncles. This shabby cottage was the nearest either she or Sylvia came to having a place of their own.

She and Mother and Uncle Aidan and Uncle Ralph formed a unit, self-contained and not unhappy, except that for the last twenty years none of them had felt love for any of the others, nor, apparently, for anyone else. They were bound together by habit and necessity, by oddness and family and the fact that all their possessions were shared, so if any one of the four had left, the remaining three would have been deprived of furniture or plates or cutlery.

Within this household she, the solitary child, had been urged to study, to train, to earn. She had always known that they would eventually depend on her for their livelihood. While she was growing up the uncles had helped with her homework, her mother had made all her clothes, and every evening after school, and later from London University, Diana had returned to their shabby semi-detached house in Tulse Hill. They had never asked about her friends and Diana, who had few enough

in any case, never brought anyone home. When, after pains-
taking hard work quite unleavened by inspiration, she had
finally secured a good degree in mathematics, it was a relief to
escape into the world of girls' boarding-schools.

At the end of the first day of term, Diana lay awake in her
narrow iron bed, although the night was silent except for owls
and the wood-pigeons' cooing. Her bedroom window was shut
and the curtains tightly drawn. She wondered whether Sylvia
was awake, and shivered.

On the other side of the wall Sylvia was indeed awake,
mentally reciting the litany of her childhood in Gower, the
necessary incantation of memory.

I brought back shells from Oxwich Bay and arranged them
in matchboxes, sorted and named; cockles and cuttle-bones
(not strictly a shell at all, but a mollusc, Dada said), lovely
spiralling whelks and the one with a funny webbed end to it
called a pelican's-foot shell. Occasionally I found a sea-urchin,
delicately green and violet, and he'd put it on the mantelpiece
until my mother got tired of dusting it and threw it away. I
gathered three different colours of seaweed from the beach to
press between blotting-paper and put into an album, labelling
the different varieties. He liked that. He liked me to be meth-
odical. I made careful drawings of wild flowers, and he taught
me their names. I didn't make close friends at school. Being
the schoolmaster's daughter set me apart. Our teacher, fat,
bossy Mrs Powell, was in awe of my father and she left me
alone. There was no one I wanted to talk to. I was happy. A
secret is a word from legend and fairy-story that keeps a child
in thrall, a magic word. He must have been, let me think, thirty-
nine then, so I was eight.

We would set off together on summer mornings and as we
walked along narrow lanes beneath tall hedgerows he'd say,
'You mustn't talk to the other children about what goes on at
home Sylvy, my Sylvy. That's private. A secret. Can you keep
a secret?' I was surprised and indignant that he could even
think I'd tell anyone about our private times, him and me and
Mother tightly enclosed in our little house that leant up against
the parson's. We were Chapel, or at least Mother was, so we

passed the time of day with the parson and his wife, but nothing else.

'I *wouldn't*. Nosy Parkers. It's none of their business.'

'There's my good girl,' he said. 'You keep close.'

Sylvia lay awake till long after the clock above the old stables that were now the garage had chimed midnight.

Two

The L-shaped wooden floor of the junior common-room was scattered with huddled groups of fourth-formers playing jacks. The tiny rubber thump of a bouncing ball alternated with the metallic swish of practised hands scooping up the star-shaped metal jacks, sweeping them into the other hand, and deftly catching the ball again. Rings of two, three or four girls sat mesmerized by the game, impervious to those who hovered behind them watching knowledgeably, to the noise of wind-up gramophones in the background, and to the deepening dusk as it flattened the long summer shadows beyond the french windows.

On a patch of rough ground in front of the pets' shed another group of girls had fed, cuddled and bedded down their rabbits and guinea-pigs for the night and were now playing Kick the Can. The girl who was It counted to fifty while the rest hid in the trees and bushes behind the shed or over towards the games field. When time was up she kicked the can as a signal and ran in search of the others. A girl who'd been seen and chased and touched was out and had to stand in captivity beside the can, unless another player could dash up and kick it, in which case she was free again. The summer air smelled fresh and sweet, for the games field had recently been mown. The game was in perpetual motion, as figures in cotton frocks ducked and swooped, giggled and ran, swerving and tripping, shrieking as their hearts and lungs pounded with the thrill of the chase. The last person to remain uncaught was It next time. Like dryads they flew, coiling themselves round trees, beckoning teasingly and laughing as they sped off. What agony if a best friend was languishing by the can; what resourcefulness in contriving to release her; what light-footed bliss as both raced off triumphantly, brimming with liberty.

Sheila and Charmian were tending their garden, a four-foot-square patch among the chessboard of other girls' gardens, enclosed within the red brick walls of the former kitchen garden. Charmian's mother had arranged for a spectacular rose-bush to be delivered by Carter Paterson. It would bear dozens of heavy yellow blooms, she had said, with a wonderful fragrance. Sheila's fingernails were black with earth. She had dug a deep hole and was filling it in around the root-ball of the rose, while Charmian watered and picked at weeds. They'd sprinkled a couple of packets of mixed seeds round the edge of their square, scooped the earth gently over the black and brown specks and watered these, too.

'Suppose we came and did it three times a week,' said Sheila, 'then there wouldn't ever be any weeds and it'd look really nice and we might win.'

'*Three* times?' said Charmian. She preferred playing jacks or listening to records and learning the words. If Sheila was so keen on the soppy old gardening prize, let *her* do it. After all, it wasn't her mother who'd bought the rose, which was much the best thing they'd got.

'Well, all right, then, why don't I come twice and you come once? And I'll help on your evening. That'd be fair.'

'They're playing Kick the Can up by Pets!' shouted a passing girl. 'You coming?'

'Stale buns,' said Sheila, but Charmian jumped to her feet.

'Wait for me!' she shouted. 'Waaaait! I'm coming!'

'But there's only ten minutes to bedtime...' pleaded Sheila. Charmian scampered off, kicking up her white-socked ankles, her short blonde bunches bouncing from side to side.

'Half a mo',' yelled Sheila, 'I'll come!' But Charmian, evidently already out of earshot, ran on.

Soppy date, thought Charmian as she accelerated, fusses me all the time. I'm fed up with her. Doing my prep as though I was a baby. She might think she's cleverer than me, but she's not half as pretty.

'Coo-ee!' she called out as she approached, for the counting had reached forty-one. 'I'm playing too, wait for me, don't kick yet.' She crouched down behind a tussock, panting.

Gosh, there's Charmie without boring old Sheil, thought Flick. Bet they've had a row. Good-oh. 'Charmie! Here – over here – quick! Anyone can see you there,' she called.

The two of them pressed close together behind the broad trunk of an oak at the edge of the wood.

'Sheila'll be in a bate with me,' confided Charmian.

'Let her. She can jolly well stew in her own juice,' said Flick, and they giggled and clutched one another's slight, hot bodies until they heard the dormitory bell jangle faintly from the main building, calling them in for 7.30 bedtime.

The ringing of the bell disturbed Constance, who was sitting in the Reading Corner trying to concentrate on *The Children's Newspaper* (every Wednesday, 3*d*.) but was really thinking about her mother. She'd just written to her parents, though you were only supposed to on Sundays after church or before Walk. 'Thanks awfully for sending me to such a good school and I know I'm frightfully lucky and all that,' she had put at the end, 'but honestly it would be much better if you took me away because it would save you oceans of money and I'm not ever going to be happy here in a million years. So come and take me away, Mummy, please.' Even to her it didn't sound convincing, but once they'd left for Kenya she would have missed her chance of going too, so the letter was urgent.

She put down the magazine and walked up the back stairs to her dormitory. The other girls came in, flushed and excited from playing Kick the Can. Their talk was muffled as they pulled frocks and vests over their heads, or stooped to undo their sandals and take off their socks and knickers. Constance felt self-conscious about undressing in front of other people, so she tried to wait until they'd gone down the corridor to the bathroom. She herself was still quite flat-chested, although some of the girls already wore what they called BBs.

She was the last one back into the dormitory, after cleaning her teeth and washing her face. Fiona stood in the midst of a crowd of girls, looking, as her mother would have said, 'hot and bothered'.

31

'Don't worry, Feeny,' one was saying reassuringly. 'You probably forgot to pack it. Bet that's what happened.'

'But I would have noticed.'

'You might not have. I bet your mother's sent it on already. You wait: it'll be in Parcels tomorrow.'

Constance gathered, although no one bothered to explain and she dared not ask, that Fiona had lost the silver-framed photograph of her parents; but as nobody was sure whether she'd had it before, or whether they were just remembering it from last term, the loss didn't seem serious. Nevertheless Fiona continued to make a great fuss, claiming she'd never get to sleep unless she could have a last look at her mother's picture before closing her eyes. Mothers were sacred, so the dormitory offered lengthy sympathy. But Constance's desperate, unspoken homesickness went unnoticed. Had she been pretty, or cried, she would have been surrounded by clinging supporters offering to be her friend; but silent, bespectacled new girls suffer alone. The others were a group and she was the outsider.

After lights out some of the girls read, propping themselves sideways on one elbow so as to catch the light from the window. Sheila got out of her bed next to Constance and walked over towards Charmian's bed. She was crouching beside it when the door opened and Matron strode in. Small, round and cheerful in her starched white uniform, Peach liked to be thought kind and wanted to be popular, but she was feared because the girls had learned that she was not to be trusted. Anyone in charge had power, and those who tried to disguise it were more unpredictable than those who simply used it, with no pretence at equality.

'What's going on in here? Who's been talking? Come on now, or everyone will be punished.'

Books slid softly under pillows and Sheila crouched unseen.

'Who's dormitory captain in here? Deborah? Who was talking?'

There was no reply.

'Right-ho, then, I shall have to punish all of you. No more sweets till Sunday. For *anyone*.'

Sheila stood up.

'Sorry, Miss Peachey, it was me. I had to tell Charmie something important. It was my fault.'

Miss Peachey looked at her, relented, and smiled forgivingly. 'All right, then, I'll let you all off this time, since term's only just begun. And it can't have been Sheila making *all* the noise. Now, hop back into bed, ducky, and not another sound.'

A sycophantic chorus of 'Gosh, thanks, Peach!' followed as she closed the door of Starlings behind her; then a brief silence, in case she waited outside before she walked away. After a safe pause, Fiona leant across from her bed on the other side of Sheila and breathed, 'Thanks, Sheil. That was jolly dee of you.'

'Shush,' said Sheila, and rolled herself into a heap facing Constance, with her head jammed into the pillow and her eyes tightly shut.

The wood-pigeons cooed outside the window. Voices carried on the still air from as far away as the tennis courts. In the senior common-room someone was playing records from *King's Rhapsody*, and the wistful notes of 'Someday My Heart Will Awake' floated through the gentle Sussex evening. The curtains shifted. An iron bedstead creaked.

When she was almost certain that everyone was asleep Constance whispered, 'Sheila?'

Sheila's eyes opened at once. 'What?' she said.

'Are you all right?'

'Why?'

'I knew you were still awake. Me too. Is anything wrong?'

'Just a bit mis, that's all.'

'Are you homesick?' asked Constance.

'No . . . well, a bit. It's not that.'

'What, then?'

'Just . . . I'm a bit upset 'cos . . .' her voice trailed off in a whisper.

''Cos what?'

'Charmian. She's supposed to be my best friend. Sshh. Don't tell.'

'Promise. Cheer up. Night.'

'Sleep tight, don't let the bugs bite,' said Sheila, and smiled at her over the edge of the sheet.

*

The early summer days were long and clear. Figures in one-piece bathing-suits walked as though on a tightrope, swaying and balancing as they hobbled along the gravel path leading to the swimming-pool, carrying collapsed rubber bathing-caps and towels. From the pool came the sound of splashing and the games mistress's shrill, abrupt whistle. After half an hour the same girls would hurry back to the changing-rooms, shivering in wet costumes. The pool was out of bounds after supper, but in spite of this girls would settle along its low surrounding wall like birds on a telegraph wire, staring into the melting ripples or watching stray leaves drift on its surface. When they were happy at school it was the unconscious happiness of times like this, absorbed in their world, and its gossip. Living in such close proximity, every shift of favour was observed, as girls wove in and out of friendships.

'Charmie's gone off Sheila. Flick's sucking up to her like mad.'

'Mouldy old Flick. More fool her. Charmie's so stuck-up. All that fiddling with her bunches and looking at herself in the mirror.'

'The way she says, "Oh, my hair's hopeless: just like Mummy's" and you're supposed to say, "Oh you're so lucky, it's really smashing."'

They giggled spitefully.

'Who's Sheil friends with now?'

'Don't know. The new girl – Gogs – asked if she could be her partner for Walk on Sunday.'

'Yes, and it was so funny 'cos Sheila said no so they both walked by themselves at the back, looking as if they were busy thinking beautiful thoughts.'

Everyone laughed.

'She's jolly clever, though,' said Madeleine. 'She must be. She got nine out of ten for bilge, even though she's the youngest in the form.'

'Lucky her, to get on the right side of Parry. Gosh, she was in a bate yesterday.'

'I'm scared of her,' admitted Fiona, 'when she's in a bate. You know the way she looks at you: as if she'd really like to

34

hurt you.'

'Well, she's not allowed to, so she can't, so hard cheese her.'

They looked up as the music monitor scanned her practising list and checked the girls round the pool.

'Fiona Cathcart . . . Madeleine Low . . . Anne Hetherington – you're all five minutes late for piano practice. Down to the music rooms *at once.*'

'Yes, Barbara – sorry, Barbara. Gosh, my watch's stopped,' they exclaimed, and then, *sotto voce*, 'Bossy boots.'

Next day in the Lower Fourth's art class Miss Emett picked Constance to pose for the rest of the form. She walked round, charcoal stick in hand, correcting the proportions of their drawings, noting the way the light fell across Constance's shiny hair, the curve of her awkward forearms and the sideways slope of her ankle and foot. Extraordinary, Miss Emett thought, how the young human figure can't help being graceful. This poor child could hardly be called pretty, but Gwen John would have rejoiced in that clumsy arrangement of her hands in her lap, the droop of those narrow shoulders.

'Girls!' she suddenly said. 'Would it be better if Constance took off her glasses? They're really hard to draw. You all make them round, and they're not if you look properly.'

'Oh, yes, Miss Emett,' they chorused. 'That's *miles* easier.'

Constance, deprived of vision as well as movement and speech, sat frozen under their stares. She tried to imagine herself as a hooded falcon chained to her master's wrist, awaiting the imperious moment of freedom; but although she summoned up images from *The Sword in the Stone,* and the tapestries from Cluny that she had seen on a postcard her godmother had sent, she could not detach herself from the humiliating exposure of the present. I hate this awful school, she thought; hate it, hate it, hate it. It's no good Mummy saying it's a *beautiful* school in the *heart* of the country. (The sound of her mother's voice rang in her ears.) I shall die of unhappiness here. I'll pine away and never grow up. There's no one I can talk to and I don't know how to be popular and anyway they're all stupid, with their stupid records and babyish books: *Dimsie* and Enid Blyton.

And now they're all doing feeble drawings of me that'll make me look even worse than I am. I want to go *home*. I want my own room. I want Felix. But I haven't got a room any more. I don't belong anywhere. When I get to Kenya in the hols I won't know anyone there either, and Stella will have made masses of friends. Everyone fusses her because she's younger than me and because she's pretty. Why can't she tell me how to be popular? It's not fair... Perhaps I could try talking to Sheila again. No, she'll only snub me like she did on the walk, with everyone watching. Oh, God, oh, Mummy and Daddy, please take me away from here! I wish I could run away. But who could I go to? No one's going to see me cry. I'll just scrunch myself up tight and clench my teeth and hold my heart in.

'Constance, dear, relax,' called Miss Emett. 'Try and keep the pose nice and loose. Only another five minutes. There's a good girl.'

The bell rang for break and they all took off their overalls, hung them on hooks and rushed out of the studio shouting, 'Fains I put the easels away... Fains I! Fains...'

Constance clambered down from the stool slowly because she was stiff and had cramp in one leg.

'Shall I help?' she asked. 'What do I do? Where do they go?'

'There's a kind girl,' said Miss Emett. 'The pictures of you aren't very good, I'm afraid. Not very flattering. Put your glasses on again and have a look.'

The drawings were worse than not very good. Some of them were positively malicious: caricatures to make the other girls snigger. Only Sheila and Deborah had captured any sort of likeness. In Deborah's drawing she saw her own unhappiness so clearly exposed that she covered it up with the next crude sketch.

'Constance,' said Miss Emett. 'Listen, try not to worry. Nearly everyone's homesick at first. It gets better – and this is a lovely term. They don't mean to be unkind, you know; they're just working out where you fit in. Girls are very cliquy at this age – do you know what "cliquy" means?'

'Yes,' muttered Constance.

'Well, then. Find yourself a friend. Don't be proud, just ask. Lots of the others are lonely too, I expect. They all crowd round Mick and Flick because they're twins. Why don't you try Deborah? She's an interesting girl, and she must feel out of things too, being American ... Look, dear: the box for the charcoal is kept here. That's right ... Why not try talking to her?'

'I must go for break now,' said Constance, knowing she sounded ungrateful when this little, dishevelled woman with the whiskery skin was reaching out to her.

'Righty-ho, then. Off you go. But mind you think about it,' said Miss Emett.

Constance's misery was crushing because she felt utterly helpless. She had no say in the adult decisions that governed her life. Do what your parents want, Constance was thinking, and you are a good child; do it willingly, like Stella, and you are a very good child: 'That one's no trouble at all,' her mother would say to friends, taking all the credit. But it was easy for Stella and much harder for her. If she resisted or even tried to tell them what she wanted, Mummy and Daddy just complained and called her ungrateful.

Constance would have been happy in Kenya, but her parents sent her to boarding-school because that was what people of their class did if they went abroad; why otherwise should the Colonial Office contribute £150 towards the cost? Everyone else's children were boarding, and being able to talk about Constance's beautiful English school in the heart of the Sussex countryside, along with rueful comments about how expensive the uniform was, confirmed their own status. A bookish elder daughter, hanging around with African servants, would hamstring their social life and highlight their failure to conform. In the face of these unspoken considerations Constance was powerless. But she couldn't contemplate the possibility that her parents might be selfish.

The life of the school ebbed and flowed. It rushed towards great events like Sports Day with communal excitement and preparation, everyone united in practising, running heats, making costumes, painting scenery and ensuring the school did itself justice. The second week of the summer term was not such a time. Parents' Weekend was still a fortnight away. The end-of-term play – *1066 and All That* – was newly cast and not yet into the swing of rehearsals. Yet beneath the tide of school routine the minor dramas of friendship, rivalry and deceit preoccupied each girl. These could stir up intense passions which were usually dismissed by the staff as adolescent hysteria or sulks.

School friendships were conducted according to a rigid code. Best friends walked in twos, sat next to each other in lessons and at meals, met each other's parents and from then on always sent their love in letters. At bedtime they said goodnight to each other last of all. With Charmian avoiding her, Sheila would have liked to respond to Constance's timid approach, but she was still Charmie's best friend. Walking with anyone else would have been disloyal. Until the breach had been established by silence, tears, sulks, sympathy and a final row, with every member of the class taking sides and new pairs of friends emerging, it would only have made her unpopular. It was different when Charmie scampered off arm-in-arm with someone else, because everyone knew Charmie was a flirt. Sheila was the solid one, the reliable one, the rock of the relationship. All she could do was stick to the rules.

Life in the Reynolds' home had been different during the last Easter holidays. Charmian didn't say so, because it was something she dared not acknowledge. Her parents had made an effort to behave normally and conceal their estrangement from her. They only had rows at night when Charmian was supposed to be asleep. Charmian had to lie to herself, ignoring what was obviously going on. It was like standing at the edge of the sea when the tide is coming in and the sand trickles away between your toes, throwing you off balance. So she turned on her friend, becoming deceitful because she was being deceived.

None of the grown-ups took these little melodramas seriously. Childhood, after all, is an innocent, unclouded time. Children are like tumbling puppies or singing birds. Even the most loving and sensitive parents, grannies or teachers assume that adolescent emotions are undeveloped and fleeting. How *could* they be serious, funny little monkeys? It was a tiresome phase and of course they all exaggerated wildly, but thank goodness it didn't last. Adults have forgotten the agony of growing up, when feelings are vast and incomprehensible, primitive and turbulent. Sheila and Constance suffered stoically and in silence, while Charmian vented her anger and pain on her best friend.

Every day was divided into meals and lessons and Rest; letters and parcels; sport and play; Prayers and mufti; hobbies, pets, bath-time, hair-washing and bed. Each segment of time was signalled by the heavy clanging of the bell.

Every week a different prefect had the job of bell-ringing. She had to walk – the school rules said girls must walk, never run, not even in case of fire – from her form-room or dormitory down to the cupboard in the Covered Way (which the squits, for this reason, innocently called the Cupboard Way) where the bell was kept. She would grasp its smooth wooden handle with both hands and hurl the sound in all directions, deafened by its great double thunderbolts. Its clangour would reach the form-rooms, the lavatories and changing-rooms, where girls were dreaming or conspiring; it would reverberate high up on the top floor and across the lawns, commanding people to return from the swimming-pool and tennis courts. Everyone obeyed, for without the bell's regular, impersonal ringing, the school would have collapsed into chaos. Everyone could chant the school timetable: Nine-oh, nine-forty, ten-twenty, they'd mutter (now comes Break), eleven-twenty-five, twelve-five.

After the bell for the end of the last period before lunch, Sylvia Parry arrived in the staff-room and searched impatiently in her drawer for a cigarette. The Lower Fifth, revising biology for their imminent O levels, were whipping themselves into melodrama. Many of them were stupid or lazy, with every reason to panic about their chances, and she had lost her temper.

'For Pete's sake, Marjorie Hilton!' she had snapped at one vacant-faced, pony-loving girl who had been gazing out of the window. (She was dreaming of riding bareback, hair streaming

in the wind, towards some ill-defined but glorious encounter.)
'If you can't understand osmosis by now we might as well all
give up. I'd like to take hold of that stupid brain of yours and
wring it out to see what, if anything, you have retained from
your years of expensive education.'

Shocked out of her fantasy, Marjorie stared at the raging
figure beside the blackboard. A hand went up.

'Well, what is it now, Wendy?'

'Please, Miss Parry, shall I show Marjorie my notes and
explain them to her?'

'Well, of course, if you feel you may succeed where I have
manifestly failed, I shall be happy to hand my job over to you.
Meanwhile I suggest we leave Marjorie to wallow in her own
stupidity and get on with the next block of revision.'

She knew she'd been unfair to them both but for God's
sake . . . As she took out a Craven A, Ginny Valentine said, 'I
wouldn't if I were you, Sylvia. There's a note in your pigeon-
hole. Looks like a summons from on high.'

Sylvia tore open the pretentious crested envelope. It bore
the school emblem, a three-masted sailing ship, and below it
the motto *Fortiter, fideliter, feliciter*, bravely, faithfully, happily –
Mrs Birmingham's dream for her school. The note inside said,
'Would you be good enough to come and see me before lunch?
HB'

Sylvia took an urgent drag before stubbing out her precious
cigarette and slamming the door.

'Come in,' called Mrs Birmingham with a rising inflection.
'Ah, Miss Parry. Thank you. Do sit down. A sherry?'

The Headmistress's study was a serious room, lined with
bookshelves and the school group photographs for the last
seven years. There were also prints of Dürer's hare and his
praying hands, which economically conveyed to parents and
other visitors an interest in religion, biology and art. Very few
failed to recognize the prints, and only the most confident could
refrain from murmuring 'Ah, Dürer, of course . . .'

Mrs Birmingham's desk stood in front of tall windows. Light
gilded her papers, the wooden IN and OUT trays, and a
rectangular blotter with leather corners. Behind the desk stood

a substantial chair that had once been her father's, more like a throne than a chair, while facing it was a much smaller chair with a high, hard back. Sylvia, motioned to the small chair, sat down with only the sherry glass to differentiate her from any girl called in for a ticking-off. Miss Roberts's desk in the other corner of the room was tactfully empty.

'I thought it time we had a chat about how things are going this term,' the Head began neutrally. She waited, her concentration fixed and her face unsmiling.

'I've just come from the Lower Fifth,' Sylvia said. 'They seem to be up to scratch with their revision. One or two failures to be expected, of course, but that's unavoidable.'

'Is it? I thought if we knew a girl was bound to fail we didn't enter her for the examination. It's bad for confidence, and bad for the school's record.'

'Well, they're not *certain* to fail. I'm being realistic. Pessimistic even.'

'Have you offered extra coaching? I would have to consult their parents, naturally, but few parents decline.'

Extra coaching, dear God. And when was she supposed to find the time for that, with over a hundred books to mark every week?

'Well, let's leave that aside for the present,' Mrs Birmingham said. 'I asked to see you because certain disturbing rumours have reached me, not for the first time, about your demeanour in class. Your handling of the girls. I thought it would be helpful to hear in your own words if there is any cause for concern. Anything I ought to know about.'

'There's been another outbreak of stealing, mainly in the Lower Fourth. Fountain-pens disappearing, the usual sort of thing.'

'I was referring to your own conduct, Miss Parry, rather than to that of the girls.'

'Girls can be very excitable. They can be – how shall I put it? – melodramatic.'

There was no answering smile.

'I was under the impression that it was you who are excitable, Miss Parry. That you frequently lose your temper. That some

41

of the girls are afraid of you.'

'No bad thing,' said Sylvia, attempting another conspiratorial smile.

'On the contrary,' said the Head coldly, 'it is a very bad
thing . . .'

Does she imagine I don't know what a very bad thing is?
Does she think I was born this caustic, dangerous spinster?

One freezing Gower winter, Mother caught pneumonia.
Small wonder, the times she stood out in the cold hanging
sheets on the line as they snapped back into her face, or trudging
along, head down against the wind, to and from chapel or the
grocer. She continued stumbling through her duties, hacking
and wheezing, and I don't remember that my father or I took
much notice. Now, as then, Sylvia was unable to feel guilt.
Finally one day we came back from school together, me bundled
up on the front of his bicycle, feeling his strong body pedalling
rhythmically against me, and she wasn't there. He went upstairs
and found her lying on their bed, frightened by her collapse,
the loss of control. The doctor came and took her off in
his own car to the hospital at Swansea. He said she was very
ill.

Then we were on our own. We divided up the chores and
kept the place spick and span. Mother would have been proud
of us. We didn't need the neighbours, though I heard them
behind my back saying I was a brave girl and the parson's wife
would bring round a cake or a pan of soup, still hot from her
own stove. We drank cups of tea together, my father and I,
just the two of us, while I listened to *Children's Hour*, and for
supper we ate the parson's soup, or bread and meat paste,
tinned sardines and hard-boiled eggs – things that didn't need
cooking. I'd clear away the table while he marked exercise
books and prepared lessons. I never asked for his help with my
school work. He was busy, and besides, I could do it easily.

When it was my bedtime he'd tap his watch and go up to
draw the curtains and run my bath. I undressed and he folded
my clothes in a tidy pile on the chair in my bedroom. I'd sit in
the bath – this wasn't every night, of course, only about twice
a week – and he would soap the flannel and wash me, making

42

swirls of lather across my skin like the patterns on the matted coats of the white Gower ponies. Then I'd step out of the bath into the towel, and he'd close his arms and hug me inside it, rubbing my back and legs.

'Are they done?' he'd say. 'No, I don't think they're quite done.'

I liked it, and giggled as he dropped the nightdress over my head.

One night when she'd been away about a week, maybe ten days, he read a story, as usual, cuddled me and kissed me good-night and after he'd gone downstairs I got out of bed quietly, so as not to hurt his feelings, because he'd forgotten my prayers. I knelt down beside the bed and folded my hands and leant my forehead on them. I shut my eyes and said, 'God bless Dada and God bless Mummy and make her better, and make me a good girl...' Even though I'd been so quiet I heard his step on the landing. I opened my eyes and saw the wedge of light widening as he came through the door.

'What are you doing, Sylvy? Naughty Dada, did we forget your prayers?'

I don't know why I felt guilty. I scrambled to my feet and was climbing hastily into bed.

'Well, we'd better have another good-night kiss, then.' He walked back to the door and closed it, so the room was dark, a line of light from the landing showing up the texture of the lino. He was still in his schoolmaster's suit, only he'd taken the jacket off and was wearing an old Fair Isle knitted waistcoat. The waistcoat crossed the room towards me, stretched across his chest. I wasn't in bed; I was still sitting on the edge with my legs dangling down.

'Haven't I been a good girl?'

'Oh, yes, a good girl, such a very good girl. Quickly now, into bed, quickly, under the sheets.'

I stared very hard at the drawn threads along the hem of my calico sheet, at the neat little squares they made, like the edge of a stamp, and I looked at the fat, faded roses on my bedroom wall-paper, because you know how it is, after a while a dark room seems to become quite light. That's because your eyes adjust.

Walking down to the beach one day by myself, through the tall sea-grass, slippery to the hand like chives, I overheard two boys as they passed me, whipped by the wind.

'That's just love innit?' the big boy said to his pal.

'Oooh-er . . .' said the other, smaller boy, screwing up his nose and stamping on something in the sand.

'Did you killed it?' the first boy asked.

I walked along the beach looking down at my feet where brownish, visceral ropes of seaweed coiled, glistening wetly on the sand. They felt squelchy if you trod on them, like something dead and putrefying, like the sheep I sometimes found in ditches, all slimy inside and covered with flies and maggots.

I still have the photograph taken of us that summer: all the village children lined up in forms outside the school. The teachers are in the middle of the group, my dada in the very middle. Some of the more daring boys have pulled a face, but most of us, conscious of the click that would freeze us for ever, are still and serious. If you made a face and the wind changed, you'd stay like that, and it was the same with the camera. My eyes are just two dark triangles – the sun is overhead and it blanks out my expression. I look like my father: the same thickset body and broad face, the same swarthy Celtic colouring. I was Dada's girl all right. My mother, who had come back from hospital pale and dry, moving slower than before, was cross when she saw the photograph.

'What were you glaring like that for? Like a real black dog was sitting on your shoulder.'

I didn't answer.

Sylvia returned from that long-ago time and place to find the Head still speaking, as though mere seconds had passed.

'. . . Girls need discipline, yes. But even more than discipline, they need kindness. I assume you entered the teaching profession because you felt, if not a vocation . . .' Miss Parry smiled in acknowledgement of the irony '. . . at least a sympathy for girls; some understanding of their problems.' Mrs Birmingham leant back, her eyes tender and reminiscent, and continued, 'Until they're ten or thereabouts, twelve if they're fortunate, little girls are privileged beings. Those years are the nearest we ever come, perhaps, to the Garden of Eden.'

'I grew up in Gower,' said Sylvia, seeing she had to say something.

'Land of our fathers, land of the free,' quoted the Head obscurely. Then, getting back to the point, 'But adolescence, on the other hand, is not always an easy time. How are we to teach them, other than by precept and example? Being seen to lose your temper is not an example you would wish to set, surely?'

In the silence that followed, Sylvia felt her gorge rise and the dark mottling began on her neck. Mrs Birmingham noticed too, and waited.

'May I know who has complained?'

'No, you may not. You may deny the truth of it, however, if it is untrue. Do you?'

'I may ... occasionally, under pressure ... speak a little harshly, perhaps. I will try to moderate my reproofs,' said Sylvia formally.

'If there is anything you need to talk over, I am always here. I am concerned about the stealing, of course. For the time being I prefer to investigate that privately. As to yourself: perhaps there are personal problems? Could you take the first Parents' Weekend off?'

'I have no personal problems, thank you, Headmistress. I shall not require the weekend off,' said Sylvia Parry.

'Very well. And now, there's the lunch bell. Thank you.'

One-all, thought Sylvia, as she stood up to leave. I have been warned. But she hadn't heard about the stealing. I've got to watch my step all the same. Self-righteous cow.

She strode into the dining-room and stood rigidly at the head of her table as one of the seniors gabbled, '*Benedictus benedicat per Jesum Christum Dominum nostrum*. Amen.' From the shelter of closed eyes and bent heads, Diana Monk looked anxiously across at her. Chairs and benches scraped the floor as the school sat down to lunch.

Girls were popular either because they conformed, naturally and without trying, to the prevailing idea of what was normal, or because they deviated from it in some remarkable way. Hermione Malling-Smith was a perfect example of normality, never harbouring a single original thought, but she also deviated because of her fragile beauty. A cloud of adoration, like a solar flare, surrounded Hermione on her elaborately modest path through the day. She epitomized sixteen-year-old loveliness, legs tapering elegantly as a pair of scissors from the neat, flat ovals of her buttocks, her body curving and budding as though it moved underwater, while the fine, pale hair looped on top of her head flowed like the air itself. She had wide eyes, wide nostrils and small, pretty ears. One in a thousand girls conforms to this universal image of young girlhood. It was Hermione's accidental good fortune to be that one.

Because Hermione looked so exquisite, so sweetly vulnerable, it was impossible not to feel that her character – her soul – must be heavenly too. The tributes beauty accepts make it easy to be generous. Hermione had always taken this attention for granted, making little distinction between the worship she received from her parents, other people's brothers, certain teachers, or her own contemporaries. At sixteen, however, she was becoming aware that the stares of men were more disturbing than those of the juniors. She was curious about the effect of her dazzling looks, the power she might wield, and impatient to put it to the test. She rather liked the idea of being cruel and seeing some young man languishing and fading away for hopeless love of her.

At school she was called 'Hermy-One', the joke failing to conceal that she was the unique, the one and only Hermione. She was not clever, but most members of staff made allowances; she was not tidy, but someone else would always gather up her discarded clothes or papers, grateful for the brief intimacy this permitted. Her personal mannerisms were mimicked throughout the school – the way she unpicked the pleats of her heavy tweed skirt so that instead of kicking lumpishly around her calves it swung coquettishly from her hips; her way of writing capital letters with a loop and a flourish. She ran like a deer, springing across the games field to a background roar of 'Oh, come *on*, Hermy One! Oh, yes! Yes! She's *done* it!' More girls had 'pashes' on Hermione than on any other senior.

In most cases a 'pash' was a safe outlet for adolescent emotion and practice for sexual encounters to come. Charmian and Sheila were united in their mutual worship of Hermione. Others worshipped her in secret, deriving a bitter thrill from denying it.

'She's not *that* pretty,' they would say, crossing their fingers.

The desire her beauty aroused was not always passive, for Sylvia Parry was in thrall to Hermione. The taut blue veins at the back of Hermione's knees, the concave upward arch below her chin, the triangular breasts that tipped her Aertex shirt into twin points as she moved; these recurring glimpses tormented Sylvia. She would enter the Lower Fifth's form-room clotted with expectation, telling herself that Hermione was just an ordinary, silly girl, vain and shallow like most sixteen-year-olds, only to be ravished by the rediscovery that she was as flawless as in memory. In class the girl seldom asked a question and, if addressed, would smile abstractedly.

'I don't know, Miss Parry. Shall I look it up?' Someone would thrust a book under her nose, open at the appropriate page.

'Oh, yes,' she would say. 'Here it is. Do you want me to read it out?'

'You're supposed to *know*, Hermione,' Sylvia would admonish, grateful for the excuse to pronounce her name and look directly into her face, gulping down its details as greedily as a pelican, to be regurgitated later for the nourishment of her ravenous heart.

'What made you want to teach biology?' Diana asked one evening, shyly curious.

'Oh, it was the place. Gower. Not a lot to do there – nearest cinema was miles away – except read books, or go for walks. Lots of wild life, though. Just sort of happened.'

Gower was still Gower, in all its beauty: self-contained, teeming with life under hummocks of gorse and in rock pools. I was wild, too – cantering off on my own, hiding in cliffs that overhung the sea above Worm's Head or Oxwich Point. I knew they were high and dangerous. My mother would have beaten me if she'd known the risks I took. Often I scraped myself against the jagged edges of rocks, or fell and grazed my knees until they bled.

'Worse things happen at sea,' my mother would say as she swabbed the cuts with Dettol, and she'd stump off, leaving my father to comfort me. He would pull me on to his lap and I could smell the sweat of his clothes and the Brylcreem on his hair, and he'd whisper, 'Worse things happen at sea,' and laugh into my ear.

I took longer and longer walks. To justify them I would say as I left the house that I was studying the plants and shore-life. I sketched and wrote down the Latin names of what I drew. So the beautiful pink and violet shell was *Gari fervensis*, the big pink scallops were *Chlamys opercularis*, and very occasionally I'd come across the rayed artemis, *Dosinia exoleta*, a round shell with markings that looked like ancient writing – Sumerian, I thought later. I learned the names of all the crabs, from the fierce, attacking fiddler crab, *Portunus puber*, to the timid shore crab, *Cracinus maenas*.

'Other children collected stamps or cigarette cards; I collected the natural history of Gower, drew it and labelled it. I became more knowledgeable than anyone, even my father, and that, I suppose, is why I am a biologist. Or at any rate, a biology teacher.'

Diana Monk had no idea that Sylvia cherished powerful fantasies about Hermione. It did not occur to her that she had the right to be jealous. She barely acknowledged her own emotions, let alone Sylvia's. As for the girls, it wouldn't have entered their heads that a member of staff might trespass into their zone; and, indeed, what Sylvia Parry felt for Hermione was not an adolescent 'pash'. Although they sometimes shocked and excited one another with smutty conversations after lights, most girls were entirely ignorant about their own sexuality. By the time they reached the Lower Fourth some had started the curse, but they couldn't have explained accurately what its function was, even though they giggled in class when the

English teacher read out, 'The curse is come upon me! Cried the Lady of Shalott.' They kissed each other good-night, but these kisses were still the smothering hugs of children and not yet the explorations of precocious young women.

Occasionally a 'pash' between a pretty junior and a receptive senior might lead to a secret meeting in the long grass at the end of the games field. They would usually just talk, unfamiliar with the vocabulary of desire, hardly knowing why they wanted to be alone, until by accident they brushed against each other's little breasts and discovered how nice it felt. But the prelude was so long and the subterfuge so elaborate that most 'pashes' were over before reaching even this innocent stage. In any case, 'pashes' were discouraged, and once a term Mrs Birmingham would talk vaguely in Prayers about being pure in mind and body and (the relevance was obscure) about the undesirability of friendships between girls from different forms. Then the school would sing 'Love Divine, All Loves Excelling'.

Very rarely was there a scandal. Letters hidden under pillows during term or sent by post in the holidays would be intercepted, diaries read; there would be a brief episode of melodrama, and all contact would be forbidden. For a while the girls concerned would whisper and cry in the dormitory at night, but it never lasted long. Sometimes a girl would develop a passion for one of the teachers, but this was ridiculed. Teachers were in the other camp, although Miss Valentine was an exception. Her face glowed with such cheerfulness, her voice was always so lilting and good-tempered, that she was generally agreed to be 'an absolute darling'.

The Lower Fourth breathed heavily over its prep.

'I saw you sucking up to Miss Valentine. Yuk! How could you? Practically slobbering all over her. It's only because she gives you good marks...'

'It's got nothing to do with you, so MYOB. If you weren't so jolly lazy, Fiona Cathcart, you might get decent marks too.'

'*I* haven't got a pash on her, so *I* don't write it all out twice and do beautiful darling little maps with lovely green and blue outlines, *that*'s why.'

'I don't care,' said Madeleine and made a face, scrunching

up her nose and mouth and poking her head forward.

'Anyway, *some* people are trying to *work*, in case you hadn't noticed. Which, 'cos I've looked everywhere and I still can't find my rotten pen, is hard enough, without your sarky comments.'

Constance looked as though she were working, but she was not writing her English essay ('My Best Friend'), which had been easy and had only taken her ten minutes, even though the best friend she described was imaginary. Now she was writing a letter. She knew it was hopeless and she was only putting herself in the wrong and sounding ungrateful. She knew her mother would tell her to make more of an effort to join in and find a friend. So she added, 'I do *try* and join in. But I'm no good at jacks and nobody ever tries to catch me in Kick the Can. Oh, well, there goes the supper bell so I'll have to stop now. Masses of best love, Constance.'

I'm going to run away and that'll show them, she thought. She made a song of it: I'll run away, far, far away, and come again another day – no, that was silly – she'd never come back. Not ever.

Sheila stared at her supper, an iridescent orange triangle of smoked haddock lying in a tepid puddle of milky liquid. She ate the bits of potato that weren't dyed yellow and put her knife and fork together.

Charmie was talking across her to Mick and Madeleine: '... so then this girl, she's an orphan you see – I think that's it – yes, and she's fallen on hard times and she has to go and be a typist because she hasn't got any money and she's so ashamed she changes her name. That's so no one will know it's her. But the boss's son – he's a lord really, only his father's making him start at the bottom – well, he keeps noticing her 'cos she's so pretty and sad and everything, and...'

The other two listened bright-eyed, eating mechanically.

'That's not how you told it to me, Charmie,' interrupted Sheila. 'You said it was her who was the duke's daughter, only...'

'Oh, shut up, who cares anyway, it's my story. *You* didn't see the film. Quick, take my fish, I don't want it.'

I don't want it either, thought Sheila, crumbling the shiny yellow flakes on her plate. She turned them over so that the black skin was on top.

'Pass your plates along, everybody!' commanded Hermione, the senior at the head of the table.

'Whose is this? Who hasn't eaten their fish?'

'Please, Hermione, Sheila hates fish. Do let her off,' said Charmian.

'Sheila Dunsford-Smith, is this your plate?'

'Yes, Hermione.'

'Well, sit here and eat it or you won't have any pudding.'

Torn between the desire to obey Hermione, thus earning her fleeting approval, and her disgust at the sight of the mangled fish, Sheila answered, 'But I don't want pudding.'

'That's got nothing to do with it. You know the rules. You can ask for a small portion, but you must eat what's on your plate.'

Conscious of having been scrupulously fair, Hermione turned back to her neighbour.

Long after the others had scattered for the last forty minutes of their day, Sheila sat over her congealing plateful. At last she was released by Diana Monk, who glanced into the dining-room and was moved to pity by her slumped shoulders and trapped expression. Five minutes later, enclosed within the warm red brick walls of the kitchen garden, Sheila knelt by their plot, turning the earth with a fork as listlessly as she had picked at the fish.

'Sheil! Sheeeeei-la!' she heard, and saw Charmie up by Pets, beckoning to her urgently. 'Quick! Only ten minutes left and Mick's just started counting. *Here.*' As Sheila joined her she smiled radiantly and said, 'Gosh, you were super to get me out of that stinky fish!' Together they raced off to crouch behind the garden shed, arms round each other's shoulders, panting and flushed under the rose-pink evening sky.

The last rays of the sun soaked into the plump rectangular cushions on the bay-window-seat. The Head and her Deputy sat in their usual armchairs over a pot of weak coffee, the wireless tuned to the Third Programme.

'You were right about Sylvia Parry,' said the Head. 'There is something threatening there. No wonder she frightens the girls. That little one – third-former, Katherine – '

'Wilson?'

'Yes, little Katherine Wilson, she'd been sent out to stand in the corridor yesterday. I happened to come across her. She was petrified. Shaking like a leaf. She isn't yet ten. I can't employ a woman who terrorizes small children. Why is she doing it? Frightening little girls ... is the woman right in the head?'

'She's responsible for more order marks than any other member of staff,' said Miss Roberts. 'And she and the unfortunate Diana Monk are up to something.'

'Well, perhaps. You could be right, though personally I doubt it. In any case one couldn't dismiss her for that. They'd both deny it.'

'But one's never very happy about it,' said Miss Roberts vehemently.

The Deputy Head's unmarried state resulted from the fact that no man had ever asked her. She liked men well enough. She thought lesbianism was unnatural and wicked, and would have preferred to dismiss staff whom she suspected of such leanings, but unfortunately the law was not on her side.

The Head continued to brood.

'She's never administered corporal punishment, as far as I know ...'

'Henrietta, she doesn't need to. She frightens them to death as it is.'

'What am I supposed to do, Peggy? I can't possibly replace her at this stage of term – not with O and A levels just coming up. I've tried to talk to her. She denies having any personal problems.'

'Diana Monk doesn't look capable of making trouble,' said Peggy, and smiled wryly. 'She'd never stand up to her. No, I think it's a matter of temperament. Parry's one of those people with more than their fair share of anger. She could fly off the handle at the slightest thing. Did you give her a formal warning?'

'Not this time. I hinted that she could do with a weekend off, but she turned it down.'

'Let's hope we don't get any parents complaining. That could be tiresome.'

'Keep an eye on her for me, won't you, Peggy?' The rain-pattering sound of applause swelled from the wireless. 'Now then, shall we listen to the news?'

Half an hour later, after the usual depressing reports from the Korean war (it couldn't – could it? – affect her boy in Hong Kong), Henrietta Birmingham sat looking out across the darkened lawns to the trees silhouetted against the slate-blue sky. Too late for the sunset, too pale for moonrise; only the evening star hung above the earth. She used to watch it as a girl from her bed in Scotland. She had had a bedroom to herself by the time she was twelve, but when the boys were away at the front she preferred to sleep in the old nursery, with its memories of the time when they'd all been children together under the benevolent eye of Nanny, rather than stay in a grown-up room empty of ghosts. How hard it is being a girl, she used to think when her brothers' stilted letters arrived. They told her nothing, hardly more than their dutiful letters home from Eton, but she read between the lines and imagined the thrill, the rivalry, the dramatic challenge of doing your best – not just in a cricket match, but for your country. She had envied them at first.

Jamie had kept his promise to write, but what was she to make of the cryptic lines which expressed no pride and delight? He was just being modest. He must be doing marvellous things. She longed for something broader and greater than her own limited horizons, for the chance to escape, to be brave and glorious, for *some*thing beyond the narrow confines of girlhood. But the world, her parents, Nanny, her brothers, even Jamie – they all thought her yearnings foolish. They told her that one day, when a good man asked her to marry him, everything would fall into its proper place and she would find her destiny.

Every evening she prayed for them, alone in their nursery with its alphabet frieze round the walls, toys tidily ranged in the toy cupboard, watching her through the glass doors, books in order on the shelves (she would take them out sometimes, wistfully – *Jock of the Bushveld, The Crimson Aeroplane*). Praying was all she could do, and so she prayed for hours: first for Jamie, that she might see him again, then for the other two, that they might not be wounded or ... or called to God just yet. She prayed for all British soldiers and airmen, and for the Canadians and Australians, and the brave Indian regiments whom she had seen marching at the King's coronation; she prayed as well for all German officers and soldiers and all poor prisoners wherever they might be; and most earnestly she prayed to God to make the generals end this wicked war. Finally, opening her eyes to the high, cold, hard-hearted moon, she prayed for their happiness. Not for her own. She knew she wasn't good enough to deserve that, and in any case she didn't know what would make her happy.

The next year her eldest brother, Alistair, died, and a month or two later Jamie was wounded on the Somme. But God answered her prayers. Jamie came back. Back, it is true, with one leg missing, a mockery of her fleet-footed young companion. When they sent him home to convalesce, she was the one who sat beside his bed all night, while the nurse or Nanny dozed next door; she was the one who listened while he moaned and twitched in his sleep. She heard his panic-stricken roars and cries, and started when he jerked bolt upright out of his dreams to clutch the stump of his knee and groan at the pain in his missing leg.

'Tell me, Jamie. Never mind how disagreeable, don't spare me. Tell it all to me, and maybe that will take away the nightmares.'

At first he would scowl at her.

'You're a girl. Don't be stupid. Get the nurse. Tell her I need morphine. *Get her* for me, Henrietta.'

After a while, though, the blackened, charred desolation in his mind began to find its way into words. Her old nightmare took on shape and detail. 'It was like roasted chestnuts on the nursery fire – when they're all burnt and black, the flesh in the middle oozing and sweet. The noise was like hell. I hear it in my head.' The sounds he made were a parody of her brothers, as boys, playing soldiers: 'Boom, bang, thump, whistle, wheee, boom-boom,' but then, 'scream, yell, moan, gasp.' They'd never mimicked the noises of pain, just keeled over and died obediently. After the bang-bangs you were dead, for a moment or two anyway.

'You've never seen . . . you can't possibly imagine our faces,' Jamie told her. 'People making ghastly grins and jokes. Bad form to show you were afraid. Ever heard the word rictus? It's in between grinning and dying. The men's faces grinding over their skulls, and sometimes just skulls. Like this – look at me, Henrietta. *Look at me.* Yes, they did that, too: eyes screwed up against the light. And then a smile, fine old boy, don't you worry about me. Don't you ever dare think war is fine and noble, Henrietta. Don't tell Mother I said so.'

She would force the nurse to let her help when the dressing on his stump was changed, force herself to confront unblinkingly the crazed red flesh that had been his leg, the seeping yellow and black lines where the wound was healing slowly, to cradle the hot, ugly stump while cool fresh gauze was wound around it, so that it looked cared-for and hygienic, hidden from fastidious eyes.

Soon he would call her at night and spew up the jagged fragments of his nightmares. 'The horses, Henrietta – have I told you how the horses stank? How the rats would crawl out from inside their bellies, after gnawing out their livers. The liver is the best bit, and the old rats knew it. We had rats in the trenches, too, and we used to stick bits of cheese on the end of the bayonet and when they came and nibbled the cheese we'd pull the trigger. Oh, we had our laughs. Do you know the colour that rotting horse turns? A sort of slimy blueygreen.'

She never covered her eyes or ears; she accepted whatever he had to tell her and still looked steadily back at him as though uncontaminated by his horrors. Their parents never knew. Her mother was relieved that Hetta's awkward desire to nurse was stilled by having Jamie to care for.

During the day she would wander exhausted over the summer hills, falling asleep with her face on her arm, waking up to find the scratchy heather embedded in her stockings and hair as the birds sang high up in the clear sky. She would plunge her arms into the ice-cold water of a lochan until her flesh vibrated from the chill, and then shake the freezing drops into the bright air. It was not a time when she could pray. She was angry with God for allowing such things. Nature became her church, the trees its pillars, the hills its altar. The sunsets were its stained-glass windows and the stars its candles. Submerging herself in the changeless calm of her surroundings, she would fall into a healing trance and go home to another night with Jamie.

A friend from school, a comrade of his called Roly, who had come through the same horrors, had been wounded but survived with all four limbs intact, came to pay him a visit. Only his mind was shattered. He watched the tall girl with grey-blue eyes and long, shining hair and wondered why the corners of her mouth trembled and why she narrowed her eyes when she looked at him. When he wanted to talk to Jamie alone she would not leave, saying, 'I have heard it all. Nothing you can say will shock me.' After a nod from Jamie he took her at her word, and she heard the familiar stories from another man's mouth. But when he began to talk about the two French girls they had rogered and she realized what that meant, she was shocked; she understood that there was even more frightfulness in this war than Jamie had told her, of a kind that she hadn't imagined, that could affect girls like herself; and that she too would have been corrupted and changed, as Jamie had been.

That evening at dinner Roly was placed beside her. She wore her hair down; they thought she was still a child. Nobody mentioned the war for fear of distressing her mother. But later they sat together on a sofa by the fire and he told her what a splendid chap Jamie was and how gallant, just as though she'd been any foolish, ignorant young sister. She looked directly into his eyes.

'Tomorrow I will take you out on the hills, Mr Graham, if you would like it,' she had said quietly, so as not to be overheard. 'My mother will not insist that anyone accompanies us. She is used to me wandering by myself. Then we will talk about my brother.'

The drawing-room carriage clock chimed ten. I will think about that another time, said Henrietta Birmingham to herself. She turned out the light that had shone down on Peggy Roberts' tapestry, and closed the door behind her.

Three

The first tidal excitement of the term mounted like a wave, crashing on the shores of Parents' Weekend. On the Saturday when they woke up it was raining. Those who lived nearby were collected by their parents and taken home to stay until Sunday evening, home with their dog or pony, sleeping in their own bedroom and eating their favourite meals. But those whose people lived far away had to choose between a picnic eaten in the car beneath dripping trees, or lunch in one of the local hotels, surrounded by other Raeburnians in clean striped dresses and newly polished sandals. They didn't clean their own shoes, of course, but laid them out in rows in the Covered Way to be polished by Waterman, the gardener, and collected them next morning.

Lunch at the hotel was an ordeal rather than a treat. The dining-room at the Spread Eagle was filled with girls and their parents, not separated by the usual hierarchies of age and form, but muddled together, so that you could find yourself at a table next to one of the seniors, and didn't know whether or not it was all right to treat her just like anyone else. However hard the girls tried to speak quietly, as a hint to parents to keep their voices down, it was impossible not to overhear neighbouring conversations. The anxious advice or pride of someone's else's mother unwittingly broadcast to the nearby tables would cause a child to cringe and blush with embarrassment. The well-meant heartiness of fathers was almost as bad.

'Working hard, old girl? Nose to the grindstone, eh? That's the stuff! Not too much athletics, if you ask me. Can't have you ruining your legs. Spot of tennis is fine, though.'

'But, Daddy, I'm in the house team.'

'Jolly good. Play up and play the game. Happiest years of your life.'

'Hum, hum, I don't think,' the child would mutter, for the benefit of those who could hear.

Everyone looked forward desperately to Parents' Weekend and it was always a disappointment. Once the holidays ended and the term began, parents and their children lived separate lives, and letters did little to bridge the gulf. They could not communicate their daily experience, except in meaningless clichés.

Charmian's mother had driven down from London with her friend in a low, shiny sports car, all scrolling curves and rich-smelling leather. Charmian and Sheila were squashed uncomfortably into the back as they drove first to the Post Office, at Charmian's insistence, to send off her parcel to Dr Barnado's Homes, before joining the lunch-time clamour at the Spread Eagle. Heads turned, Charmie noticed, as her mother walked in. In a clinging crêpe-de-chine dress, with the ends of her plump fur stole thrown carelessly across one shoulder, she was the best-looking mother in the dining-room, Charmian thought. Uncle Dickie looked proud of her too, pulling out a chair and settling her first, and then making an elaborate pantomime of doing the same for Charmian and Sheila.

'Have you got a nice part in the school play, darling, so we can all come and watch you?' asked Charmian's mother, fluffing up her own hair and then smoothing Charmian's down.

'She's the King of France's page,' said Sheila eagerly. 'She's on nearly all the way through.'

'Have you got a lot of lines to learn?' asked Fay Reynolds, addressing herself directly to her daughter, and ignoring her tiresome plain friend. She had hoped for the opportunity for a little chat. Now that the divorce was agreed, the time had come to drop a few hints.

'Why hasn't Daddy come too?' Charmian said.

'Well, now, young lady, your father's a very busy and important man, and he's got lots of things to do, so you'll have to put up with me instead,' Dickie said.

'Aren't *you* a very busy and important man, then?' said Charmian.

'Now, now...' began Dickie, but he was interrupted.

'Wasn't it sweet of Dickie to drive me down?' said Fay Reynolds to her scowling daughter.

'Oh, it *was*!' simpered Sheila.

'Waitress!' Dickie raised his hand and a girl in a black dress hurried over, fishing in her apron for a pad.

Across the other side of the room Constance had placed her knife and fork neatly together next to the fat and was talking to her parents in an urgent whisper, trying to get them to meet her eyes. Her parents thought fondly how smart she looked in her cotton frock and clean white socks, the straw hat with its blue hatband that showed she was in Drake House hanging over the back of her chair. What a good thing they'd got her into such a nice school, where she'd keep her English ways and make suitable little friends. Perhaps someone would invite her to stay next Easter holidays. She couldn't fly out to Kenya three times a year – it was too far and too expensive. An invitation from some nice girl in her form would be a weight off their minds.

'Daddy, you've got to *listen* to me – '

'*Got* to, Constance? I don't think I've *got* to listen to you.'

'I mean, *please* listen to me. It's no good Mummy keeping on just saying it's a beautiful school in the heart of the country if I don't like it.'

'Your mother and I decide what's best for you. Remember what I told you? If at first you don't succeed...'

'Try, try and try again,' said Constance, her voice as bored as she could risk sounding, since this was what her father always said.

'Right, Constance. Good. Now, you can have your say. What makes you think you don't like it?'

'I've been here a month now, so it's not as if I'm just homesick. But none of the other girls like me and nobody wants me to be their friend, and come to that I think some of them are awfully soppy, with their teddies and glass animals and all that, and kissing their mothers' pictures goodnight...'

'Oh, darling, do they really? I think that's rather touching,' said her mother.

'Well, I don't kiss *your* picture goodnight,' said Constance ungraciously. 'I don't see the point.'

'I expect you seem a bit stuck up,' said her father. 'Nose buried in a book, reading all the time.'

'What's wrong with reading?'

'It would be better if you joined in a bit more, tried to share their sort of hobbies and interests, instead of being snooty about them. Don't be such a chump, Constance. You're not the only pebble on the beach. School is about learning to muck in, to share and share alike. Teamwork and so on.'

'Collect postcards of the Royal Family, you mean, or china horses, or read soppy stories and swoon over Richard Todd and Jean Simmons and thingummy Peck – whatever those film stars are called. You hardly ever let me go to a film – '

'Darling, that's not true!' said her mother. 'You saw *Scott of the Antarctic*.'

'Not the sort of films *they* see, so I've no idea what they're talking about. I couldn't care less anyway. Oh, but that's not the point.'

'Darling, we're being very patient with you,' said her mother. 'We've driven all the way down here to visit you, even though we're off on Thursday and there's still a great deal to be done, because we wanted to see you happy and settled. It's too bad when all you do is complain.'

'Buck up now!' said her father. 'Shoulders back – big smile – remember the Brownie code? A Brownie is cheerful and does her best at all times. Try to remember that. It'll see you through.'

Constance shut her eyes and clenched her teeth and jaw and fists (I am a tree, I am a tree) and said in a passionate monotone, 'The point is, I'm not happy here and I never will be, because you'll be in Kenya and it'll all be too difficult to arrange from there and if you make me stay I'm going to be frightfully mis and I shall run away – oh, crumbs, it's all so *rotten*...'

She looked up. Her parents weren't looking at her, but at one another. Her mother was making an apologetic face and she caught her father's indulgent smile. Nothing, she saw, would make them change their minds.

'I've got a jolly good idea!' said her mother brightly. 'Let me have a word with the Simpson twins. I'll explain that you're not very happy and ask if one of them will be your friend, just to help you settle down. Hmm?'

'Good idea, Paula,' said her father heartily. 'Now: pudding for a growing girl. What's it to be? Ice-cream?

'I need to spend a penny,' said Constance. Abruptly, without asking their leave, she got up from the table. Straight-backed, Mowgli banished from the Council Rock, the little mermaid entering a strange element where every step was torture, she walked through the crowded hotel dining-room and went to the ladies'. She sat down on the lavatory and listened to the rain. A cheery line from *1066 and All That* sang in her head: 'Oh, we don't want to leave you, but we think we ought to go . . .' Her head and neck and shoulders were hunched forward until only the cracked tiles on the floor met her eyes, but still she could not cry.

Sylvia Parry and Diana Monk were making the most of Parents' Weekend. They'd spent the rainy Saturday morning marking prep books and now they had all Sunday free. The morning was as hazy and fresh as a watercolour. Straight after church they had driven down to Brighton in Sylvia's Austin Seven. There they had had lunch in a smoky, grubby café on the front and now dawdled bare-footed through the cold shingle on the beach, sandals swinging in their hands, gazing at the rhythmical greeny-grey swell of the sea. It rose and fell against the pebbles with a soft, steady furling and unfurling. Small children in ruched seersucker swim-suits ran shrieking after each retreating wave and scrambled back, shrieking louder, as the next wave rose up the beach and spent itself. Dogs bounced and yapped, leaping for driftwood and rushing back to have sticks flung again.

'Monsters,' said Sylvia. 'Look at them: all wet and mucky.'

'Dogs always get like that. They like it.'

'Not the dogs: the children. Now they're going to have tar

all over their hands and feet and some poor bloody woman has got to clean them up and listen to them whining all the way home. Or back to their miserable boarding-houses.'

'Did you ever want children?' asked Diana.

'Fat chance of that! No, thank God, I never did. I'm not that stupid. Don't tell me you did?'

'Not exactly. It wasn't until a couple of years ago that it dawned on me I wasn't very likely to have them. I think you take it for granted, when you're growing up, that you'll get married and have a family. I mean, most girls do. It's either that or be a spinster.'

'I never did. But then I knew all along I'd never marry, ever since I was about twelve, anyway.'

'You don't talk much about your childhood.'

'No bloody wonder. What do you want to know? I've told you we lived by the sea in Wales – the Gower Peninsula. Have you ever been there? It's beautiful, I'll give it that. There are wild ponies and rare birds and ruined castles and prehistoric stones. Best of all, miles and miles of beaches, and sort of moor and scrub where you could just walk all day without seeing hardly anyone. I miss that – being alone.'

'Sorry.'

'I didn't mean anything personal.'

'It sounds bliss.'

'The place was. I'm only talking about the place. The sea had buried villages and you could see the ruins at low tide. But as for the Welsh . . . tough, sentimental, Chapel . . .'

'Heaven.'

'No, definitely not heaven.'

They walked along in silence, their skirts swaying against their legs in the breeze, their bare arms goose-pimpled. The air was bitter with the ozone smell of the sea, and gulls cried plangently on the slant of the wind.

'Don't let's go back yet.'

Prayers on the Monday morning after a Parents' Weekend were always tricky. The school routine had been disturbed, some of the girls who'd gone home were now homesick all over again,

63

while the rest felt a sense of anticlimax. Mrs Birmingham had a couple of tiresome interviews with parents to brood over. The Cathcarts had given trouble with some tale of a lost (she heard the implication that it might have been stolen) photograph frame. Privately she blamed them for putting temptation in the way of the domestics by giving the child a solid-silver frame to take to school, but she had promised to investigate. Peggy would look into that – she was in charge of all the domestic arrangements – but she herself would need to make inquiries in case it could be one of the girls. Her mind ran over these necessary steps as her voice intoned the prayers. 'Give us Thy goodness and truth, O Lord. Make us pure in heart and honest in thought, word and deed. For Thy sake...' The school breathed a respectful 'Amen'.

Peggy Roberts scanned the Lower Fourth from under downcast eyelids. The King child's parents had said she was slow to settle down: could she be stealing? The Cathcarts were not absolutely sure that the frame *had* been stolen, but a silver frame was probably worth five or six pounds. She hated to have her cleaning staff accused. They were simple Swedish country girls, known by the school as 'the Scandies', and the last people she would suspect of dishonesty.

'You may go to your classes now,' said Mrs Birmingham. 'Michaela Simpson, will you come and see me during Break? Thank you, dear.' She smiled to show it was nothing unpleasant. No need for the girl to worry all morning. As she and Miss Roberts processed out of prayers she paused by Miss Valentine.

'Can you spare five minutes before your first lesson?' she murmured.

The three women sat in the Head's study. Beyond its closed door they could hear the clatter and squeak of the girls surging into their first class. Miss Valentine's usually cheerful face was anxious. The rumours and suspicions that buzzed covertly through the school and staff-room whenever there was a bout of thieving were dreadfully upsetting, and the recent incidents had been happening in her own form, the Lower Fourth. So far it was just the photograph frame, someone's leather writing-case and a fountain-pen that were missing. But you couldn't watch 120 girls every minute of the day; she couldn't even watch the twenty-three in her own form, and lockers, despite their name, were not locked. She ran through possible culprits in her head. Sheila Dunsford-Smith wasn't looking at all happy this term, though it was hard to associate her open face and stocky figure with ideas of deceit. Her friend Charmian was too stupid for the necessary subterfuge.

'What about the new girl, Constance?' the Head was asking.

'Constance King? A very intelligent child, but a bit of a loner. I'll keep an eye on her. Deborah Brewster looks a bit sly, though it's unfair to judge by appearances. She's another outsider.'

All three knew how difficult it would be to find a determined thief. The staff could threaten or hint that they knew the identity of the culprit and it would be best if she owned up. Then they could warn that the whole school would be punished unless the guilty child came forward, and this sometimes worked if she had confided in someone else. But if a girl had the wit to keep her mouth shut, they were powerless.

'There is, of course, no proof that the thief is a member of my class,' Miss Valentine added hopefully.

'No *proof*, no... Of course not. Well, for the time being I don't think we say anything publicly. It may all blow over. You might just ask Anne Hetherington whether she's found her pen yet.'

'Right. Well, the O levels will be waiting for me.'

When she had gone the Head and her Deputy looked at each other and sighed. Stealing, like poison-pen letters, was one of those adolescent crimes that broke out from time to time, but it was bad for the school's reputation and for their authority.

'Let's hope that pen turns up,' said Peggy Roberts.

When Mick emerged from the study during Break, Flick was waiting for her in the Reading Corner. Together they vanished through a side door and took the long way round back to their form-room.

'She swore me to secrecy,' said Mick.

65

'Cross my heart and hope to die.'

'Someone's stealing.'

'Well, we knew *that*. Stale buns. What else did they think had happened to the photo frame and writing-case and all that? Just vanished into thin air? But *who*?'

'Haven't the foggiest. They don't know either. They asked me if anyone had been' – she mimicked Mrs Birmingham's weighty, aristocratic voice – '"behaving in an unusual fashion".'

'In an *unusual* fashion? So you said, yes, everyone!'

'Shut up, Flick, don't be daft. It is serious, actually.'

Their sandals scrunched across the gravel. Secretly they were excited. This was a drama, and they were the first to know about it. Apart from the thief, of course.

'Old Ma B doesn't want me to say anything about it yet. Our best hope is to lie low and watch.'

'Who do *you* suppose it is?'

'Haven't a clue. Could be Gogs. She's in your dorm.'

'She's always writing secret letters after lights and things.'

'Well, watch her, OK? That's your job. Watch her. Who else? Has anybody got a grudge against Anne? Her pen's missing.'

'I thought she'd lost it.'

'Well, perhaps. Or perhaps someone's pinched it.'

'She's got a Parker 51. Like Gogs.'

'And hang on to all *our* things. I'll be livid if anything of ours gets pinched.'

The twins joined hands and ran back to their form-room, their short white socks flashing, their bunches bobbing stubbily.

The summer days became warmer, started earlier and ended later. The school settled into its disciplined routine and even Constance found herself adapting, despite herself, to the pattern of days divided into forty-minute sections. The teachers began to emerge from anonymity and assemble themselves as distinct figures, those she liked and those who liked her. They ceased to be merely 'grown-ups' among a crowd of hostile girls. In the first week of term she had learned to recognize their faces and put names to them, then to identify their handwriting, and finally she was able to anticipate what a lesson would be like – who was strict and made you sit still and keep quiet; who let you muck about; who gave generous marks and who jumped on every weeny mistake or untidiness. The English mistress, Miss Worthrop, was her favourite, and not just because she praised Constance's work and encouraged her to read. She suggested it was time to move on from animal classics and stories of happy families to more rewarding books like *Jane Eyre* and *Wuthering Heights*. Constance devoured these in greedy gulps.

'I envy you,' Miss Worthrop had said, 'reading *Jane Eyre* for the first time. Don't forget to tell me what you think of it.'

Serious but with shining eyes, Constance had told her.

'And did they write any other books?' she had asked.

'Quite a lot, yes. But you may find them a bit difficult for the time being.'

Constance, to prove her wrong, had started *The Professor*, and found that Miss Worthrop was right; the story seemed turgid by comparison. But it didn't stop her reading. She dived into books as though entering another world, one in which she could blot out her loneliness. She could forget her surroundings more easily in the pages of a book than in becoming a tree. Tree-ness was becoming harder to achieve. She was no longer simply instinctive, able to tune in to anything at will. Instead she browsed in the school library; she read *Pride and Prejudice*, *Sohrab and Rustum*, and *Salome*, as Miss Worthrop had recommended, but also the *Herries Chronicle* and Mazo de la Roche, *Peter Abelard* and Georgette Heyer, and *Green Dolphin Country* by Elizabeth Goudge, which she loved. She devoured them all, following them like pageants, incorporating them into her mental furniture. She no longer hung around the junior common-room, or bothered to go up to the pets' shed in the hope of being asked to join in a game. She spent her evenings sitting under, or in, a tree, looking up from her book to see wild rabbits venturing out in the early dusk or the seniors frowning over their mottled brown revision files as they crammed for their imminent exams.

From a perch above their heads she would hear snatches of conversation as people passed below: 'Promise you won't split?' and 'Cross your heart and hope to die and I'll tell you who *I* think...' She learned that she was a prime suspect for the thefts. This stung, for Constance had been brought up to be scrupulously honest, according to her father's old-fashioned code, and would no more have touched someone else's things than made an apple-pie bed – the trick that was played on her one evening. Too proud to complain, and unable to make a joke of it, she spent the night curled up in the top half of her bed, cramped and uncomfortable, but with the satisfaction of knowing that the girls who had done it derived no pleasure from her humiliation. 'Spoil-sport,' someone muttered, but Constance knew it was one up to her.

The books saved her from the misery which had smothered her first three weeks at school. In fact, to her surprise, she found that it was easier once her parents and Stella had left for Kenya, extinguishing the last small hope that she might somehow, miraculously, go with them after all. It even made the loss of her pen easier. The knowledge that her mother wouldn't hear about it for weeks was better than having to confess within days. Constance said nothing, just in case it should somehow turn up in her desk, her locker, or blazer pocket, though she had searched them all.

It had still not turned up when the Head summoned her.

'Ah, yes, Constance King,' said Mrs Birmingham as Constance entered and sat down nervously on the far side of her imposing desk.

'You've made a very good start, my dear, and your teachers are very satisfied with your work. Well done. You seem to be settling in.'

'Yes,' said Constance, for it was true.

'Let's see... English, history and geography seem to be your best subjects. Maths not so good, Latin not bad, considering you've never done it before. Biology not so good. Art...'

'I'm hopeless at art,' said Constance. 'I can't draw for toffee.'

'Well, if you can't draw pictures you'll have to learn to write vividly, won't you? I expect you'll manage that. You seem to be good with words. But you ought to do something creative with your hands. There's needlework, or dressmaking, or ... would you like to take up pottery?'

'Yes,' said Constance. She had looked through the windows of the pottery hut and seen girls with squelchy worms of wet clay oozing through their fingers, and it looked fun. She'd seen their absorbed expressions. Yes, she'd like to have a go at that.

'Now, games. Good at athletics, not good at team games. Why's that?'

'I don't know,' said Constance. 'I've never played rounders before. Or tennis. But I like swimming.'

'I should hope so too,' said Mrs Birmingham. She smiled. 'Everyone likes swimming. Now, what about your parents?'

Constance, startled, drew down the shutters.

'They're all right.'

'I'm sure they are. What about you? Still homesick?'

'I'm all right,' said Constance, adding unexpectedly, 'I've lost my pen. I'm dreading telling them. They're going to be absolutely livid.'

' "Livid" is a much misused word. Its dictionary definition is dark blue, purplish. A bruise is livid. Do you mean your parents will be angry?'

'Furious,' said Constance. 'It was fearfully expensive.'

'I'm sure they won't be furious. Perhaps it wasn't your fault.'

'Last Monday I couldn't find it, but I know it was in my pencil-box on Sunday because I used it to write home. It must have gone after that, and I've looked everywhere.'

'I'm sure you have, dear. Keep your fingers crossed that it'll turn up. Have you tried looking in the confiscation cupboard?'

'No.'

'Well, then. Now, what about friends? Have you made friends?'

'Not really. Sort of, a bit, with Rachel and Jennifer. They're jolly decent to me but they're friends with each other. They don't need me.'

'Nonsense. We all need friends. "No man is an island, com-

69

plete unto himself." You wouldn't know who wrote that?'

'No.'

'John Donne. A very great poet and preacher of the seventeenth century. You'll enjoy reading him one day. I think you'll find poetry a friend.'

'I do already.'

Mrs Birmingham looked up, and saw that the child was serious.

'Good. Try Browning. Not Elizabeth Barrett. Robert. Look up a poem that begins, "Grr, there go, my heart's abhorrence! Water your damned flower pots, do!"'

'Didn't he write "The Pied Piper of Hamelin"?'

'Good *girl*. That's right. This is a few steps on from that. Run along to the library now, and look it up before you forget. We'll have another chat in a few weeks' time.'

As the door closed behind Constance, Miss Roberts said, 'Another pen missing?'

'Yes. She hasn't lost it, poor little mite. It's been taken. So have a silver photograph frame, a leather writing-case, another pen, half-a-dozen glass animals, and a ten-shilling note pinned inside a birthday card.'

'Will you talk to the school?'

'I suppose it's time I did.' Mrs Birmingham sighed heavily. 'There's always one rotten apple.'

'She's a clever child, Constance King. She'll be a credit to the school one day. Pity she's not getting on with the Lower Fourth.'

'Well, she is a bit of an odd-bod. What can I do, Peggy? I can't possibly move her down, but I can't put her up with the fourteen-year-olds, either. She'll just have to find her level. Shame about her pen – but a bit of a relief as well. It means she is unlikely to be the thief.'

'That seemed unlikely anyway.'

'You're right, though. It's time to talk to the school.' *Dear God*, prayed Henrietta, *show me Thy wisdom, give me an understanding of the hearts and minds of others. Fill this my school with Thy goodness...*

*

70

'Fill this Thy school with Thy goodness and fellowship, that it may be an example of a Christian community to all who live and serve within it. For the sake of Thy son, our Lord Jesus Christ . . .'

'Amen,' intoned the school.

Once they had left the common-room, teachers and girls, safe from being overheard by one another in form-room or staff-room, began to speculate.

'Poor girls,' said Miss Worthrop. 'It's horrid when everybody's under suspicion. They all looked guilty.'

'If you ask me, it's Charmian Reynolds,' said Sylvia.

'We've got absolutely *no* evidence about anyone so far. Let's try and remain fair and open-minded,' said Miss Valentine. She hated her own form being under suspicion and privately thought Charmian far too vapid to carry out a series of thefts. 'You are only accusing Charmian Reynolds because you don't like her.'

'That's untrue and uncalled for. I think you should withdraw that remark,' said Sylvia.

'Withdraw, withdraw. There goes the bell. Into the fray, everyone!'

Waiting for the first lesson, the girls buzzed with drama and outrage.

'No sweets for anyone!' said Fiona. 'Gosh, I think that's a swizz.'

'Me too,' said fat Rachel.

'Won't do *you* any harm,' said Charmian.

'Mean pig,' said Jennifer.

'*My* pen's gone too,' ventured Constance, admitting it for the first time.

'Are you sure?' said Flick, nastily.

'Of course I'm sure.'

'OK, OK, keep your hair on. Hey, quick, shut up everyone, here comes Batey Parry!'

'What do you make of this?' asked Henrietta Birmingham, passing a letter across to her Deputy. Peggy read the letter rapidly: ' "Deeply distressing time for all of us . . . despite our best efforts ... forced to the conclusion ... fear I must ask you to break the news to poor Charmian... bound to be terribly upset at first ... probably best if she can spend half-term with a friend to help her get over the shock ... sending her to my sister for the summer... Yours sorrowfully" – Sorrowfully! She's got a nerve! "Fay Reynolds." '

'What are *we* supposed to do about it? It's not Charmian I'd like to talk to, it's her mother!' said Henrietta.

'That goes for many of the parents,' said Peggy Roberts. 'There's several I wouldn't mind having a word with. Paying off guilty consciences or just plain indifference by sending their daughters here. And then they tell them they aren't really homesick and furthermore how *lucky* they are.'

'They are lucky, in many ways,' said Henrietta. 'When I think of my own education ... crumbs from my brothers' table.'

'Will you break the news to Charmian?'

'It looks as though I shall have to. I'll think about how best to do it for a day or two first.'

'You don't think she could be stealing, as a reaction to what's going on at home?'

'How could she? She doesn't even know about it yet. No, she may be a silly child, but I don't think she's a wicked one. Much more likely to be one of the lonely or unpopular ones.'

'Sheila?'

'Could be. Who knows? It could be almost anyone. Well, I must tidy myself up. I'm expecting a couple of prospective parents in ten minutes.'

Constance had finished her prep ahead of everyone else and gone to sit in the tiny library, where she knew she could be sure of being alone for twenty minutes before the supper bell rang. She had discovered *The Rubáiyát of Omar Khayyám* on the shelves, drawn by its exotic title (what *was* a Rubaiyat?), and was entranced by its lush and sensuous language. 'And Wilderness is Paradise enow...' *Enow*: somehow it's far more mysterious than enough. At table you've had enough, but enow... I'll never have enow.

Why, she thought, *why* is everyone happy except me? How do they do it? They giggle and chat and muck about. They do things together – pets and gardening and things – and they all sort of belong, all except me. Why is it so hard to be happy? She remembered the simple, light-hearted time when she was living at home and going to the school up the road, when she too had skipped and played and joined in. During special treats with Mummy and Daddy, when it was all too wonderful for her to take another breath, she used to shut her eyes and try to blank out for minutes on end, thinking, I'll store this; I won't enjoy it now, I'll put it away for later, when I need it.

Now, she tried to summon up those stored moments – at the circus, or on Christmas Eve after she'd heard her father tiptoe in with the fat, crackling stocking and pin it to the end of her bed; or when her parents were playing tennis with friends and she was ballboy and her father had said 'Well *done*, Constance! You *are* a good ballboy!' She'd wanted to burst with pride at hearing him say it in front of everyone. Sitting on the floor, an open book on her knees, she twined her arms round herself, put her head down and shut her eyes, breathing deeply to bring back those precious, stored moments. Nothing came.

'Well *done* Constance!' she whispered, trying to recapture Daddy's voice. 'Well *done*, Constance!' but it was her own whisper she heard inside her head. The lovely moment was gone. Her bottom was cold on the stone floor and the book was sharp against her cheek and no happiness came flooding back.

Someone was running down the stairs. Into the library, light and airy, all trailing tendrils and swinging skirt, came Hermione. She stopped when she saw Constance.

'Gosh, you do look mis, poor old sausage. Cheer up! What's the matter?' she asked.

'Sorry – aren't I meant to be here?' said Constance.

'I've no idea. I don't know who you are, but so long as you're not a squit you're allowed to be in here. Anyhow until the bell goes.'

'I'm not a squit, I'm in the Lower Fourth. I'm Gogs,' said Constance.

'Poor you.'

'Well, I'm Constance King really, but they call me Gogs.'

'Never mind; they call *me* Hermy-One.'

'I know,' said Constance, not daring to add, 'Do you mind your nickname?'

'Oh, gosh, I haven't a clue where the soppy old poetry books are,' said Hermione, with an appealing air of helplessness. 'I can't think why Miss Worthrop sent *me*. I'm the last person who'd know.'

'Here,' said Constance. 'Are you looking for anyone special?'

'Michael Arnold? Malcolm Arnold? Arnold somebody-or-other.'

'Matthew. Here.'

'I say, well *done*, Constance!' And Hermione smiled her careless, magic smile as she pranced out.

'Her*mi*one' murmured Constance to herself, pronouncing it right. Not Hermy-One! How wonderful she is, how kind and lovely. I shan't tell anyone. Her*mi*one.

Opening the door of the staff-room on her way to marshal the supper queues in the Covered Way, Sylvia Parry was rewarded by the sight of Hermione Malling-Smith cantering along the corridor towards her. She is like a young racehorse, thought Sylvia; her beauty compels devotion, it is so perfectly appropriate.

'Sorry, Miss Parry,' said Hermione, slowing to a walk and flashing a perfect smile as she passed.

Is it possible for people to be happy? wondered Sylvia. Suppose my wildest dreams were realized and that beautiful creature belonged to me, would I be happy? No, because in my dreams I want her to love me and me only, for ever; to live with me and cherish me; to depend on me and cleave only unto me, as long as we both shall live. She stood motionless in the corridor as other girls hurried past. Well, all right, if *that* happened, would I be happy? Yes, but I have designed for myself an impossible happiness, in which there is no secrecy, no jealousy, no change, no boredom: just an eternity of loving

Hermione. It is impossible. Other people can be happy, but not me.

She began to walk slowly towards the queues lined up for supper, their high-pitched hum of talk and giggles muted by her arrival.

'Silence!' she shouted at the top of her voice, entering the Covered Way. 'The next person to speak has an order mark. I want total, complete and utter silence until the bell goes. Is that quite clear?'

Under their breath, one or two girls muttered, 'Batey-*batey*!' or, 'OK, OK, keep your hair on . . .' but fortunately Miss Parry didn't hear them.

Mrs Birmingham, after a difficult and tearful half-hour with Charmian, told the child to go to Matron and say she'd been sent to lie down. Matron had been warned of this possibility and would, she knew, give her a 'tonic' to make her drowsy. Best to sleep off the immediate effects of a catastrophe.

Why do people expect to be happy? wondered Henrietta. Why should that flighty, fading little woman, Charmian's mother, believe she has any right to happiness? How dare she send her daughter adrift, distress her husband, abandon her home and ensnare another man, in the belief that she has any entitlement to happiness? They have everything, these women – husbands, children (how many of my generation missed out on *those*?), wealth, comfort, attention; and in spite of all that they are bone idle and mindlessly greedy. With their fastidiously painted finger-nails they constantly reach out for more.

Happiness is not our lot in life. Love of God and our neighbours, being true to our word, doing our duty, *that* is our lot. Happiness has nothing to do with it. Was my beloved brother Jamie ever happy? No. Or my parents, with half a son left out of three? No. Is Lionel happy? No, alas. James . . . ? *O dear God, let my son James be happy, of Thy goodness and mercy I pray Thee. Not for myself I ask it, but of Thine own great love for Thy son.*

Have I ever been happy, she wondered, other than through my brother Jamie, for such a little time when we were children together, and for a long time now through my son James?

Certainly I was not happy as a young girl. That day on the hills with Roly. Blot out the images, Henrietta, blot them out. Such a gentle, companionable beginning, as she had shown Roly her favourite walk to the still, shining lochan near the top of Ben Mor. They had walked easily together while he told her about his long friendship with Jamie – for they had met and become friends in their very first half at Eton. Then he had reminisced about triumphs on the cricket field, long reading holidays, mutual discoveries of Lucullus, Ovid and Donne, of Macaulay, Browning and a poet she'd never heard of then, called Gerard Manley Hopkins. He had walked and quoted and she had walked and listened until, with the sun high and hot, they had stopped to eat their picnic in the shade.

Cook had packed cold chicken and cold beef, fruit pie and a bottle of father's good claret. Henrietta drank water, watching Roly with the wine bottle tipped to his mouth, his lips squashed around it, his throat swallowing strongly. He smiled at her, then settled himself down into the heather saying, 'Will you be all right if I sleep for a little – half an hour – before we go on?' She sat a little distance apart from him, watching the hawks circling lazily high up in the sky as they waited for some unwary small animal to betray its presence as it scuttled hundreds of feet below. Insects buzzed and twittered, but otherwise there was a great stillness all around. She could see deer on the opposite hillside, grazing and lifting their heads and dropping them to graze again. She herself was not drowsy but alert, for once full of serene thoughts about Jamie's brilliant schooldays. At least he'd had that, she thought; he has good memories, too. Her heart, which had been hard as marble, warmed for the first time in weeks to a sort of passive restlessness that could not be called happiness, but was not icy either. She could not understand herself, but she saw a glimmer that promised light and warmth one day, and maybe even fire – not the fire that in her dream had annihilated Jamie, but a thrilling, life-giving fire. She looked towards Roly, to see if he still slept.

He was not asleep, but looking at her.

'Come here, Henrietta,' he said, his voice very steady and neutral. He sat up. 'Come here.'

'Shall we go on?' she said. 'It's another good hour if you want to look at the view from the top.'

'How does a girl like you, a sheltered young miss who hasn't yet put her hair up or her skirts down, a gently reared, devout girl, know about rogering? *What* do you know?'

She was afraid. Men should not say such things, no, nor do them.

'I heard the word yesterday for the first time. I didn't understand at first. Mr Graham, shall we go on? Or shall we at least talk about something else?'

'Henrietta, whatever is the matter? Why are you frowning like that? My dear, are you all right?' asked Peggy Roberts.

'Why,' said Henrietta Birmingham slowly, 'why do people expect to be happy?'

Four

'... Eleven ... twelve ... thirteen ... FOURTEEN!'

On the last count Fiona Cathcart, still in her pyjamas, flew into the air, tossed upwards by the energetically heaving arms of the four girls who were giving her birthday bumps. She landed in a heap on her bed as the others in her dormitory began to sing, their excitement overtaken by the almost dignified clarity of their strong, sweet voices:

> 'Happy Birthday to you,
> Happy Birthday to you,
> Happy Birthday dear Feeny,
> Happy Birthday to you!'

Then they clapped and gave the ritual call for 'Speech!' Fiona stood up on her bed and, grinning with joy and embarrassment, was just starting off, 'Friends, Romans, country – I mean, fellow members of Starlings...' when the door opened and Miss Peachey walked in.

'I know,' she said, to their cries of protest. 'I know perfectly well that it's Fiona's birthday – many happy returns of the day, dear – but that's no excuse for you all to be late down to breakfast. No she may *not*, Charmian, she can open her cards later. Now then, there's only five minutes to the bell: get a move on, all of you!'

At eleven o'clock when the bell rang for Break, half the form ran to the Covered Way with Fiona to look for her name on the parcels list. Birthday presents were always held back until the actual day, even if they'd arrived earlier, so she had the satisfaction of seeing Fiona Cathcart (5) on the list for everyone to read. She and Anne Hetherington collected her parcels together and put them up in the dormitory, to be opened during Rest. It was generally considered better to wait, even though you didn't see your birthday presents till two o'clock; but it meant you enjoyed the luxury of anticipation, and of being able to unwrap them slowly.

While they were upstairs, Constance was opening a letter. She didn't know the writing on the envelope, nor was the postmark familiar, so she turned it over for a while, savouring the mystery. Inside she found a letter from Mrs Simpson, the twins' mother, inviting her to spend half-term with them. She pushed the straw through the hole punched in the cardboard milk bottle top and sucked as she read.

'Your Mother tells me you've taken to the school like a duck to water and I'm sure the twins will be glad to have someone to play with over half-term,' wrote kind, misguided Mrs Simpson. 'You'll find us pretty dull I expect – don't pitch your hopes too high! I'll drive down and collect the three of you on Friday at lunch-time. Don't worry! I won't be late!'

Constance looked around for Mick and Flick in case they'd had a letter by the same post, but they were whispering together with Deborah, empty-handed. Her face and shoulders sagged, but she knew it was best to get it over with, so she walked across to them. They looked at her with closed expressions.

'What d'you want?' said Flick.

'Nothing. Sorry. Well, actually it's just that your mother's been smashing and she's, um, invited me to spend half-term with you.'

'Oh, super,' said Mick, flatly.

'How jolly dee,' said Flick.

'Yes, um, thanks very much. It's terrifically kind of her . . . of you.'

'Not *us*. First I've heard of it,' said Flick.

'I say, hard *luck*, old beans,' Constance heard Deborah say as she walked off. 'What a mouldy rotten chiz. Your half-term too . . .'

The bell rang, piercingly imperious in the confined space of the Covered Way, and everyone began to move towards their form-rooms, some dawdling with their heads still bent over a letter, others in cheerful groups. Sheila and Charmian walked together, Charmie jiggling impatiently, Sheila flat-footed and solemn. Hermione came running lightly down from the music rooms, her smile like a flag waving its impartial brilliance. Charmie and Sheila straightened up and walked on with self-conscious deportment, turning to each other with excited whispers as soon as she had passed.

'Hello, Hermione,' said Constance, shyly, as Hermione drew level.

'Oh . . . er – h'llo.' And the beautiful smile flashed again.

Oh, gosh, she is terrific, thought Constance, and forgot Mrs Simpson's troublesome invitation.

'I feel sick,' said Charmian, staring at her untouched pudding. Her cheeks were bloodless but her eyes glittered as though reflecting candlelight. 'Please, Miss Monk, I think I'm going to be sick.'

'You don't look very well, dear. Do you want to leave the table?'

Charmian gulped, nodded and looked appealingly at Sheila. Miss Monk, who had heard about the Reynolds divorce at the latest staff meeting, had been expecting something like this.

'You go with her, Sheila,' she said kindly.

As soon as they had made their conspicuous exit from the dining-room, Charmian said, 'Quick, the lavs! Run!' But when they got there, she wasn't sick at all. She kicked open the lavatory doors one by one to make sure they were empty and dragged Sheila after her into the changing-room next door, where rows of blazers hung from row of pegs and beneath them rows of shoes nestled in individual wooden lockers. She pulled Sheila into a corner where the two of them were hidden behind long green capes and there, smothered in a thick darkness that smelt of wool and gym shoes, she said, 'Sheila I'm in trouble. You've got to help me.'

'What on earth's wrong? I thought you wanted to be sick.'

'Much, much worse than that. I do feel sick in a way but not like you think. Cross your heart and hope to die you promise not to split on me?'

'Cross my heart and hope to die.'

'Swear on your mother's life you'll never ever tell?'

With sinking heart Sheila repeated solemnly, 'I swear on my mother's life.'

In the enveloping darkness Charmian put her arms round Sheila and whispered hotly into her ear: 'It's me, Sheil. *I* took the things. It's me that's the thief. And what's more, I ran up to the dorm today just before lunch to pinch one of Feeny's parcels – I don't know why! I just did! – and as I was coming out with it stuffed into my knickers Peachey saw me. She asked what I was doing so I said I'd come to get a hanky. So then I went into the bathroom and pretended to wash my face and when she'd gone away I hid the parcel in my sponge-bag. And now Feeny'll notice and I'm terrified there'll be a search. Sheila, you've *got* to help me. How can I get rid of it? What if I'm caught? Oh, I wish my mummy was here!'

Charmian began to cry, and Sheila held her steadily while she tried to be calm and grown-up, to think clearly and responsibly about what was the right thing to do.

'Why don't you just run up now – there'll be nobody about, they're all in lunch – and put it back?' she suggested. 'Or I will, if you like.'

'No!' said Charmian with amazing vehemence.

'OK, OK, keep your hair on, I'm only trying to help. Now listen, shut up crying and let me think. Look, all right, this is what I'll do. I'll go and get it from your sponge-bag. I'll hide it somewhere else – I don't know where, I'll think of somewhere – while you go back in. Rinse your mouth with soap or something first so they'll all think you've been sick, and then I'll come in after you and say I had to clean up the aunt.'

'Okey-dokey. Good idea. Gosh, thanks, Sheil! You are a sport.'

'Count up to fifty while you wash your face, to give me time . . .'

Sheila ran up the back stairs, her legs trembling. Two flights up – Starlings' bathroom – Charmie's sponge-bag. There it was: a neat, rectangular parcel, criss-crossed with string and sealed with a blob of red sealing wax. She grasped it, zipped up the sponge-bag, rearranged the towel over it, and stood stock-still on the slatted boards of the bathroom, trembling with fear and indecision. Why didn't she just put it back? That wouldn't be breaking her promise to Charmie, and no one would ever know what had happened. She remembered Charmie's passionate '*No!*' and her mind raced on. At the darkest end of the corridor, high up on the wall, was a wooden box with the electric fuses. It was locked, but there was a narrow gap on top between the box and the ceiling. Sheila grabbed a chair from the end of her bed, ran into the corridor, stood on the chair, pushed the parcel in as far as it would go, put her chair back and then forced herself to wash her hands and walk slowly and deliberately downstairs back into the dining-room.

Lunch had just finished, and chairs scraped as the school stood up for grace. 'For what we have received may the Lord make us truly thankful,' piped one of the squits and the school sighed, 'Amen'.

In the dormitory after lunch, puzzlement turned into disbelief, then accusations, denials, threats and finally tears, before Fiona settled down to open her remaining four presents. When the bell rang for games, the members of Starlings dispersed with new suspicions. Constance, knowing herself to be shunned, left the dormitory first. Let them talk about me behind my back, see if I care, she thought mutinously.

On their way to the changing-room before swimming, Charmian whispered fiercely to Sheila, 'What did you do with it?'

'Don't worry,' said Sheila soothingly. 'It's quite safe for the moment. No one'll find it.'

'Well done you!' said Charmian admiringly. 'So where did you hide it?'

'You know that box thing in the corridor, where all the electricity goes? On top of that.'

'Good for you! Whoof!' She heaved a deep sigh of relief, and Sheila was glad that she'd been able to help her troubled friend.

'Now look here,' Charmian went on, 'I've got to talk to you!

Make an excuse to get out of swimming and I will too. We'll meet behind the pets' shed. Come on, Sheil, you've got to! You promised!'

For Charmian, subterfuge was simple: not only because she lied fluently, but also because the staff had been advised to go easy on her. Sheila, however, was obliged to tell Mrs Whitby, the games mistress, that she was 'off' games, with that special look and emphasis that indicated she had the curse; and since it was not an excuse she had ever used before – she didn't yet have the curse – the lie was compounded by Mrs Whitby's kindly inquiries as to whether she 'knew what to do' and assurances that she needn't worry, it was perfectly normal and just showed she was a big girl now. Sheila then had to make her way to Sister's room and request a packet of STs (furthermore, she knew she would have to try to remember to ask for them every month from now on) before finally racing up to the pets' shed, where she found Charmian cuddling their wide-eyed, palpitating rabbit.

'Oh, what a tangled web we weave . . .' began Sheila, for that was what her father used to say when he caught her out in a fib.

'You're barmy,' said Charmian. 'I haven't the foggiest what you mean.'

'Oh, forget it. Doesn't matter anyway. Though you might at least be nice to me, after all I've been through for you. Now listen, honestly, Charmie, you've got to tell everything.'

'I told you. It was me. I took the things.'

'What, all of them? The Parker pens and everything?'

'And the photograph frame. And the ten-bob note. And Fatty's writing-case,' said Charmie smugly.

'You must be stark raving bonkers. Whatever for?'

'To send to Dr Barnardo's. For the orphans.'

'For what?'

'You know. Orphans. Poor children with no mothers and fathers.'

Charmian began to cry, clutching the rabbit tightly. It trembled in her arms, its long transparent ears flat against its back.

'Oh, Charmie, for heaven's sake don't cry. Look, we'll sort

it all out. Tell you what, *I'll* go to Old Ma B and own up. I'll say it was me that took the things and give them back, and the worst she can do is give me a stripe and I don't care.'

'You can't,' sobbed Charmian.

' 'Course I can. Where are they? I mean apart from Feeny's parcel.'

'I told you. I sent them to Dr Barnardo's.'

'To Dr Barnardo's? Posted them? *How?*'

'Simple. Easy as pie. The first lot I posted on Parents' Weekend and I waylaid the postman with the rest and gave them to him.'

'Well, then I'll take the parcel and make up something about the others.'

'I've already gone and got the parcel. That's why I asked where you'd hidden it.' She grinned.

'Charmie! You really are – well, I'm sorry to hurt your feelings and so on, but I think you're *wicked*. What've you done with it?'

'I'm not telling.'

Charmie's fair hair fell across the soft grey-and-white fur of the rabbit. They were both trembling now, and Charmian began to cry again. Sheila stroked her friend awkwardly and after a while Charmie shuddered and looked up. She fished a letter out of her pocket with her spare hand.

'Anyway the stealing's nothing. I couldn't care less about the stupid old things. Here. Go on, you read this.'

The letter was in such extravagantly looping handwriting that Sheila couldn't decipher it, so she handed it back and said, 'You'll have to read it to me, I can't. I haven't got a hanky. Do you want a dock leaf?'

Charmian wiped her nose and dried her eyes on the leaf, pushed her fringe back from her forehead and read her mother's letter aloud, pausing from time to time to utter a great gasping sob:

'My own bestest little girl,
    I'm afraid this is going to be a terribly difficult letter for Mummy to write 'cos she's got very bad news for you

84

and she wants you to promise to be brave and sensible and a really big grown-up girl. I expect the Headmistress has had a word with you already, so perhaps you know that Daddy and I don't feel we can go on being married any more. You remember nice Uncle Dickie who drove me down last Parents' Weekend, don't you? He liked you so much. Well, when this beastly divorce...'

Sheila gasped. '*Divorce?*'
'Yes, divorce, OK? Now be quiet and let me go on reading.

'When this beastly divorce is all over, Uncle Dickie and I are going to get married, and of course you'll come and live with us. I wouldn't lose my little girl for anything in the world. I know it must all seem like a dreadful shock to you just now, darling, but I promise you it'll be all right in the end and everyone will be much happier. You and me and Uncle Dickie will have such *fun* together, poppet! If you want to go on seeing your father we shall have to try to work something out for you, and if you decide it would all be too upsetting then Mummy will quite understand. One day you might even be able to think of Uncle Dickie as your Daddy! Poor baby. I wish I was there to give you a great big hug and make it all better.

Meanwhile I think it's probably best if you spend half-term with Auntie Barbara, don't you? One last thing my pet, don't talk about this. Anyway, I don't suppose you feel like it much. Remember I shall be thinking of you specially just now with bestest mostest love blah blah blah from your Mummy.'

'See?' said Charmian triumphantly. '*Now* you know why I couldn't care less about the stealing.'
'Oh, Charmie, you poor, poor thing,' said Sheila fervently. 'I'm most dreadfully sorry.' She had heard her mother say that and it always sounded as though she'd dragged it up from the bottom of her heart.
'No need for *you* to sound so pleased with yourself,' Charmian sneered.

'Why? What makes you say that? I think that's really foul.'

'Grown-ups do slushy, soppy things to each other in bed at night when they're married and if they sleep in different beds it means they don't want to do those things any more, and you said once that *your* parents don't sleep in one bed, so they'll have to get divorced too.'

'You're making it up. I bet you haven't got the foggiest clue. Anyway, let's change the subject. I'm frightfully sorry about your parents and all that, but we ought to think of what to do with Feeny's present. I bet someone's been to Old Ma B about it by now.'

'They do dirty things to each other underneath the blankets, and then the lady has a baby.'

Sheila's sex education was non-existent. If she gave the matter any thought, she assumed babies came out of their mothers' tummy-buttons. It made her feel squeamish to think about it, and she hadn't cared to speculate about what went on between grown-ups. Once last term, one of the girls in the dormitory had been persuaded, after mock hesitation, to sing a song called 'Mademoiselle d'Armentières' and Sheila had cringed with shame at the words. Some girls had giggled knowingly, but most of them had been embarrassed and rather disapproving, and the song had never been sung again. It sounded disgusting. Was that what grown-ups did to each other underneath the bedclothes? No wonder her mother wanted a bed to herself.

'I don't believe you. You're making it up.'

'What a baby you are! You don't know *any*thing. Mummy's little baba. Bye baby bunting...' Charmie chanted mockingly. 'Your father and mother must have done it too or you wouldn't be here.'

'Oh, do shut up. I don't like talking about it,' said Sheila, primly.

'You've gone all red.'

'I haven't.'

'Yes you have. Bright red. You're blushing, la la la-*la* la, Sheil's blushing, 'cos she's embarrassed,' said Charmian in a sing-song voice.

'Charmian, you're being a really mean pig and if you won't talk about Feeny's parcel, I shall go away and leave you on your own. Then *you* can jolly well sort it out.'

'I won't be on my own. I've got Flopsy.'

'I'll go and tell Miss Valentine.'

'You wouldn't. You promised! You swore solemnly on your mother's life that you wouldn't.'

'That was before I knew what you were going to say. I wouldn't have sworn if I'd known. Anyhow I take it back.'

'If you take it back, then it'll mean something awful's going to happen. Your mother'll die or your parents will get divorced like mine,' said Charmian, her eyes hard as little pebbles.

Sheila's face drained, leaving it as white as milk. Charmian grinned defiantly. 'There! That shut you up!'

'Charmian Reynolds, that's a wicked thing to say. You ought to be ashamed.'

'Says who?' said Charmian. 'Fat lot of good you are, when I tell you all my secrets. You're supposed to be my friend. You're the one that ought to be ashamed. Oh, yuk! How foul! The rabbit's done a poo on me!'

She jumped up, grabbing the rabbit by its ears, and ran into the pets' shed. A moment later she emerged and raced off towards the swimming-pool, her pony-tail swinging: a carefree, pretty child.

Sheila stayed where she was, unmoving, turned to salt. Impossible to believe that this very morning she'd been throwing Fiona up in the air to give her birthday bumpsies, and now... Now she was in Charmian's power because of that frightful threat, and only by keeping her secret could she prevent it from coming true. She put her head on her knees, clasped her arms over her head and wept, to the faint background noise of high-pitched shrieks from the swimming-pool.

After a while she heard the bell ring, far and sweet, signalling the end of games. She waited till all the voices from the tennis courts and the swimming-pool had receded. Then she got up, shook her legs because she'd got cramp, and walked down the hill towards the form-rooms. She looked into the swimming-pool as she passed. The water was still lapping gently against

87

the side from the movement of the last bodies that had scrambled out, dripping and glistening. In the middle of the pool a bee was buzzing frantically, turning in a desperate circle that grew slower and slower. Sheila stopped and watched it. When at last it floated motionless on the still surface of the pool she walked away.

At half past five the bell rang for the end of prep. Miss Valentine stood up and raised her hand, interrupting the slamming of books and desk tops and the murmurs of 'Will you hear my French vocab?' and 'Does anyone know why Sheil's in a foul mood?' which would erupt into cacophony the moment she left the room.

'Girls!' she said. 'I want to hold a form meeting. Yes, now. Stay in your places everyone, please, and Michaela, will you come up and stand here. Now then. As you all know someone, probably in this class, is stealing. This affects every one of us, and is something that I, personally, feel deeply ashamed about. You have been a good and happy form so far this year, and I have been proud of you. It makes me very sad' (Mick lowered her eyes and looked sad too) 'that my form should be the centre of suspicion and, probably, wrong-doing. Now then, I have Mrs Birmingham's word that if we can sort it out between ourselves, if the culprit will own up, then whoever she is (or it may be more than one person), she will be punished privately and nothing more will be said. This is your last chance to clear things up. Otherwise I'm afraid it may end in someone being expelled.'

She paused to let the full weight of this sink in.

'Michaela, is there anything you would like to add?'

'No, Miss Valentine,' said Mick, nervous and self-important. 'Except that I feel awfully ashamed too and so please, whoever you are, do own up.'

'Right. Now then, I'm going to go round the form asking each of you two questions in turn. Do you know anything at all about this stealing? And is there anything you would like to tell me in private? All right? Good. I'll start with you

Madeleine, since you're at the front: do you know anything at all about these thefts?'

'No, Miss Valentine, honestly.'

'Is there anything you'd perhaps like to say to me in private?'

'Umm, no, thank you, I don't think so.'

'You're on your *honour* all of you: remember that. Next. Deborah?'

Round the desks she went: the front row, the second row. Fiona Cathcart thought she might like to have a private word with Miss Valentine – it was easy for her, *she* obviously wasn't the thief – and so did Anne Hetherington.

'Sucking up,' mouthed Fiona silently.

Next row. 'Charmian Reynolds? What about you, dear? Is there anything you know? Anything you'd like to tell me?'

'No, Miss Valentine . . . except, oh, gosh, it's all so *rotten!*'

'I'm sure every single one of us feels that, Charmian,' said Miss Valentine, kindly. Poor child, she had enough on her plate already.

'Sheila Dunsford-Smith? Do you know anything, anything at all about the stealing? Or is there perhaps something you'd like to discuss with me alone, just the two of us?'

Charmian turned her wide blue gaze sympathetically upon Sheila. There was a pause of one, two, three heartbeats.

'No, Miss Valentine,' said Sheila quietly. 'No to both questions.'

Only when Miss Valentine had moved two desks further on did a blush begin to suffuse her face and neck.

The staff-room was a hot, female fug of powder and cigarette smoke. The women were sprawled in sagging armchairs; one or two sat at the table trying to mark prep books; all wore relaxed, unguarded faces in this brief interval away from the scrutiny of the girls. As Ginny Valentine walked in, her shoulders drooped and she slumped into the nearest chair.

'Fag, someone, for Christ's sake,' she said.

'Any joy?'

'None whatsoever. Two or three sycophants want to talk to

me in private; otherwise nothing. Frankly, I haven't the faintest idea who it could be. I seriously begin to wonder if it's someone from outside my form, laying a false trail. God, I hate this business.'

'Girls are sly at that age. Nobody even looked guilty? No shifty eyes, twisting hands, nobody blushed?' asked Sylvia.

'They blush out of sheer embarrassment, I think. Yes, some of them blushed. Flick . . . Jennifer and Rachel . . . Sheila. What can you read into that? Damn and blast it, let's talk about something else.'

'You're on supper rota,' said Diana.

'Oh, *no*. That's the last thing I need.'

'Shall I take them for you?'

'Sweet of you. No. There's the bloody bell. I'll go.' She stubbed her cigarette into a ring of coffee in the nearest saucer and left.

'Poor cow,' said Sylvia. 'Rather her than me.'

The drawing-room bay-window was clouded by a light summer drizzle. From the junior common-room came the sound of two or three gramophones playing at once. Tchaikovsky's Piano Concerto mingled its sweetness with 'Stranger in Paradise', and a subdued buzz of voices underlay the clear enunciation of the Head and her Deputy.

'I think it's a waste of time getting cross,' said Henrietta Birmingham. 'It would simply be seen as a loss of control which will upset everyone and undermine my authority. Besides, what can I back it up with? I'm not going to threaten to cancel half-term or the school play unless I mean it. I'm left with pointless tyrannies like stopping swimming. How can it be fair to punish a hundred and twenty girls in order to catch one or two? It's even possible that it isn't one of the *girls* at all.'

'Well, I've talked to the Scandies,' said Peggy, using the girls' name for the Scandinavian maids, 'and I'm reasonably confident it's got nothing to do with them. They might just steal a photograph frame while cleaning the dormitory, I suppose; but at lunch-time, when Fiona Cathcart's parcel disappeared, they're all busy in the kitchen. Besides, they're decent, healthy, industrious, *honest* country girls. That's why we engage them.'

Henrietta sighed. 'I agree. I think you're right.'

'What about the teaching staff?' said Peggy. 'Sylvia Parry, for example. Now there's a bitter and very angry woman.'

'In a *dormitory*?' said Henrietta.

'Unlikely. I take the point. But not impossible.'

They relapsed into silence. 'All lost in a wonderland/Of all that I've hungered for . . .' crooned the gramophone. 'When I stand starry-eyed . . .'

'That terrible song!' said Henrietta. 'Why must they play it the whole time? And that other frightful thing I hate even more – you know the one – 'Sugar Bush' . . .'

Miss Roberts smiled thinly. 'Sugar Bush, I love you so' was hardly a sentiment to appeal to Henrietta. The Head saw the smile, and returned it disarmingly.

'I know, I know. Must move with the times. Turn on the wireless, Peggy. I'd rather think gloomy thoughts against a classical background. Oh, look. According to the *Radio Times* there's a Kathleen Ferrier recital. They say she's gravely ill, you know. *Such* a beautiful voice.'

The liquid notes freed her mind. The strong, pure-throated contralto lifted her spirits. She leaned back in her chair and smiled at Peggy Roberts.

'Sorry I'm so irritable,' she said. 'Wretched girls.'

The rain had settled into a steady downpour by the time Diana Monk and Sylvia walked across to the cottage. The staff-room that evening had been full of speculation and concern. Diana was sympathetic and longed to contribute some insight; Sylvia was dismissive and scornful. 'Lot of fuss about nothing!' she had said as soon as they were on their own.

'You wear such lovely clothes,' Diana said, to placate her and change the subject, watching as Sylvia ironed a silk blouse, taking pride in doing it to perfection. 'You are lucky to have such good taste. I don't know how you can afford it. My mother makes most of my stuff. She buys remnants in sales and makes clothes for both of us. It keeps her occupied, and it would hurt her feelings if I didn't wear them.'

'Of course,' said Sylvia non-committally. The iron slid smoothly across barely damp silk and she reflected on her incongruous passion for expensive clothes. I couldn't look like a frump, she thought. No matter who had made them, I couldn't wear cheap dresses.

When I started at the teacher training college I'd chosen in Twickenham, near London, I spent as much money as I could afford on dressing myself – *more* than I could afford. I bought lengths of beautiful, luxurious materials and found a woman who made them up for me into soft, swaying garments that half-disguised my stockiness and were long and low to hide my thick legs. It became an obsession, collecting beautiful clothes with the same care that I'd once tracked down shells and flowers. I never spent money on going to films or the theatre. I didn't send money home, though I dare say my mother had hoped I might. I lived in cheap lodgings, and once I began to teach my accommodation was free, more or less. Gradually I built up a magnificent wardrobe. I bought only the best, saving for a whole year, if necessary, so as to be able to spend seven guineas on a lizard-skin handbag or twelve guineas on real crocodile shoes. And of course, good things last. I have that handbag still.

You develop a feel for quality; your fingers know blindfold the difference between handwoven fabrics and factory lengths of stuff. I learned to play up my swarthiness with jewelled colours – purple and rust, deep Persian blues and forest greens. I had my hair professionally cut so that instead of sticking out in a frizz round my head, it was shaped into a cap that curled over my ears. This was just after the war, and good clothes were scarce, but good materials could be had. Liberty's in London was a treasure-house.

I had to wait till I was twenty-two before I made love to a woman, and the odd thing was, she seduced me. I hadn't noticed her, fixated as I was on the impossibly feminine creatures who had more men than they could juggle. My clothes made her notice me.

'Do you dressmake professionally, Miss Parry,' she asked, 'or are you just vain?'

Twenty-two, in my first teaching job, and someone had noticed me. We were in bed together that same night. I never stopped to wonder whether I was attracted to her; the miracle was that she had fancied me. All the staff slept on the top corridor, in adjoining cubicles that must once have belonged to the servants. She and I slipped in and out of each other's rooms in the dead of night, and I acquired a taste for making love in silence. I grew to judge by the quickening of her breath, or my own ... not that what I was registering was love; lust would be more like it, and for me, the explosion of appetite.

Diana grew uneasy at the long silence.

'Do you want a coffee?' she asked. 'Shall we listen to the recital on the wireless?'

'Please yourself,' Sylvia answered abruptly, thinking, For you'll never please me.

An hour later, having passed one another in silence on the way to and from the bathroom, they lay in separate beds listening as the rain lashed softly, coolly against the window: a sound so lonely when you are alone, so comforting if you are not. In the darkness, quietly so as not to be heard through the adjoining wall, Diana wept. On the other side of the wall Sylvia listened to the soughing of the rain and the stifled sobs and thought, I'll have to make it better with her tomorrow. Poor, virginal, empty, frustrated Miss Monk.

The school tide swelled and gathered and swept towards half-term. Whirlpools of effort concentrated here and there. Athletic girls trained hard for Sports Day or tennis matches against neighbouring schools; some ran their lone course up and down the drive each morning in preparation for the 100 yards, the 200, the 440 or the relay; others lobbed or served balls diligently for hours on end, persisting, never bored, until they had mastered the correct delayed-action drop, swing and follow-through.

From the amphitheatre, a natural green bowl hidden among the trees behind the swimming-pool, came the voices of other girls rehearsing the play for Speech Day. Singing lessons would send high, clear notes spiralling upwards, to break free at the level of the tree-tops and float downwind. They practised sweet, old-fashioned songs like 'Time, you old gipsy-man/Will you not stay?' and 'Nymphs and shepherds, come away, come away, come away...' Their voices carolled and sang, unself-consciously pastoral. 'Come follow – follow – follow – follow follow – follow me!' And on fine, calm evenings the Lower Fourth forgot its secrets and suspicions in the darting energy of Kick the Can.

Nowadays Sheila, like Constance, seldom played. Instead, she bent over her garden each evening, pulling out weeds when they were only an inch or two above the earth; spraying with the finest rose on the watering-can so as not to inundate their delicate seedlings as they grew tremulously towards the light. Charmian had given up any pretence of helping, yet they were still bound together by secrecy, and Charmian had become bolder now that she had an accomplice and alibi. She seemed to delight in her cunning, and would steal pointless, useless things – a prep book in which someone had been marked 10/10 for a careful piece of work; a letter from someone's mother, left lying for a moment in the Covered Way. Out of the corner of her eye, Sheila would see Charmie's little hand dart out to pocket it. She would stroll away, taking her time, and be in the lavatory before its loss was noticed.

'Hey! Where's my letter from Mummy?' the girl would ask a moment later; and Sheila would mutter sullenly, 'Crikey, don't look at *me*. I haven't got your silly old letter.' And there would be an argument.

When the first pale-blue airmail letter arrived from Kenya, it seemed very foreign to Constance. Her mother could hardly suppress her excitement at the new life she had found out there, a world of swimming-pools and sundowners, cocktail parties and black house-servants. 'The laundry boy is marvellous,' she wrote, 'and irons Daddy's shirts far better than the laundry at home used to, and as for my summer dresses, you won't recognize your smart new Mummy!' Often she described outings they'd enjoyed together. 'We three...' these descriptions began, as though she and Daddy and Stella were some holy trinity from whose face Constance felt herself to be cast into outer darkness. 'We three are going on a "safari" soon, just for the weekend. Stella's a bit young really, but you can imagine how she begged, and in the end Daddy gave in.'

Constance's own letters back were flat and pedestrian. She had given up begging, for she knew now that Daddy would never give in. Instead she made up songs about running away, using the tunes of hymns they sang in Prayers, or songs they were rehearsing. 'I'll run away, I'll run away, They can't make me, I won't stay!' she scanned awkwardly; or, 'Constance King has run away, run away, run away; Constance King has run away – No one could stop her!' These rhymes jiggled in her head and were obscurely comforting. Does everyone hear tunes inside their head, she wondered sometimes, or am I going nuts?

She walked around with a vacant expression, her mind and her senses turned inwards. Her work remained excellent. The teachers were pleased with her and had no reason to question her absent manner. Blue-stockings were notoriously awkward. Girls weren't meant to be brainy and if they were, it was bound to cause difficulties.

The Lower Fourth had fragmented into half-a-dozen cliques, all with elaborate theories about the guilt of the others. Constance, with little alternative except to be a loner, found herself bracketed with Rachel and Jennifer. She didn't like either of them. Rachel was fat and Constance thought she didn't wash very often, for she always seemed to smell: a rank, womanish sort of smell, like her mother after a game of tennis. There were often damp crescent-shaped patches under her arms, and a wave of what the others, with a snigger, called 'BO' would emanate when she put her hand up in class. Constance wondered if she too had 'BO' without knowing it, and would surreptitiously lift her arm and give a quick sniff, but all she could smell was cotton starch. All the same, she wished her mother had bought some Odo-ro-no on their last trip to Boots. Several girls in the dormitory made a great show of dabbing it into their armpits and then waving their arms around while it dried. Dusting powder was another favoured remedy. It came in small upright tins shaped like hip flasks, with holes punched into the lids, and sent a cloud of Cussons' French Fern, Apple Blossom or Lilac over the dormitory. Some girls used a solidified, ice-blue stick that you pushed up and stroked across your forehead or wrists to keep them cool and fragrant on hot days. These items were considered essential, and using them marked you out as someone feminine and well-groomed. Constance wished her mother had known this.

The girls were preoccupied with smells. Farting was sure to prompt an outcry of disgust, an exaggerated pantomime of nose-holding (the left hand held the nose while the right pulled an imaginary chain) and unpopular girls would be accused of having 'let off and made a foul pong'. More often than not Jennifer was responsible. Her stomach was evidently delicate – she would confide, breathily, the details of what happened 'on the lavvy', and once invited Constance to inspect the result for worms. Constance shrank from these intimacies; but she shrank even more from the public disgrace of always being seen to be alone. Besides, she was useful to Rachel and Jennifer. She helped them with their prep, explained the simple things they failed to understand during lessons, and part of her enjoyed the superiority this conferred. Jennifer invited her to stay for half-term, but Constance knew that, however relieved Mick and Flick would have been to be spared her company, a rebuff would make her more unpopular still.

Unpopularity followed her like a shadow, dragging at her heels, slowing her step and distorting her face. It bowed her shoulders like a physical weight. Only in rare, sunny moments could she forget it. She discovered she was good at sprinting and long jump and the shouts of 'Gosh, well *done*, Gogsy!' from fellow-members of her house made her smile with secret delight. She was in Drake: named after Sir Francis Drake and identified by a blue hatband on felt and straw hats, and a diagonal blue ribbon worn across Aertex shirts for Games. The other houses were Rhodes (Cecil), which was red, and Clive (of India), whose band was yellow. Intense rivalry was encouraged between the houses and Constance's surprising talent for running was her only source of popularity.

Another delight came from an accidental moment of perfect co-ordination when she swiped at a tennis ball and felt it spring lightly off her racquet to soar in a strong arc over the net and land beyond her opponent's reach. But in the ordinary daily routine, queuing for milk or post at Break or waiting by a basin to clean her teeth at night, she knew she was shunned. Getting changed in front of other people was even more of an ordeal now that small folds of flesh had begun to point her nipples outwards, and she walked with her arms crossed awkwardly over her chest to try and conceal the horizontal fold they made in the front of her dress. Her physical development was slower than that of the other girls in her form, most of whom were a good year older, and she was torn between wanting to wear a 'BB' – brassière – and dreading the day when someone would point out that she needed one. She heard them whispering about the curse, which she only half-understood; when she asked what it meant even Rachel said sharply, 'Mind your own beeswax!'

Constance's unpopularity handicapped her efforts to be normal and unselfconscious. It surrounded her like a miasma, invisible but repellent. She constantly asked herself how other people managed to be liked. She knew she could never aspire to be like Hermione, loved for her floating beauty and effulgent smiles. But Madeleine was popular, despite her sharp tongue and temper; even Charmie was popular, though everyone knew she was horrid to poor, dogged, patient Sheila. What was the secret? She tried to learn the funny voices in which they talked. Hubble-bubble language, in which every word was gargled with double ells, was easy to pick up and perfectly com-prehensible – but still they turned away from her. She sat in the library in case Hermione might come leaping down the stairs again, but she never did. Constance learned to imitate her handwriting to perfection, and as her hand reproduced Hermione's pudgy, wide-open letters and the figure-of-eight loop of her Gs and Ys she felt herself transformed into Her-mione – but only briefly. The magic eluded her.

*

Charmian gloried in her ability to devise new plots, scent new suspects. For several days she made Constance, Jennifer and Rachel seem the most likely culprits, so plausibly that the three of them went about their daily routine like lepers, shunned and yet watched by everyone else. The story spread that Constance had hidden her own pen so as to deflect suspicion, and once she came up to the dormitory at bedtime to find everything in her locker disturbed.

'It was me,' Charmian said brazenly. 'They voted me the one to look through your locker for that pen *you* say is missing.'

'I didn't just *say* it was missing: it *is* missing, so sucks boo to you. Well, did you find it?' said Constance.

'You're too clever for that, aren't you?' taunted Charmie. 'Clever dick, dirty trick, when you're found we'll make you sick!'

This period as a double outcast culminated in the disappearance of Rachel's precious album of Royal Family photographs. She and Jennifer had spent Rest sticking in three new postcards (of the Queen and the Duke of Edinburgh with the golden-aureoled, smiling royal children) and fawning over their handiwork. That evening when they came up to the dormitory at bedtime the album had gone. Rachel's face, already glistening from her strenuous run in response to the dormitory bell, was now streaked with tears, her sticky body heaving. Charmian, who normally avoided any physical contact, put her arms round Rachel's chunky shoulders and said, 'Poor Rache, how absolutely mingy! Everyone knows how you feel about that book. Well, the thief's gone too far this time! Now there's going to be trouble. Right, let's all think back. Where was everyone after supper? Let's start with me, I volunteer.'

Sheila and Jennifer and Rachel herself could vouch for Charmian's presence in the gardens, at supper, in prep. It seemed that she had not been unobserved for a moment. Rachel and Jennifer were of course exonerated, but not Constance. Each member of Starlings had to give a detailed account of her afternoon and anyone who had spent even ten minutes alone was made to feel uncomfortable.

The next day at Prayers Mrs Birmingham announced that

the Lower Fourth would have to miss their first lesson. She wanted them all to wait outside the study, and she would see each girl separately, in alphabetical order. They sat in the Reading Corner, Anne and Fiona flicking through *Horse and Hound* with expert comments until it was Fiona's turn to be summoned. Charmian seemed absorbed in *Riding* ('Oh, Sheila, look at that adorable pony – 13.2 hands – just the right height for me!') and Constance, who'd read the magazine already, sat and stared at the beaky profile of Mr Punch and the wispy fairy figures floating round the edge of the magazine's cover, like illustrations from a Victorian children's book. After about twenty minutes her name was called and she went in.

'Sit down, dear. There's nothing to be frightened of as long as you tell the truth,' said Mrs Birmingham. 'I want you to think very carefully. Remember that God hears what you say, and then tell me what you know about these recent thefts.'

There was a pause, during which Constance was very conscious of the Headmistress's watery blue eyes watching her. She met them steadily, noticing the flaky texture of the Head's skin. Her complexion was bleached of colour to a sort of bluish-grey, the more so because it was overlaid with a layer of white powder that had lodged in the creases around her nose and mouth, where it flaked like the skin itself. The veins on her cheeks had broken, making a tracery of tiny red lines. Constance could not have said whether Mrs Birmingham was fifty or eighty; she seemed the embodiment of age and grandeur, carved in delicate skin and fine white hair, but as solid and unchanging as the figures chiselled out of Mount Rushmore that Constance had seen in the *National Geographic* magazine.

'I don't know anything about it, Mrs Birmingham, honestly and truly. And my pen still hasn't turned up either. I suppose it must have been stolen, like all the other things. But I've no idea who by.'

'Very well, Constance. If you're quite, quite certain there isn't anything else you'd like to tell me . . . ? You needn't worry; nothing will go beyond this room.'

'I would, but I can't. I don't know anything.'

'Thank you, Constance. In that case you may go. Would you ask Madeleine Low to come in next please?'

One by one, they went in and, after a few minutes, came out again. Rachel cried. Mick and Flick went in separately. Everyone was aware of the drama of the occasion. When they had all been seen, Mrs Birmingham opened the door to the drawing-room and said, 'I would like you all to come in here and sit down while I saw a few words to everyone together.'

They trooped into the warm, scented room and squeezed together round the window seats and on the sofas. The last half-dozen or so sat on the floor. Miss Roberts sat in the wing-chair beside the fireplace, but Mrs Birmingham remained standing. Her eyes went from one face to another in silence. Finally she said,

'I had hoped, indeed I have prayed, that the culprit would own up this morning of her own accord. Nobody has done so. I have heard a number of names mentioned whom other girls suspect. I have heard no firm evidence that would lead me to take any notice of these suspicions. This is a very serious thing to have happened, and a very sad thing for whoever is responsible. I have no alternative, for the time being, other than to punish you all. Sweets have already been stopped. Now, I intend to stop all parcels...' there was a low murmur of complaint '... except on birthdays, when they will be opened under the supervision of a matron; and from now on there will be no more playing outside in the evenings, except at weekends.'

A gasp of disappointment ran like a current round the group.

'If the thefts continue, I shall have to consider what else must be done,' said Mrs Birmingham. 'And now, I'd like you all to close your eyes and bow your heads. We shall end with a prayer. O Almighty God, to whom all hearts and minds are open...'

Her voice was precise and sombre and at the end the girls mumbled a shame-faced 'Amen'. They scrambled to their feet as she dismissed them, and hurried back to their form-room. Sheila took Charmian's arm, but Charmie shook it off furiously and spat at her, 'Leave me alone! I don't want to hear about who you suspect! Old Ma B's right ... all this is horrid. Just shut up about it.'

Oh, Mummy, help me, thought Sheila. I don't know what to do and I feel so ashamed and I'm scared. Oh, Mummy, Mummy, tell me what's happening. Don't leave me alone. Please God, don't let Daddy leave us. Don't let Mummy and Daddy divorce and I promise never to do anything wicked again; ever, ever again.

Next morning Constance, in her Aertex shirt and brown-pleated shorts and plimsolls, saw the postman bicycling down the drive as she ran up it doing her daily athletics practice. On the way down again she was puzzled to see Charmian, who didn't usually go for early-morning runs, giving the postman a parcel and some money and then scampering back to her dormitory. She didn't stop to wonder why. In her mind she was Mowgli, loping easily across the plains of the Deccan beside the long, lithe stretch of Bagheera.

Five

Half-term had emptied the school. The buildings lay becalmed under a cloudless sky. Jack Waterman, the gardener, cut the grass on the games field and dragged the paint-roller across its newly shorn surface, laying a complicated pattern of white lines in preparation for Sports Day. A flattened oval marked out the 440-yard track with staggered lines at the start to compensate for the outside bends, while down the centre of the field ran four parallel lanes for the 100 yards. The edges of the sandpit, landing ground for the high and long jumps, were trimmed and tidied, and a load of fresh yellow sand tipped into its greyish centre. Having thrust a handful of freshly mown grass into the cages of various hamsters, guinea-pigs and rabbits and topped up their bowls with oats and clean water, he called it a day and went home to listen to the cricket commentary. Denis Compton was on the point of scoring his 100th century and Jack wanted to hear history being made and the great roar when the crowd saluted their hero. As a little lad, Jack had dreamed of being a cricketer, but the war and his gammy leg had put paid to that. Refereeing the girls' cricket matches was as close as he ever got these days.

Most of the staff had taken the long weekend off, glad of a respite from patrolling and controlling, and from the claustrophobia of the staff-room. Sylvia and Diana had not. They were happier in the cottage than either would have been in the airless boredom of their own homes. It was a luxury to relax, uninterrupted by the clamorous bell that punctuated their lives, to talk without being overheard, to stroll or swim in privacy, sunbathing on the hot tiles around the swimming-pool and hearing the distant purr of the motor-mower like the buzz of cicadas in the south, where neither of them had ever been.

On the Saturday evening they sat in the thickening light of dusk on the lawn behind the cottage. Normally they would have been in full view of the girls' dormitories, but tonight, they had taken the kitchen table and two chairs outside and eaten salad and cold meat with a celebratory bottle of wine, followed by strawberries with condensed milk. Diana, who had scarcely had a drink in her life before meeting Sylvia, was emboldened by two glasses of wine to ask questions.

'Sylvia,' she said. 'It's a lovely name. Why did your parents call you that? Bit un-Welsh, isn't it?'

'My father's idea. He used to be an English teacher. Very keen on poetry.'

'It is a poetic name.'

'It was one of his typical jokes to show up my mother's ignorance. Apparently when I was born he came into the nursing home and said to my mother, "Who is Sylvia? What is she?" He'd hoped for a boy, you see. I was a disappointment. But my mother didn't understand the reference and just thought he wanted to call me Sylvia. So she did.'

'Your father's not alive any more?' Fatherless Diana shrank from the word 'dead'. In her family they always spoke of her father, who had been killed on the Somme, as having 'passed on' or 'given his life for his country'.

'No. Oh, Diana. You *are* an innocent, and there are so many things you don't know. We've finished the wine, haven't we? Pity. Get the cider from the larder.'

What have I started? thought Diana, as she fetched the bottle of cider from the cool, tiled floor of the larder. I must be very calm and not let her realize that she upsets me. I don't want to set her off on one of her rages.

'Was it very hard for you? Knowing he'd wanted a son?' she said carefully, after a silence.

'Oh, I think in the end he was quite glad I was a girl.'

'So that was all right, then.'

Sylvia looked across the darkened lawn. On evenings like this, at home, you could always hear the sea swishing softly in the distance.

'I was quite a sweet child, believe it or not. Very anxious to please. There were just the three of us, but I liked being an only child. When I felt like running wild I could go along the beach, collecting my shells and things. Roam across the moor. I wasn't lonely. School was a bit tricky, my father being a teacher, but he was respected. You know what children are like. Fair play. We were an upright family. Everyone knows you in a small Welsh community. A nice, safe little world, it felt like. Pass me my ciggies.'

She smoked in silence a while and Diana didn't like to interrupt.

'When I was small, my toys were the rocks on the beach near our house. They were gnarled and beautifully shaped, with holes that the wind poured through and I peered and clambered into. I played quite happily all by myself. The sea came galloping across the sand towards me and I used to stand my ground, until it collapsed at my feet. I'd be holding my shoes by their straps, and the water round my toes made them numb with cold. I played every day on the long, empty beaches, even in winter, when the sky seemed to have closed down over the horizon, cold and black. The reflection of the clouds darkened the water. I didn't need a bucket and spade or a rubber ball like the children who came on holiday. All I needed was a big stick to draw letters and patterns in the sand. I'd watch the sea wash them off, just like one of those magic slates on which you could draw things and then, swish, they'd vanish.

'I learned to write when I was very little – my father taught me – and I carved huge, wobbly words in the sand: SYLVIA, of course, and MUMMY, but mostly DADDY. Once I wrote MY DADA, and he saw it when he came looking for me at tea-time, and teased me. But I meant it. He was my dada and no one else's. I thought he was so strong and clever and good. I knew he went to school every day to teach other children but I wasn't jealous of them, only of my mother. What about you, Diana? Did you love your father very much?'

'He died just before I was born,' said Diana. 'I'm sure I've told you that already. I didn't love my uncles, exactly, but my father...? I think when I was very little my mother made me kiss his photograph good-night. But there wasn't much kissing in our house. We weren't a huggy family.'

'My father kissed me all the time.'

'You must have adored him.'

'Yes and no,' Sylvia said. 'Luckily I remained an only child. I wouldn't have stood for a baby, I would have drowned it, so it was just as well none ever came along. Mother was just *there* – washing and ironing, cooking and cleaning, reading the Bible in odd moments, trudging off to chapel with her hat on, twice a day on Sundays. They never seemed to do things together much, except share the great big double bed with iron railings at the head and foot.

'We had a lot of books and my father often read to me. *Little Grey Rabbit*, *The Wind in the Willows*, *The Water Babies*. Even when I could read for myself he went on sitting on my bed at night, one arm round me, the other balancing the book on his lap, rolling out the stories in his strong Welsh schoolteacher's voice. *Children of the New Forest*, *The Mowgli Stories*, *Coral Island*, *Treasure Island*. No, those must have been later, I suppose.'

Why am I telling her all this? Must be the drink. Bet she's bored. I remember it all so clearly, not as though it had happened to me but to some other child. There I am, see me, a tiny figure on a great expanse of empty beach, below an even huger expanse of sky. I am crouching over trails left by water in the sand. Pools collected round the rocks and flowed away in little streams which soon gave out, leaving twisting, plaited patterns that looked as if a snake had slithered by, or like the footprints of some bird. There were patterns on the wild grey ponies, too. They had close, dense hair and after rain it would form matted whorls across their flanks. They were tame, you could pat them. I wasn't afraid.

Yes, I am lucky to have had that freedom, and the security and routine of home, which I took for granted, never thought about. It was an idyllic start in life for a clever, solitary child.

'Yes, I was lucky, I suppose.'

The sun was dropping low, dodging behind the tall trees, flickering through their branches as it had flickered on the surface of the swimming-pool earlier in the day. The air grew cool and the wood-pigeons murmured and squabbled. Smoke from Sylvia's cigarette inscribed a pure calligraphic line wavering slightly at the tip.

'I don't know why my parents married. I never saw them be demonstrative. I was the same. Never cuddly or anything. Welsh as slate.' Sylvia didn't smile. She finished her cigarette and smashed the tip into the lawn, grinding it under the sole of her shoe. A long silence divided them. Diana's colour was high and she felt blood pulsing in her cheeks and neck. The veins stood out on her hands. She could hear, as well as feel, her heartbeat.

'I'm going for a walk now,' Sylvia said abruptly. 'On my own, do you hear? On my *fucking* own! I don't like all this reminiscing. It's pointless.'

Diana watched her head off quickly into the smoky dusk, then she stood up and carried the supper things indoors. She washed up and put everything on the draining-board. She carried the cumbersome table back into the kitchen, and the chairs, dried the plates and cutlery and put them tidily away, then closed her bedroom curtains and sat behind the open window, waiting for the sound of Sylvia's returning footsteps.

Henrietta Birmingham carried the tray into her bedroom, placed it on the chest of drawers and helped her husband to sit up. He leant forward while she plumped the pillows, then sank back into them with a wheezy sigh.

'No skin on the cocoa today,' he said.

'That's because I made it for you. It's Saturday, remember? Ridley's evening off.' Goodness, she thought, how rare it is to see him smile. 'After church tomorrow, would you like a little drive?' she suggested. 'We needn't go far.'

'I'd have to get dressed up,' said Lionel. 'All that palaver.'

'It's going to be another hot day,' Henrietta coaxed. 'Just a shirt and your linen trousers. I'd give you a hand.'

'Has it come to that?' he asked. 'Can't even dress myself?'

'You could try, and then if you needed me, I'd give you a hand.'

'Lot of fuss and bother for nothing,' he said sulkily. 'Not worth the effort.'

He means he can't face the humiliation, thought Henrietta. He doesn't want to admit how weak he's become. Should I try to persuade him?

'Would you rather I asked Peggy for a drink before lunch? She often says how much she misses talking to you.'

'Withered old trout. I'd rather talk to the trees.'

'Think about it, dear. The fresh air and a change of scene would do you good, I think. And it would please me.'

'Long time since I've done *that*,' he said, and gave her another thin smile.

She put out her hand, and closed it over his grey one, its bluish veins shockingly gnarled. Her hand was warm, his cold and flaccid. Did he ever please me? she thought. She stared at his hand and her eyes glazed and locked as she withdrew from him, deep into the privacy of thought. It was our wedding night that gave him a hold over me. It made us equal, in his eyes. We are all equal, in the eyes of God, she thought, and her hand tightened over his. She squeezed it briskly.

'We'll see how you are in the morning,' she said. 'Try and sleep now.'

By Sunday Constance knew that half-term wasn't going to be nearly as bad as she'd feared. The twins, away from school, were actually being quite nice to her, and their mother was a darling. She fussed over Constance as though she were a third daughter, chattered enthusiastically about her parents – 'Dear Paula, she's divine! *Such* a good sort! And your father ... what a wonderful man he is! I'm quite in awe of him, you know!' – and encouraged her to eat large, delicious meals.

'It's lovely, your house,' Constance had said shyly to the twins on Friday morning, after Mrs Simpson had shown her the sprigged, cosy attic room where she was to sleep. Mick and Flick were bouncing on the beds in the room next door, shrieking, confident and unfamiliar in their mufti. 'Really cosy and homely.'

'It's not *ours*,' they said scornfully. '*Our* house is much nicer.

Daddy's just rented this one, for Mummy, for the Season.'

Constance thought 'season' was a funny way to describe the summer, but all she said was, 'Well, yours must be pretty smashing then.'

Gradually they thawed and became more friendly and inquisitive. Constance dropped her guard and basked in the family atmosphere and the knowledge that, for the first time in weeks, she did not have to be perpetually on the defensive.

That afternoon, as Mrs Simpson dozed on the terrace in her sun-dress and the girls lazed about, half-heartedly trying to catch butterflies and grasshoppers in the unkempt paddock, Mick took her by surprise.

'Who d'you think's the thief, Gogsy? Go on, say . . .'

'Haven't an earthly. I thought you might know.'

'Some people say it's you.'

'I know and I think it's foul. Obviously it's not me. I wouldn't steal my own Parker 51.'

'Charmie thought you had, and hidden it.'

Stung by the injustice of this, Constance said, 'Well if you really want to know, I think Charmie's the thief herself.'

'Charmian Reynolds?' said Mick.

'You don't!' said Flick.

'Why? Go on, tell us why.'

Constance withdrew her confidence from them, pulled at a long grass stem and sat chewing its sweet, pointed end, her teeth leaving flattened marks.

'Don't be so *mean*, Gogs,' they wheedled. 'It's not fair. You're staying with us, aren't you? We wouldn't tell anyone, honestly. Cross our hearts and hope to die.'

'I just made it up,' said Constance, after a pause. The fine fluff at the top of the grass drifted between her fingers and she scattered it on the wind.

'Bet you didn't,' said Flick. 'You wouldn't. You're not such a clot.'

Constance was worried. It was true she suspected Charmian of stealing, mainly because she was always inventing suspicions that diverted attention away from herself and on to others, but she couldn't justify her theory to the twins, and she knew that, in the last resort, they'd take Charmian's side.

'Did you say anything to Old Ma B?' Flick persisted.

'No.'

'Who then? Miss Valentine?'

'I haven't told anyone. I said, I was making it up. It was just the first name that came into my head.'

'Liar! Liar! Your house's on fire!' chanted the twins.

From the terrace Mrs Simpson shaded her eyes with her hand and called,

'Are you all right, darlings? What are you playing?'

'Nothing. Just mucking about...' yelled Mick.

'Good girls...' drifted on the wind. 'Lovely to have you here.'

Constance lay back in the long grass, letting the sun beat down on her closed eyes. The twins sat cross-legged, but although Mick said once more, 'You are a swizzler, Gogs. You might *tell*...' the dangerous moment had passed. Insects buzzed through the grass, the sun rode lazily through the midsummer sky, and the three girls gradually fell silent, and slept.

That evening after supper Mrs Simpson taught them all mahjong and they sat on scratchy white-painted garden seats out on the verandah, the small bamboo tiles clicking like insects, until the light failed and they went indoors.

In her attic room, stuffy with the drowsy heat of the midsummer weekend, Constance undressed as far as her vest and knickers and went to the bathroom one floor below. Pulling her knickers down, she gasped and stood stock-still, looking at the stained cotton between her legs. Last time she spent a penny she had noticed a reddish-brown patch, a bit unusual but nothing to worry about. Now it had grown to a large, sticky area of dark blood. Constance stood rigid with embarrassment and panic. How could she wash her knickers? What with? Soap? How? Where would she hide them while they dried? A thick blush suffused her face, until her cheeks seemed to bulge with blood and her neck swelled and felt thick, as it did when she was being a tree. The curse. This must be the curse. This was what the whispers and giggles were all about. *This* was 'STs, if needed.'

The twins would be wanting the bathroom. Constance took a towel and wrapped it round herself, then hobbled quickly back up to her room; aware for the first time of the prickly stickiness between her legs which, come to think of it, had been there all evening, every time she shifted her bottom on the flaky paint of the wooden chair. There must be a mark on her dress! Everyone must have seen! She snatched up the cotton dress from the back of the chair. Inside the skirt there was a faint brownish stain, but from the outside it was practically invisible. Someone knocked at the door and Constance dragged her cotton nightie over her head before asking, 'Who is it?'

'It's me, dear,' said Mrs Simpson's voice. 'Come to kiss you night-night.'

'Um. Yes. Sorry,' said Constance.

'Are you all right, duckie? You look a bit shaky. Anything up?'

'No, nothing ... important ... Just' – she tried to sound offhand – 'started the curse.'

'Poor old you, what a bore.'

'Yup.'

'Have you got your doings with you?'

'Have I got *what*?'

Mrs Simpson looked at her. 'I say, it's your first time, isn't it? Oh, my *dear* ...'

She stepped forward and hugged Constance; then said briskly, 'Right. Got some clean knickers? No? Never mind – I'll go and hunt out a couple of old pairs of the twins'. You get out of those things and I'll rinse them through for you.'

Tactfully she disappeared.

Constance sat down on the edge of her bed, got up again hastily, took her knickers off, peered at the sticky dark-red substance again – it smelt funny, not like ordinary blood, more sort of zooish – and folded the knickers carefully into a tidy white parcel with the stain hidden inside. She waited. She put her foot on the end of the chair and picked a scab on her knee with elaborate care, enjoying the tweaks of pain and the beads of blood that grew into a tiny trickle. She pushed the blood aside with her fingertip and sucked the finger. It tasted sweet and bitter. She squeezed the scab between her thumb and finger, watching the irregular brown crust split and ooze more blood. The sound of footsteps on the stairs made her straighten up quickly as Mrs Simpson walked in.

'Here we are! Three pairs. They're pretty shabby, so just chuck them away when you've done with them. Here's half a packet of STs as well. You fix them on to this belt...' She held up a tangled, droopy piece of elastic. 'Just like suspenders, really. Don't put your STs down the lavatory, there's a good girl. They clog up the works. I'll leave some brown paper bags in there. Now, what have you got to give me? Dress OK? Well done.'

She stopped talking and looked into Constance's face. 'Don't be frightened. You'll soon get used to it. Happens to us all. You're a young woman now. Tummy hurting? No? Here's an aspirin, just in case. Night-night, dear. Sleep tight. Don't let the bugs bite.'

She closed the door behind her, and Constance picked up the twisted sanitary belt and the squashy packet called Dr White's. It said 'sanitary towels' on the outside. She took out an ST. It was soft and smelt of nurseries, a long pad of cotton wool covered with a layer of gauze. It looked nice. She bent her knees outwards and held the pad between her legs. It felt nice. Now I need STs, thought Constance.

The next day Mrs Simpson had arranged a lunch party for two girls who lived nearby and had been at the twins' former school. They arrived with their mother, a plump, shiny little woman called Priscilla Kenworthy-Browne. She wore a tight dress that emphasized her stomach.

'Do you *love* your new school, darlings?' she asked, and didn't wait for their answer. 'I'm sure you do. I bet it's super. Wizard. We're having such problems finding somewhere suitable for these two. Darlings' – she turned to her listless daughters – 'wouldn't you like to go to the same school as the twins and, what was your name, dear? Never mind. Wouldn't *that* be fun? You could all be chums and get up to all sorts of mischief. You can't fool *me*, I know what you naughty girls are like...'

Everyone else ate steadily through their cold ham and salad blobbed with Heinz salad cream. From time to time one of the girls would mutter, 'Mummy I don't feel well,' or 'I'm not hungry,' which Constance interpreted as, I'm bored, can we go home? Not until the lunch was almost finished did their mother notice that they had eaten almost nothing.

'So ungrateful of you both! Whatever will Mrs Simpson think? My dear, you must forgive their disgraceful manners. I can't *imagine* what's wrong. They're normally such good eaters.'

'Mummy, we *told* you,' said one of the girls wearily. 'Me and Patsy don't feel well. Our legs hurt. And my head aches.'

'Nonsense, darlings!' said Mrs Kenworthy-Browne, and laughed merrily. 'A nice walk in the sunshine, that's what you two could do with! Mick and Flick will take you down to the meadow, won't you, darlings, show them the pony ...'

Glumly, the five of them trooped out.

Six

The Lower Fourth sat bolt upright. They were tense and quiet. Their classroom had been animated and buzzing with half-term gossip when Miss Parry marched in. As she strode up to the desk, her highly polished Elliott sandals slapping over the parquet floor, the gored pleats of her brown linen skirt flapping against her sturdy legs, the whole form braced itself. She banged a pile of biology prep books on to a desk in the front row before seating herself at her table next to the blackboard.

'Hand these out and NOT A WORD!' she ordered.

Her gaze travelled from one scared face to another. Nobody met her eyes. Sheila was trembling; Charmian was composed and demure. Mick was rigid, the form captain on the alert; Flick looked down at her books. Constance was sucking her finger. While the books were distributed, Sylvia continued to observe them all. She knew her anger was very close to the surface, knew it was not their fault, and she was struggling to master it. If only she could have a cigarette! Osmosis. She must pull herself together and think about osmosis.

A hand went up. Fat, spotty, greasy-haired Rachel. God, the child was ugly. Stupid too.

'Put that hand down! Even you should have the wit to understand that I want NO TALKING.'

The trembling hand was lowered. Osmosis, thought Sylvia Parry again. Like the edge of my skirt in a rock pool, absorbing the sea-water, the colour gradually getting darker as it became damp, then wetting the back of my legs as I stood up and looked for seaweed to pop. She took a deep breath, turned to the board and wrote with firm strokes of the chalk, OSMOSIS. She underlined it, and the lesson began.

Mrs Birmingham returned to her study from a divinity lesson with the Upper Fifth. As she walked in, Peggy Roberts said, 'Telephone call for you from Mr Dunsford-Smith. He wouldn't tell me what it was about. Said he needed to talk to you.'

'Did he leave a number, or is he going to phone again?'

'Here's his number. He's waiting by the phone for you to ring.'

A moment later Henrietta Birmingham listened, appalled. There'd been a car accident, in the south of France. No, not he himself; once half-term was over, his wife had gone away for a few days with her sister, Sheila's Aunt Muriel. They'd taken a train down to the Côte d'Azur, and hired a car there. Not used to driving on the right. French such bad drivers. Police looking into it. The bodies were being flown back. Sheila would have to be told. Didn't think he was quite up to doing it himself.

Mrs Birmingham replaced the receiver and sat for a few moments with head bent and eyes closed. *Give her Thy peace; may she find rest and forgiveness for her sins. And forgive me my intolerance and malice against the mothers of these girls. I too have sinned, above all the sin of pride. Grant Thy comfort, Lord, to this motherless child.*

She looked up at last.

'Bad news. The worst possible. Sheila Dunsford-Smith's mother has been killed in a car crash. I shall have to tell the child myself. Her father feels he can't. Not that I blame him. Peggy, my dear, can you find someone to bring Sheila to me? And if you could perhaps . . .'

'Of course. Do you want to talk to her in here or next door? I'll make myself scarce.'

Proud of her errand, the self-important third-former trotted into Austen where the biology class was rigid with concentration. Miss Parry wheeled round from the blackboard.

'What on earth is the matter now?' she exploded. 'Is it quite impossible for me to teach for ten minutes without interruptions? Will you LEAVE MY CLASSROOM! Now!'

As the little girl checked her step and hesitated, Miss Parry seemed about to run through the room and chase her out. The child fled.

Moments later the stately figure of Mrs Birmingham appeared at the door of Austen. At the sound of the handle and the latch Miss Parry had turned, her face dark with rage. She saw the Headmistress and her hands dropped to her sides.

'I sent for one of the girls a moment ago, Miss Parry. Was it not possible to release her from your lesson?'

'I didn't realize, Headmistress – the child didn't explain...'

'Never mind. Can you spare Sheila Dunsford-Smith for the rest of this period, please?'

'Certainly. Of course. Yes.'

The Headmistress walked calmly through the room to Sheila's desk and laid a hand on her shoulder.

'Miss Parry will excuse you. Come with me, dear.'

She looks like the pope giving his blessing, thought Constance. She is so kind and yet so awe-inspiring. Even Batey Parry's scared of her. Poor old Sheil. Wonder if it's about the stealing? The girls met each other's eyes briefly and questions danced like motes through the bright air.

'May I have your attention please girls?' asked Miss Parry, almost deferentially, and the lesson continued without any more interruptions.

Sheila sat down opposite the Head and met her pale-blue, watery eyes, noticing the tiny tributaries of lines and folds and the way her eyelids drooped at the corners, and the eyelashes, white, like her hair. The Head smiled gently and laid both hands palms upward on the blotter in front of her.

'Sheila, dear,' she said. 'I've just been talking to your father on the telephone.'

From the third-floor bathroom window that overlooked the drive and main entrance, three heads craned out for a last look. They saw Matron hand a suitcase to Miss Roberts, who stowed it away in the boot, and then the small figure of Sheila, her face hidden by the brim of her straw hat, got into the front. Miss Roberts closed the car door softly behind her, got in on the other side, and gravel swished under the tyres as they drove off.

'D'you think she'll ever come back?' Fiona asked Charmian.

'Doubt it,' said Charmian authoritatively, though in fact she had no idea. As the only person who had been allowed to say goodbye to Sheila, she was the sole source of information, and she intended to guard her precious hoard and only release it slowly, letting the rumours and speculation go on as long as possible in order to savour her power over them all.

Mrs Birmingham sat in the pale turquoise and beige serenity of the drawing-room, marvelling that such horrors could happen under a clear blue sky and a steady sun. The Somme had been like that, Jamie told her; astounding, flaming sunsets of utter glory, so that it seemed impossible that the guns didn't stop for everyone to admire the brilliant colour lighting up the undersides of the clouds. Or so he had thought at first.

She had asked him once if he'd actually killed a man, and he had said after a pause, yes. She didn't ask how many. But she did want to know what it was like, and he said it was like pushing a knife into earth. Not nearly as bad, he thought, as watching the gamekeeper finish off a wounded stag.

Today was high summer, nature flaunting its perfection, and only man is frail. There was a knock at the door, and she tightened her hands and feet together and straightened her back as Miss Parry entered. Her thoughts rumbled a coda to her words, like a drum or double bass adding its muted thunder to the clear notes of the piano. *O God, it is hard to do my job. They all expect me to be strong and omniscient, and sometimes I feel quite at a loss. Give me Thy wisdom, Lord . . .*

'Miss Parry, I wonder if you can explain this morning's incident?' she said, her voice calm and steady.

That poor child. What will happen to her? Bring her Thy peace, Lord, and the comfort of Thy everlasting arms . . .

'I am not aware of any incident,' replied Sylvia Parry. 'A child interrupted my lesson without explaining herself, and I dismissed her. I was not to know you had sent her. She burst in . . .'

'What was it that stopped her, I wonder, from telling you her errand?'

How the hell should I know? thought Miss Parry.

'I'm afraid I don't know, Headmistress,' she said.

It is an emotional day, Mrs Birmingham thought. I must collect myself. Speak only of what I have seen. Do not make unsubstantiated accusations.

'When *I* entered your classroom, the figure you presented might well have silenced a little girl. You looked upset about something. Your class seemed nervous, too. Had something happened to distress you?'

'On the contrary. It had been a very orderly lesson.'

'In that case perhaps you could offer an explanation.'

Silence. Sylvia's hands were stiffening unconsciously into fists.

'You may sit down, Miss Parry.'

Her movements minimal, concentrating on seeming impassive, she walked smoothly forward and seated herself in a deep armchair. On the occasional table beside it was a highly polished silver ashtray with an inscription in the centre. *Presented to the Rt Hon. the ...* She forced herself to meet the Head's eyes as Mrs Birmingham began to speak.

'The children in this school are placed in my care and under my responsibility. But I am concerned for all members of staff as well. Your teaching is satisfactory, Miss Parry, but your demeanour is not. Let me be frank. You give the impression of a very angry, deeply unhappy woman.'

Their eyes locked in silence.

'If I can help or advise you in any way I would like to be given the opportunity to do so. You may speak to me in perfect confidence. I hear many people's secrets.'

Silence. Several minutes passed. The bell for the end of Rest clanged in the distance. Mrs Birmingham drained her cup of cold Camp coffee and looked frankly into the closed face opposite her.

'I have no secrets, Headmistress. But my private life, such as it is, must remain private.'

How dare she snub me? Her colour is rising again, almost

imperceptibly, mottling her neck. She has great self-control, but that she can't hide.

'Miss Parry, you are at least twenty years younger than I, and doubtless more familiar with the modern treatments available from psychiatrists and suchlike. I believe they can be extraordinarily efficacious. Would you like me to ask my personal doctor if he can recommend a good man? Please do not be offended.'

Now Sylvia flinched; a tiny shudder, as though a dart the size of a pin had embedded itself in her cheek. At last she spoke.

'You are quite right, Mrs Birmingham, in assuming that I did not enjoy an altogether happy childhood. I trust that I have dealt with it in my own way. May I say that I regret the manner in which I dismissed your messenger this morning?'

Oh, the proud, silly woman! *Lord, Lord, help her, help me, for we are both Thy servants.*

'Very well. But remember that the children here are my first responsibility. It is my duty to protect them. It is yours to keep your anger in check, whatever its origins. And now, I am afraid this conversation must count as a warning. If I hear of any more such episodes we may have to consider your resignation ... or dismissal...'

She stood up. Sylvia Parry stood too, turned her back and walked to the door, her face grimacing wildly, hideously, in the few seconds before she reached for the handle.

As the girls queued up in the Covered Way for supper, forming lines according to which table they were assigned to for the week, Charmian contrived to lean across to Constance and hiss, 'Gardens! Afterwards! Meet you there!' before resuming the expression of patient grief which she had worn all afternoon.

Constance arrived first, and picked at weeds or poked the earth with twigs until Charmian flopped down beside her.

'They all keep asking me questions!' she said. 'How should *I* know?'

'What *has* happened to Sheila?' asked Constance. 'Is it her parents?'

'Her mother's dead. Got killed in a car crash. Last night, I think. She said to give you a message to ask you to look after her garden for her. I mean, it's my garden too. We share it. That and the rabbit.'

'Do you want me to look after the rabbit as well?' asked Constance.

'Pore ickle wabbut!' said Charmie, in the quacky Donald Duck voice that some of the girls used when talking about things that were 'sweet' – baby animals, tearful children, or beaming, white-haired old people.

'What's his name?'

'Flopsy. Don't ask me why. It was Sheil's idea.'

'Flopsy, Mopsy, Cottontail and Peter,' said Constance.

'No, just Flopsy. Shall I go and get him and you can hold him?'

She dashed to the pets' shed, and Constance stared into the dry soil of Sheila's well-tended garden. Would Sheila come back after her mother's funeral? Everyone would be frightfully nice to her, and soft-voiced, and put their arms round her. In the meantime it was clearly her own fate to act as a replacement. She'd wanted a friend so badly, but she wasn't sure if she wanted Charmie, especially now that she was getting on OK with the twins. She crouched down and the warm ST shifted stickily between her legs. Her nostrils flared as she tried to detect its strange, visceral smell.

'Here you are!' said Charmian, and she plonked the shivering grey-and-white rabbit into Constance's lap. Constance stroked it, marvelling at the soft sheen of its fur and the corrugated boniness of its spine, before placing it on the grass.

'She also said you ought to be my friend now. Till she gets back,' said Charmian.

'Oh.'

'You haven't got a best friend. Some hope.'

'No.'

'Well then?'

'I might, but first you must tell me about the things that are missing. Do you know who took them?'

' 'Course. You do, too, don't you? You're not dim. But if I tell, you've got to cross your heart and hope to die.'

Gradually, defiantly, the story came out. Charmian revelled in her stealing, but she couldn't do it without an ally – someone cleverer than she was, who would protect her and cover up for her. Sheila had fulfilled that role and now the lot had fallen to Constance.

'Charmian, I won't. I can't do it. It's wrong.'

The rabbit had relaxed at last and was whiskering the grass edging their garden, its long ears upright and alert. Charmian grabbed it and smacked its nose.

'Naughty Flopsy! Mustn't eat our nice garden!' Then she looked at Constance. 'You can call me Charmie, if you like. Sheil used to.'

'Lots of people do.'

'So what?'

'I'm friends with the twins now anyway.'

'No, you're not. Shall I tell you how Sheila's mother got killed? She was riding along in this open-topped sports car and her long silk scarf got wrapped around the wheels and strangled her to death! Isn't it ghastly?'

'I don't believe you.'

'Don't, then. See if I care. No one else knows 'cept me and you. It's our secret. I bet even Sheila doesn't know.'

As the bell clanged for bedtime, Charmian was showing Constance her hiding place behind the sacks of oats. Blithely she offered to steal another Parker 51 but Constance knew that would create more problems than it would solve. Let Sheila come back soon, she thought, as they ran down the path past the swimming-pool towards their dormitory.

Starlings was emotional that night, looking at Sheila's neat counterpane and hearing Charmie's inconsolable weeping. Ignoring the promise of secrecy which had finally persuaded Constance to join her in the conspiracy, Charmian had given them all a dramatic account of Mrs Dunsford-Smith's fatal accident, complete with dark purple bruises on her long white throat. The nearness of sudden death touched them all. Constance offered to tell a story, and they lay quietly in the deepening dark as she began.

'Once upon a time there were two famous warriors called Sohrab and Rustum. They lived far, far away in Persia, long before Jesus was born, near a river called the Oxus. The Persian army had a champion, sort of like Goliath, and Sohrab was the champion of the Tartars, sort of like David. Their two armies had been fighting for a long time and were very well matched, so neither side could win.

'Sohrab's terrifically young and handsome, but really he's only gone to war because he's looking for his father, who he knows is called Rustum, but he's never met him. His mother told him stories about how Rustum was a great warrior, and he wants to find him and say, look Father, I am your son and I've tried to be worthy of you.

'So he decides the best way to do this is to issue a challenge to the enemy's, i.e. the Persians', bravest man, to fight him in hand-to-hand combat. Then whoever wins it'll mean their army has won the war. So he goes and tells the king of the Tartars and the king sadly agrees. Well. The two armies are camped on the plain beside the River Oxus, and the king goes out in front of them all and says to the Persians, who're the enemy, "Choose a champion from among your lords to fight our champion, Sohrab, man to man."

'Now the Persians get scared, because they've heard of Sohrab and how young and brave he is, and they've got nobody who can beat him. But they have to agree to the challenge, so they do. But what no one realizes is that an old warrior, who's just arrived to join the army, is actually Rustum – that's Sohrab's father. He himself thinks his son is lost or dead or something. So when he hears of the young man's challenge, he says, "Yes, I'll fight him, only on one condition, that I fight in plain armour." So they agree, which means that, unbeknownst to them, father and son are going to fight one another to the death ... and I'll go on with the story next time.'

They pleaded for more, called her a spoil-sport and said it was a swizz to stop when it was just getting exciting, but Charmian took Constance's side and told them all to shut up and anyway *she* wanted to sleep now before she started to think of Sheil and get mis again.

'Night, Constance!' she called across the dormitory.

'Sleep well, everyone,' Constance replied.

Some of the girls prayed ostentatiously beside their beds for longer than usual, but one by one they dropped into bed and into sleep.

Half an hour later Henrietta Birmingham sat alone in her drawing-room thinking about death. *Sheila at thirteen is younger than I was when I first heard that Alistair had been killed. It was 1916. I was sixteen. I remember the grief, how it came in waves, so that I'd wake up after no matter how bad a night with temporary forgetfulness, and for a few blessed seconds the fact of death would be far away. But then, like a car travelling along a dusty road, the great thunderous cloud comes rolling towards you, and from out of it appears this roaring black monster. He is dead. He will never be alive again. Not when I'm grown up, not for my birthday or Christmas, not once the war is over. He's dead for ever. And then the wave would recede – during a lesson when I was concentrating on French with my governess, or when I was lost in a book, or on my best behaviour at table in front of guests – until once again the memory would envelop me. Nor was it any better when Hugo died. Worse, if anything, because he had survived three and a half years of the fighting and we were beginning to believe he must lead a charmed life, that no harm could come to him. And then came the telegram, like an electric shock.*

Now Sheila will have to learn the facts of death. *Grant Thy Grace and give Thy comfort, Lord, to this child, Thy servant. May she in this time of sorrow be granted Thy peace that passeth all understanding. And grant too that father and child may draw close and honour her mother's memory. For we are all sinners. Amen.*

Look, the waves do eventually recede. I have thought of my brothers without grief and even without praying. But what consolation would that be to Sheila, to know that in thirty or forty years' time she may think of her mother in tranquillity?

The Head stood up slowly and with an effort, the creases deepening around her thick ankles as her feet took the weight of her bulky body. She smoothed her cardigan with one hand and with the other she turned off the table lamp. In near-darkness she inhaled the summer smells – the great round bowl of roses on the book table, the fresh green night air crowding in from the trees outside, and the faintly dusty odour that came from her own body and permeated her clothes. In the midst of life we are in death. A rose petal or two lay beached on the polished surface of the table, rocking in the draught that breathed through the room when she closed the door behind her.

As Henrietta Birmingham drove her car past the cottage she could see its lights still burning and hoped that timid, gawky Diana Monk was not bearing the brunt of Miss Parry's dangerous anger.

'Monkey, get the sherry out,
Monkey, get the sherry out,
Monkey, get the sherry out,
We'll both get squiffy!'

Diana heard the sharpness concealed within Sylvia's nonsense words, and closed the book she was marking with a decisive slap, as though she had finished with it.

'Perfectly timed!' she said. 'I couldn't half do with a glass myself. Why don't we go one better and broach the gin?'

'Naughty, naughty Monks! I'm corrupting you. Now I'll educate you. Don't say "couldn't half". It's common. Mustn't give the game away.'

They drank their pink gins in silence until Diana said, 'Tell me about Old Ma B. I need to know.'

'I'm in trouble. She caught me in a rage. She saw my face. I could tell she was shocked.'

'How did you get out of it?'

'Ducking and weaving as usual, ducking and weaving. It can't last.'

'Should you see a doctor?'

'Christ Al-bloody mighty, you're almost as bad as her. *She* said psychiatrist. Trick cyclist, looney-bin. You both think I'm barmy.'

'Why today? What made you blow up?' asked Diana, ignoring the gibe.

'Haven't the foggiest,' said Sylvia, and thought, Here's to the gin bottle, drowner of sorrows; here's to my childhood, which killed my tomorrows; here's to my mother, what would people think; here's to the bitters that make my drink pink. Really I'm quite brilliant when I'm pickled.

'Time for bed, Monkey. I mean, sorry, *Miss* Monk. I mean, of course, Diana, the huntress with the silver ow and barrow. Who said that?'

One day it'll be Hermione, thought Sylvia Parry in the watches of the night. If it's the last thing I do before I leave this place.

Seven

It was Hermione's week to be meals monitor. Graceful in her impartial sweetness, she was marshalling everyone into orderly queues between the first and second gongs. The prefects, as one of their privileges, were allowed to stay in their common-room until the second gong, so she was single-handedly in charge until a member of staff came to lead them into the dining-room. Hermione enjoyed the attention which this duty focused upon her.

She had already decided to be an actress after leaving school, although her parents would disapprove. They just wanted her to come out, be presented and everything, do a Season, perhaps six months at a smart secretarial place, and then marry the first suitable man who came along. She and the rest of the fifth-formers attended regular dancing classes to learn 'Strip the Willow', 'The Dashing White Sergeant' and other Scottish reels, as well as steering each other round the gym in a parody of the foxtrot or, to the staccato rhythm of *Jealousy*, the tango. On these occasions Hermione never had to be the man and lead. That was left to the strapping girls with beefy arms who would be greatly handicapped when the time came for their first dances. They would discover that the transition to mirror-image dancing, one hand resting lightly on a partner's shoulder rather than steering firmly behind her back, was never easy. But Hermione, quintessentially feminine, was never one of these substitute males. Skilled though she was at dancing and small-talk, Hermione felt she deserved a wider audience than that of her social peers.

She stood at the top of the Covered Way subduing the impatient girls by the direction of her eyes and smile. Elaborately ordinary, as only the self-consciously extraordinary can be, she threw an admonishing frown towards a late comer, raised one crescent eyebrow at a whisperer, pretended to count heads as a pretext for displaying her long fingers and oval nails, buffed to a sheen with chamois. Her audience hung on each look and gesture and when she finally turned to greet Miss Valentine, a wave of emotion shimmered like silent applause. Hermione, buoyed up by worship, feigned the utmost humility.

'Everyone's been frightfully good, Miss Valentine,' she said, as though thanking them. 'I think we're all here.' Her cotton frock moulded her thighs for an instant like marble drapery as she turned to precede them all down the corridor leading to the dining-room.

Before grace was said, the Head called for silence. 'I am sorry to say,' she announced in slow, authoritative tones, 'that news has come of another theft, and the most serious yet. Someone has entered a room belonging to a member of staff and removed valuable items of jewellery. This matter is going beyond the bounds of the school and I shall have no alternative but to report it to the police. The staff member concerned believes she saw the culprit leaving her room. I am prepared to give her one final chance if she will come and speak to me in my study before tonight's bedtime. Otherwise outside agencies will have to be called in. Meanwhile I have given instructions that, as well as cancelling all sweet allowances, there will be no more puddings at lunch or supper from now on.'

A groan arose and heads turned as the girls grimaced at one another.

'And now, may we have grace, please?' said Mrs Birmingham.

The wooden forms rocked and chair-legs scraped as the school sat down to lunch.

'Whose were the things that got stolen?' said Charmian, her eyes shining, eager for information.

'How should I know?' said Rachel.

'Must've been one of the matrons,' said Mick. 'They're the only ones anywhere near the dorms.'

'Not necessarily. Could've been Miss Roberts,' Charmian said.

'Nobody'd dare,' said Rachel.

'Wouldn't they?' asked Constance. 'Someone might. Someone's taken awfully big risks already.'

Charmian's mind sang in triumph at her own bravado. She felt vivid and important, and the fact that no one knew – except Constance, who would now be more stodgy and disapproving than ever – didn't diminish the bright flame that she carried like an Olympic torch. It was so easy! You just needed to be bold and quick. She'd been in and out of Peach's room in moments. It wasn't for the sake of the miserable little string of greyish seed-pearls or the silver cross and chain – she knew perfectly well that they were just cheap necklaces – it was for the thrill of getting away with it. No one had seen her; she was certain of that. Mrs Birmingham was bluffing. She'd slipped in after seeing the doctor on a pretext, knowing quite well that Miss Peachey would have to stay with him for another twenty minutes. Then she had gone late into class with the truthful excuse that she'd had to see the doctor. It had been brilliantly planned and carried out. She would get Constance to hide the trinkets, so that she herself was ostentatiously accounted for all afternoon.

After Rest Charmian cornered her.

'Say you've got the curse and you're off games,' she gabbled. 'The stuff's in the bottom of my pencil-case. In my desk. Hide it – you-know-where...' she would have scampered off, but Constance caught her arm.

'*No*,' she said fiercely. 'I can't. I had the curse last week.'

'Oh, you're so *wet*,' said Charmian. 'Botheration! You are a flipping nuisance. Now I'll have to think of something else. If I can...'

Later, as Constance sat on the tiled wall surrounding the swimming-pool, her towel on her lap, pulling the tight rubber bathing-cap over her hair, the games mistress blew her whistle shrilly and beckoned her over.

'I thought you weren't swimming, dear?' she said. 'I thought you had a tummy-pain and wanted to lie down. I told Charmian to say that would be all right.'

'No, I ... I'm O K now. Honestly. I feel fine.'

'Well, better not to take any risks. Sit on the side for now and just watch.'

The afternoon clouded over and without the rays of the sun it became quite cool. Constance sat with the towel round her shoulders, shivering.

Mrs Birmingham was in her study, talking on the telephone.

'I expect that was wise,' she said sympathetically. 'A funeral is very distressing for a child. It might only upset her further ... Do you discuss her mother with her? Not at all? And she doesn't seem to want to ask any questions? ... Very well, then. A fresh start. But I don't think you should assume she will forget, you know, Mr Dunsford-Smith ... Well, you must be relieved that she seems to be taking it so well. We shall miss her, of course. I'll ask Matron to send her things on, by Carter Paterson. Do give Sheila our love. Tell her the girls are praying for her ...'

She replaced the telephone heavily in its black cradle and looked across at Miss Roberts.

'I wonder if parents are right to try and hide death from children? I know he means well, but being wrenched away from school and all her friends at a moment's notice, suddenly given a series of expensive treats in London ... the poor child must be very confused and unhappy.'

'*And* it forces her to pretend she's having a wonderful time! I think it's totally misguided,' said Peggy Roberts. 'Sheer madness. She's lost her mother, poor little soul, and no amount of ice-creams or visits to the circus can alter that. Why didn't you tell him so?'

'I don't feel as sure about it as you do. He may be right. She's only thirteen. She can't have been close to her mother in the last two years, except in the holidays. I don't know. Perhaps it *is* the best way to help her get over it.'

'On the contrary. Now she has to make a secret of it. She can only cry when she's by herself. In a year that child will be unrecognizable. Withdrawn. Defensive. Her father will marry again, I suppose. Well, it's none of our business any longer. Does he want a refund for the second half of term?'

'Half a term's notice must be given,' quoted Mrs Birmingham, 'though it seems rather mercenary to insist. I'd better talk to Miss Peachey about packing up her things. I'll have Waterman look out her trunk.'

Later Miss Peachey emptied Sheila's drawers, throwing away a few papers hidden under her knickers and the tightly folded notes that had presumably passed between her and Charmian in class. She read one which said, 'I'll be friends again if you solemly sware to be loyl. Anyhow, I've got something to tell you. So don't be soppy and suck up to Gogs, OK?' She didn't bother with the rest. She hesitated over a couple of letters from Sheila's mother, finally placing them between the pages of Sheila's Bible. The child would need this evidence, in years to come, that her mother had loved her.

She filled the trunk rapidly; books and shoes and sheets at the bottom, ornaments wrapped carefully inside vests and pants, the photograph of Sheila's mother tenderly folded in tissue paper. She tied the two diagonal straps on top and lugged it down to the back door herself, to wait for collection.

As she did so she wondered whether the Head was right not to involve the police in discovering the identity of the school thief. They could have taken fingerprints, traced the culprit – maybe even got her precious pearl necklace back. On the other hand, from Mrs Birmingham's point of view, one had to consider the scandal. Police turning up and then gossip, local people asking questions; it would be in the paper quick as winking. No, she could see they wouldn't care for that.

The school dragged through the bright days of high summer. At the outset the seniors had treated talk of stealing with dismissive irritation – 'It's just the blinking squits being tiresome again!' – but now it impugned their own effectiveness as prefects and moral arbiters. Hermione had taken aside one or two juniors with 'pashes' on her, only to find that, despite the special favours she'd hinted at in return for disclosure, they seemed to know nothing. Once she caught Constance gazing at her with such perturbing intensity that she nearly summoned her too; but Gogs was a new girl: no one would confide in *her*.

The school limped on, suppurating inwardly. In the school photograph for that year the staff looked tense, and Mrs Birmingham's normally benevolent expression was equivocal. The straight lines of girls – juniors cross-legged and adorable at the front, seniors buxom and reliable at the back – hid a shared guilt, a mystery unsolved, a culprit whose face and frock were as clean as everyone else's.

At the staff meeting on the first Friday of the month they talked about the need to crack down on incidents of fainting in church, which were clearly hysterical in origin and distracting to the rest of the congregation. Finally the Head raised the subject of theft.

'I confess myself entirely baffled,' she said. 'We know – we think we know – that the culprit is in the Lower Fourth, because most of the stealing has taken place within that form, though even that isn't certain, and there was, of course, the matter of Miss Peachey's jewellery. I have spoken to each girl individually. Miss Valentine and I' – she glanced towards the form mistress – 'have spent many hours discussing it. I am inclined to think we are not dealing with one thief, but at least two, possibly several, all shielding one another; but even that is just a guess. I have not one shred of evidence. Everyone's locker has been searched, and all the desks. Nothing. So, as we're driven to desperate measures, I am going to do something that makes me feel very uneasy. I should like each of you to write down on these scraps of paper the name of the girl *you* think is most likely to be responsible. I will then interrogate, there is no other word for it, those whose names appear most often. It is not fair, but I simply don't know what else to do.' She handed round a neatly torn fan of paper slips.

'I agree with the Headmistress,' said Miss Valentine. 'I don't like it, but I have no better suggestion to offer.'

Heads bowed, the staff each scribbled a name, folded the papers and placed them in a large platter which Miss Roberts handed round.

For Diana it was a worrying decision. She knew the golden

languor of the summer term had been overshadowed for the girls, and she pitied them. She didn't want to accuse anyone, for she had no real suspicions. An unreliable moment of intuition told her it might be Mick and Flick, but perhaps this was just the fantasy of the only child, whose deepest desire is always to be a twin. It couldn't justify naming them. In the end she wrote 'I don't know' and folded the paper.

Sylvia's memory travelled along the lines of desks, recalling two girls who'd giggled, one who had blushed when startled out of a daydream, another who'd covered her paper as she approached. (It had been revealed as an elaborate piece of calligraphy forming the words I LOVE HERMIONE FOREVER.) It could be any of them – stupid, giggling, spoiled brats! Fat Rachel, oozing her shame in spots and pimples? Cocky little Mick and Flick flouncing around arm-in-arm? Hang-dog Constance, trailing around at Charmian's heels now that Sheila had gone? Charmian herself, tarty little blonde . . . ? In the end, because she didn't like Americans with their cocky voices, she wrote down Deborah's name, followed by that of Charmian. Her pulse raced and she had to force herself to write with slow and controlled strokes. That should give them a nasty quarter of an hour each! She pursed her mouth and folded the paper into a tiny rectangle.

Mrs Birmingham's device was unproductive. Two of the staff had written 'I do not know'; Miss Emett had written 'I object on principle' and signed it S. Emett; and the only names that occurred more than once were those of Constance, Charmian and Michaela Simpson. *O Lord*, she prayed, *give me the courage to admit that I have made a mistake. I have always been puffed up with pride and unable to retreat from a path once embarked upon.*

Steering her car up the drive through the long dusk of early July she remembered Lionel's proposal. Touched by his humility and the shameless pleading in his eyes (which she took to be love) she had unexpectedly said, 'Yes, yes, I will – dear old Lionel. Yes, I'll marry you.' That night she had told her mother, who was sitting in the great canopied bed while her father nodded with his brandy and his dogs before the library fire; she had told her mother that she had accepted Lionel Birmingham's proposal.

'Hetty, darling,' her mother had said guardedly, 'are you sure? This *is* a surprise. He should have approached your father first for his permission, you know. Papa will be quite put out. I had no idea you loved him, or indeed that matters had gone so far between you. Are you *really* sure this is what you want?'

Stung by the clear implication that Lionel wasn't good enough for her – which she knew to be true, less for her mother's reason, that his family was socially inferior, than because his mind and spirit could not match her own ardent energy – she had said emphatically, 'I *want* to marry him, Mama. I'm sure I can make him happy. There's more character to him than you realize. He is shy – you and Father overawe him – but...' But? But what? But he is a surviving man, he wants me for his wife, he is not maimed or hopping on a wooden leg, and he will not cry out and curse in the night. Because he is older than I am, and grateful that someone will be his wife and make him a home, and not bring to it a clutch of another man's fatherless children. Because he is made bold by my necessity, because he is a snob, because he is fearful and he clings to my strength.

Had she really known all this at the age of twenty-five, thinking herself destined for spinsterhood like so many others, or was it with hindsight that she believed she had steered so confidently into her great mistake?

'I love him,' she had insisted to her parents. 'I love him,' she had said after the first lamentable family dinner, when Jamie had looked at him with contemptuously narrowed eyes. 'I love him,' when Lionel had misattributed the ancestral portraits, and her parents had not bothered to correct him. So they had put the announcement in *The Times*, the date was fixed, and she began to be fitted for her wedding dress and the trousseau she would wear in Egypt. Lionel professed a great interest in archaeology. They were to sail down the Nile and see the Valley of the Kings.

A week before the wedding, she and her mother were in London doing last-minute shopping. From the house they always rented in South Kensington they made endless trips to Harrods and Barkers and Debenham & Freebody, buying what to Henrietta seemed pointless objects at enormous cost. She had already received sufficient wedding presents to furnish in Scottish baronial style the modest house that she and Lionel were to occupy. Lionel pretended to find them inappropriate, but she guessed that secretly he was pleased by these outward signs of the elevation of his status. His mother and sisters lived modestly in a rambling house north of the park, and Henrietta flinched from their evident awe of her. But the transition to married woman was an elevation in status for her, too, and she stowed away her fears behind good intentions and lengthy prayers.

After an evening at the theatre (they had gone to see *Hay Fever* and were emboldened by its daring informality) her mother had tactfully left them to dine *à deux* at Boulestins, after a quiet word with the head waiter. Over dinner, warmed by a glass or two of wine, Henrietta had felt honour-bound to confess. She had tried to explain that she was not – she thought she might not be – she was uncertain, but... He had looked at her in a bewilderment which grew to dismay and, finally, when she didn't know whether to expect anger or sympathy, into gloating triumph.

'*You!*' he'd said, and his hands clutched his knee gleefully. 'The cherished virgin daughter of the clan Campbell-Leith: not a virgin at all, eh? What a turn-up! Well, I'll be damned!'

She shrank from his vulgarity.

'I'm not sure. It was only once. I was just a girl.'

'Once is enough. Either you are or you aren't! No, don't tell me how it happened, I don't want to know.'

There was still a week left. She could have changed her mind. Was she sorry? Looking down the twenty-seven years of their marriage, Henrietta Birmingham surprised herself by thinking, no, not really. I am not sorry. I feared much worse. Without him there would be no James. Without him, the parents of these girls would despise me, as I see them despising Peggy, for being a spinster. With a husband and son I am the equal of any of them. It was not such a mistake after all. No,

I do not regret my marriage. And with a flourish she turned into the Lodge, braked, yanked at the hand-brake, heard it squeak, felt the car throw its bonnet up like a startled horse, and turned the engine off.

'Darling!' she shouted up the stairs as she entered the house. 'Lionel! It's me! I'm back! Coming!'

Constance had escaped from Charmian that evening by hiding in the spreading cedar that shed its greeny-black shadow across the cool green turf. Her senses were scratched by its rich smell, and her skin by its rough bark. Scared by the drop, paralysed for moments at a time, she had climbed higher than ever before, till she could straddle a branch twenty feet above the ground and lean back against the uneven trunk. She fished her mother's latest letter out of her knickers, sniffing the delicately crackling paper, inhaling deeply as though there were some faint memory of her mother's hand resting on it; but all she could smell was the sticky resin on her own fingers.

Darling Constance,

I'm just snatching a quick twenty minutes before I have to get dressed, as Daddy and I are going out to dinner, but it's cool enough for me to sit on the verandah with a nice pink gin and write to you. Oh, darling, we're leading such an exciting life out here! People are simply too social for words – parties, parties, all the time – and as we're quite new, they pump us for the all the gossip from England. (Not that I've got any, of course!) I could have done with twice as many cocktail frocks. Even though you know in advance it's going to be hot, you don't really understand until you get here. We've all picked up lovely tans already – we look like Riviera folk, imagine!

I'm so pleased to read between the lines of your last letter that you're cheering up. Trust us, darling, we knew you'd be happy there. Once you find a nice friend to confide in and share secrets, the way girls do (well, I did, anyhow!) you'll wonder what you ever thought you had to be miserable about! Stella's settling in very happily too, except that she's a bit too 'chummy' with the Africans. Poor pet, she isn't used to servants!

Well, Connie dear, I must go or Daddy will be cross with me for making us late. Work hard and play hard, and make us both proud of you. A big hug and lots of kisses from your loving Mummy.

Below this her father had written 'and Daddy'.

Constance shifted her bottom on the roughness of the branch as she hitched up her skirt and tucked the letter back into her knickers. The dormitory bell would be going soon, and she hadn't had time to think what to do about Charmie. She was tempted to confide in Hermione – being a senior and a prefect, she would know what to do – but when she had caught her eye, Hermione had looked away.

Is Charmian my friend? Must I be loyal to her? Is it always wrong to tell tales? Would they call me a sneak? I bet nobody would believe me.

People were strolling beneath the tree. She stayed quite silent and held her breath. The chattering voices passed and in the silence that followed, Constance recognized the tree sensation stealing through her, more powerfully than ever . . . I am a tree, strong and dark and green and eternal, I am a tree, my limbs thicken, I am this tree, my tongue thickens, I cannot speak, my head swells, I cannot hear or feel, my eyes close, I cannot see, I am a tree, a tree I am.

Charmian had had two letters that day, and was wandering round by the game field looking for Constance. She meant to read her mother's letter to Constance. Not the other one; Gogsy mustn't see the other one. Her mother's letter said,

My dearest darling little Charmie,

How is my pretty baby? Not too sad, I hope. What *shattering* news about Sheila's mother. I remember your friend, of course, but did we know her mother? Was she anybody? You must tell me their surname in your next letter. Perhaps I ought to send a little note of condolence to Sheila's Daddy. What a shock all this must have been for you, my precious. I'm sure you're being very brave and strong. Mummy is having to be brave, too. It's all so difficult, and Daddy doesn't try and make it any easier. But Uncle Dickie has been an absolute tower of strength and he takes me out and about and tries his very best to cheer me up.

That's all for now, darling, don't worry about me, keep your chin up.

Lots and lots of love and a great big hug from Mumsie.

Her other, secret letter was from Sheila. It said,

Dear Charmie,

Thank you very much for your letter. It's very sad that Mother is not with us any more but I'm sure she has gone to a better place. I have been to lots of theatres and films but I miss you and even miss *school!* I've been thinking, I should write to Old Ma B and tell her it was me that took the things, 'cos she'll forgive me now, and then it will be all right again and the school needn't be punished any more. You said something awful would happen if I told. Well it already has. So this is to say don't take any more things and I'll own up and then you'll be let off. Don't tell anyone it was you all along. Promise on your word of honour. Sorry to be so bossy but I've been thinking about it a lot. Tell Mick and Flick I miss them and blow a kiss to Hermione (ha ha, bet you don't dare) and please look after Flopsy and give him a cuddle from me.

Lots of love, Sheila.

She'd have to answer her mother's letter, but she wouldn't write back to Sheila. What cheek! Just because her mother was dead she thought she could say anything she wanted, and get all uppity.

'Gogsy!' yelled Charmian. 'Gog-sieeee! Hey' – she appealed to a passing girl – 'have you seen Gogs? Tell her I'm looking for her if you see her. *Go-ogs.*'

But Constance, high up in her tree, didn't catch the voice that drifted downwind. Charmian stood still, unaware that what she wanted was her mother. Then she went off to torment the rabbit. She'd pull another of its whiskers out, she thought, and watch it wriggle. She skipped along to the pets' shed.

Later in the dormitory Charmie cried again at the sight of Sheila's smooth, unnaturally flat bed, and the others clamoured for more of the story. Charmie said it would cheer her up, so Constance went on:

'So you remember from last time, Sohrab and Rustum are getting ready to fight each other without knowing who each other really is. Rustum's in plain armour with just a scarlet plume on top of his helmet, but his army, that's the Persians, know him because of his horse...'

'Tell us about his horse,' said Fiona, forever homesick for her ponies.

'Well, he's got this awfully famous horse called Ruksh, who follows like a dog at his heels, because Rustum found him when he was just little, just a baby, a colt beneath its dam – '

'Isn't that a bit cruel?' whispered Fiona, but was shushed.

'What sort of horse was he?' asked Anne.

'All it says is that he was a bright bay with a lofty crest,' said Constance.

'Arab,' said Anne. 'Obviously. Must have been.'

'Well, anyway, don't interrupt. I'm telling it. Rustum walks out in front of the Persian host, followed by Ruksh, his faithful Arab, and none of the Tartars know who he is. And at the same time Sohrab comes out of his tent all done up in magnificent armour and then there's a wonderful bit where it says' – Constance shut her eyes to remember the beautiful words exactly – 'oh, yes, I've got it:

For very young he seemed, tenderly reared
Like some young cypress, tall and dark and straight
Which in a queen's secluded garden throws
Its slight dark shadow on the moonlit turf,
So slender Sohrab seemed, so softly reared.'

There was no reaction from the others and, slightly embarrassed, she went on: 'And he looks so young that Rustum feels sorry for him, so he beckons him over and warns him not to fight. He asks Sohrab instead to come back to Persia and be

137

like his son, which is kind of funny, you see, him not knowing. And Sohrab is so touched by this that he actually falls down before this old unknown warrior and says, "But aren't you Rustum?" Only this makes Rustum suspicious, and he thinks, maybe it's all a trick for him to beat me without having to fight, and then the Persian army would have been shamed. That's why he refuses, and they have to fight. And there's another good bit, listen, when Sohrab says, "For we are all, like swimmers in the sea,/Poised on the top of a huge wave of fate,/Which hangs uncertain to which side to fall."'

'Are you sure this is a proper story?' demanded Charmian. 'It sounds more like a soppy old poem to me.'

'It's a *story*,' said Constance firmly. 'And they're just about to fight, father and son, and I'll stop now or Peach'll catch us.'

'There, Charmie, look what you've done...' somebody grumbled; but it was late and they soon slept, even Constance.

Mrs Birmingham slept too, and dreamed of chandeliers; of chandeliers and smooth parquet floors, of young men who moved stiffly and smiled vacantly; of dance floors and night clubs, frenetic with chatter and malachite cigarette-holders; of flappers, thin as waifs, insubstantial; or herself, always a weighty woman, sitting at the edge of the floor under the circling coloured lights, left out, watching as the maimed young men and sparkling girls receded further and further into a haze of jazz and cigarette smoke.

'Come back!' cried Henrietta, 'Don't go!'

She woke to hear Lionel muttering uneasily, 'What is it?'

She reached a hand across to him. 'You're there. Never mind. Just a dream. Go back to sleep, dear.'

In the darkest and most silent dead of night, when the house within which children and teachers, matrons and servants, the happy and the unhappy, all slept deeply, when the very house seemed to breathe evenly in and out, Constance clambered up through layers of sleep woken by something at the edge of her consciousness. Her eyes opened, closed; opened, and then, like a kicked swing-door, were suddenly wide and staring.

Silhouetted against the deep dark-blue of the night she could see Fiona on her hands and knees, while behind her, also on her knees, Anne rocked rhythmically back and forth. Tiny snickerings were being forced out of Fiona, which Anne, stifling her giggles, tried to hush. She seemed to have one hand under Fiona's tummy. They were obviously playing horses, but why in the middle of the night?

Constance was about to sit up and say, 'Hey, you two, what's going on?' when for some reason the words of that horrid song Charmie had told her went through her mind – 'He jumped on her till her tits bounced out' – and she blushed so deeply in the darkness that she could feel herself getting hot and tingly all over. Ugh, she thought, how horrid! and shut her eyes firmly.

The noises went on for a bit, till Fiona made a sort of long, whinnying 'Whoo-hoo-hooo...' and then Anne squeaked several times, excited squeaks, after which she got back into her own bed and everything fell silent.

Constance stayed awake for a while, trying to work it out. Somehow she couldn't get out of her mind the idea that it had something to do with the curse, which was what made you a woman. Anne and Fiona both had the curse, so they were both women, so they played these peculiar games. Mummy and Daddy had always been modest and none of them ever saw one another naked around the house. In fact until she came here, no one had seen her without her clothes on since she was a little girl and Mummy used to bath her. She had been taught to knock on her parents' bedroom door and wait for them to say 'Come in', and Daddy never came into the bathroom when she or Stella was in there. She knew that bodies and what they did were often indecent, although it was never discussed at home, just as you didn't talk about what happened in the lavatory. She felt that if she let herself go on thinking about it she would be led down strange paths of the imagination into the future, and she preferred not to follow them. Yet the sight of Anne and Fiona playing horses had stirred something deep and uncomfortable, and it was quite some time before she could get back to sleep.

Eight

'You know, Charmian,' began Mrs Birmingham, 'why you are here? Why I have asked you to see me?'

'Yes, Mrs Birmingham.'

'Why?'

'Because someone thinks it's me that's been stealing things.'

'Yes. Have you?'

'I don't know.'

This was a surprise. The other two had both said no, Michaela Simpson with proud indignation, Constance King with a clever and convincing analysis of why she might be suspected (new girl, hence outsider, hence victim and scape-goat). The Head was beginning to wonder herself if the evidence might not point to Charmian as the culprit. She was prepared for the child to deny it with a flourish of offended vanity, and yet she had allowed herself to hope she might confess, in a storm of tears and remorse, after which they would pray together for God's forgiveness. Then Charmian would repent; would agree to confess, first to Miss Valentine and then to her form, and then...

'You *don't know*, Charmian? You must *know*...'

'Well, of course I don't *think* I took them. But if the staff say I did, and I know some people in my form, like f'rinstance Constance King, if they think I did, and now you believe I did – well ... I don't know. I just can't say absolutely no any more. 'Cos if everyone thinks I'm the thief, them maybe I *am*. Maybe I did it and forgot. Maybe I sleep-walked. Maybe the devil tempted me...'

This is hysteria, thought Mrs Birmingham. The child sounds as though she has stepped straight out of the witches of Salem.

This kind of thinking is dangerous. If it spreads, then I'm facing something a great deal more serious than childish stealing.

'Charmian!' she said abruptly. 'Stop this silly nonsense *at once*. I asked you a perfectly straightforward question and I want a simple, straightforward answer: yes or no. Did you steal Miss Peachey's necklace, and the photograph frame, and the pen, and the scrapbook and so on, or did you not?'

There was a pause. Charmian's turquoise-blue eyes looked blankly back at her. Then she heaved her shoulders up and down once, and sighed.

'I don't *think* so,' she said. 'But it's all been so sort of muddled this term. I mean, what you told me about Mummy and Daddy, which I don't understand a bit, I still don't, and then the awful thing of Sheila's mother, which is all so ghastly, and oh, Mrs Birmingham...' Charmian blinked several times and began to breathe fast and heavily.

'Sit down, dear. On that chair there. That's right. Sit down. Have you got a handkerchief? Good girl. Blow your nose.'

Charmian took her handkerchief and shook it as she had seen her father do, into a large, all-enveloping square, and buried her nose in it. Behind its folds she thought, Shall I cry or not cry? She thought of the rabbit's bloodshot eyes every time she jerked a whisker out, and of how its front paws scrabbled frantically, and her own eyes seemed to swell and overflow.

'Is there nobody you can talk to?' the Head asked.

'I used to talk to Sheila,' said Charmian. 'We used to meet up by Pets...' and her eyes filled up again.

Dear God, who knowest the heart of this Thy child, prayed Henrietta, *give me Thy wisdom and Thy infinite understanding, that I may help her find her way down this troubled path.* She smiled with great tenderness at the bowed little figure in front of her.

Charmian watched the smile and thought, Phew! Done it! She stored away the knowledge, for the rest of her life, that even the apparently omniscient couldn't tell if you were lying, as long as you kept your nerve. She smiled tremulously back.

Ten minutes later, having listened wide-eyed to the Head's attempt to explain why some mummies and daddies couldn't

stay married, and had to get what was called a divorce, Charmian escaped from the soft pastel warmth of the drawing-room.
As she walked sedately down the hall she thought to herself,
She doesn't know much about it! She didn't say anything about
them not having the same bedroom any more. She hasn't the
foggiest clue. On an impulse, she turned and raced up the three
flights of back stairs to a top-floor dormitory. In seconds she
had swept half a dozen bulging-eyed glass animals off the top
of lockers, stuffed them into her handkerchief, and was walking
sedately down again. This is fun, she thought, and it's easy-
peasy. You just need to believe no one will see you, and they
don't. And even if they did, I'd say I'd been to see the Head
and she told me to go and get a clean hanky. Which is true
anyway. Easy as pie.

The staff-room during Break was a hubbub of nerves and
noise. It smelt of cheap clothes, warm bodies, powder and
chalk dust. Untipped cigarettes added their stale grey smoke to
the thick air. Miss Valentine's clarion indignation cut through
several flustered conversations in different corners of the
room.

'I think it's disgraceful!' she said. 'Nothing more or less than
a witch-hunt. On the basis of a whole lot of unsubstantiated
allegations, three of my form are given the third degree, including my form captain. When she walked into their geography
class after seeing the Head the poor child looked devastated.
As for Constance King, that's all the good of the last eight
weeks undone. She's a highly intelligent, sensitive girl – shut
up, Sylvia, I don't want to hear your bitchy remarks – and a
great deal of damage has been done.'

'And Charmian?' said Sylvia Parry. '*Do* let's hear your perfectly splendid defence of Charmian.'

'All right. O K. So you think she's the culprit. Give me one
single shred of evidence. *One.*'

'God, you're so self-righteous it makes me sick! If we had
any fucking evidence – '

'Language!' admonished a voice.

'If we had any *fucking* evidence, I said, we wouldn't all be
acting like a bunch of amateur sleuths.'

'Yet you wrote her name down, didn't you? As chief suspect?'
Ginny Valentine said

Sylvia Parry's voice grew dangerously soft, like the wolf
who's eaten chalk. 'The names we wrote down were con-
fidential, or so I was given to understand. May I have *your*
evidence for that remark?'

Diana interrupted. 'Ginny, you don't know and how could
you, so drop it. I know it's twice as unsettling for you, what
with it being your form, but do let's try and talk about something else for once. Who's going to win the Ladies' Singles?
Five bob on little Mo, anybody?'

'I'm glad you've got five bob to chuck about . . .' said 'Bibs'
Whitby; and conversation veered to the standard complaints
about how badly they were paid, compared with men, and the
iniquities of the Burnham scale, until the bell rang. All but one
headed off to their classrooms, books clamped under one elbow.

Only Mrs Whitby, the games mistress, was left behind in the
staff-room as the others dispersed to teach. She had not been
at the previous evening's staff meeting, for it was assumed that
she didn't know enough about individual fourth-form girls to
have any basis for suspicion. She'd come in earlier than usual
to draw up a detailed timetable for Speech Day's exhibition of
swimming and diving.

The one member of staff who lived at home with her husband
and children, Bibs Whitby had a sense of proportion that the
other teachers lacked. In the cramped staff-room each tremor
of favour or success was elevated into melodrama. Everyone
took sides. Gossip ricocheted off the walls, as fact was overtaken
by the wilder constructs of rumour, malice and invention,
passing from girls to staff like Chinese whispers. By now the
building itself seemed to emanate guilt to such an extent that
if in years to come someone with second sight were to walk
through its rearranged rooms, the sense of that guilt might
touch them too. Charmian's unhappy, pointless thefts – such
small crimes, she would say later, laughing, as she told some
man a pretty tale about her schooldays – the grit of those small
crimes now permeated the bricks and dust of the building.

The teachers, in this hermetically sealed, stuffy domain, knew nothing about the rituals of courtship and marriage. Worse than that, thought Mrs Whitby, they were completely ignorant of the realities of bringing up children. It showed in how much store they set on imposing authority and commanding obedience, and the footling methods they used to boost their own self-confidence and punish any child who showed spirit: the pompous ritual of order marks that had to be written in a book and verified with the teacher's initials. She'd seen the book. SP, SP, SP, SP the initials ran down the last column. And the crimes? Running down the corridor. Interrupting in class. Whispering in class. Coming late to the lunch queue. There was something wrong with any child who *didn't* behave like that, and something wrong with a system that regarded it as right and proper for children to be grave, slow and deferential.

Her own twin sons were ten, her daughter twelve, and she focused attention upon them with an intensity far greater than she gave to all the lumpy girls in the flapping shorts and Aertex shirts. Comparing the other teachers' lives with her own, she knew that she was lucky. They had scores of girls in their charge, but at the end of each day only she read her three children a story, inhaling the smell of Pears' soap and warm Viyella: her *own* children, not some other woman's. The unmarried teachers had missed out on a woman's proper destiny, and she felt a thread of contempt for them. What did they know of bed, poor spinsters? As for that unstable pair, Sylvia and Diana, Bibs disliked even being in the same room as them.

There was a knock on the staff-room door, but before she could call 'Come in!' the pert face of Charmian Reynolds, framed by blonde bunches, looked round it..

'Oh, Mrs Whitby, sorry!' she said. 'I didn't think there'd be anyone here.'

'Why did you knock, in that case?'

'Well, I don't know, um, just habit . . .'

'What do you want?'

'Nothing. Gosh. Sorry I disturbed you. It doesn't matter.'

She would have shut the door and slipped away, but Mrs Whitby got up and led her into the room.

'Come in. I know it's not allowed, but there'll be no one

here for at least half an hour. Sit down.'

'I can't. I only asked to be excused. I have to go back.'

'All right, dear, run along, then. Only remember: if you want to have a chat with me, just ask. I believe your parents are getting a divorce? I know how upset you must be. I'm married and have children of my own. I can imagine what it would do to them if Mr Whitby and I were to separate. I do understand how you feel.'

'It's awfully kind of you . . .' said Charmian, but Bibs could see that she was itching to get away.

'Remember, then. Any time.'

'Yes. I've got to go now. To the aunt I mean. Thanks anyway.'

Bibs Whitby closed the staff-room door thinking to herself, Now what on earth was all that about? Charmian Reynolds, what are you up to?

Charmian, as she raced back to her classroom, thought, That is my first mistake. It makes it all the more exciting, somehow. Then, from behind her, a voice called out her name.

'Well, that didn't get us very much further,' said the Head to Peggy Roberts. From their imposing desks in the study they looked bleakly across at one another. 'And I have received the first parental letter this morning, asking what's going on,' Henrietta added.

'Whose?'

'Hermione Malling-Smith's.'

'Well, there you *do* surprise me! I would not have thought that young lady capable of writing an articulate letter.'

'Peggy! You do make me laugh with that voice. You mustn't be so cutting. Oh, dear, you're quite right, though. Just because she's nice-looking.'

'Not "nice-looking", Henrietta. Be fair. She *is* a beauty.'

'Handsome is as handsome does, as my Scottish nanny used to say.'

'Yes, and handsome does very well in a boarding-school. And everywhere else, for that matter. Well, what are you going to do? Get her in?'

'Why not? Anything's worth a try, and I don't know what else to do.'

After the next bell, a junior was despatched to find Hermione and bring her to the study. She entered guiltless and easy, flashing the same glorious smile with which she favoured everyone. It was not returned.

'Sit down, Hermione,' the Head said. 'I have had a letter from your parents. I gather you have told them about the episodes of stealing that have bedevilled us all recently.'

Peggy Roberts smiled inwardly. Bedevilled, she thought. That'll fox her.

'That's all right,' the Head went on. 'You have a perfect right to tell your parents whatever you think fit. I wonder, however, if there is anything you should be telling *me* about these thefts? Perhaps one of the juniors has confided in you?'

'No, Mrs Birmingham, unfortunately not. I wish they had. I'd love to be able to help.'

'And you haven't noticed anything unusual? No special behaviour?'

'No, Mrs Birmingham.'

Not likely to, either, thought Peggy Roberts. There was a silence.

Most girls, after a silence had lasted longer than a minute, would become uncomfortable and volunteer some remark, even if it were only 'Shall I go now?' But Hermione sat, apparently perfectly relaxed. She was watching the gardener's boy, sleeves rolled up to reveal his muscular arms, riding the mower across the lawn. It made a distant grinding sound. Then she realized that she could look at her reflection in the side window, beyond which a dark tree acted as a mirror. She studied herself tranquilly, devoid of thought, until Mrs Birmingham said, 'All right, Hermione, you may go. You will be a prefect next term, I expect. I hope you take your responsibilities seriously. It's time you put something back into the school.'

'Yes, Mrs Birmingham,' said Hermione prettily.

As she walked along the corridor from the dining-room towards the Covered Way, Hermione saw Charmian coming out of the staff-room; definitely coming *out* of it.

'Charmian!' she called. 'Charmian! What were you doing in the staff-room?'

'I don't know, Hermy ... sorry, Hermione.'

'You don't *know*?'

'Well, I mean, Mrs Whitby called me in. I don't know why.'

She is an attractive child, thought Hermione unexpectedly, and that's why she's having problems. Old Bibs must be after her. She looks pale.

'Are you all right, Charmian? Are you sure? Has anything happened?'

Charmian had never seen Hermione's face so close, bending anxiously to look into her own, a long curl swinging beside her ear. Her skin was faintly translucent, with an almost bluish sheen through which her veins showed up in lilac tracery. She smelled of Elizabeth Arden's Blue Grass. Charmian had a sudden vision of herself being picked up by Hermione, of being carried away, of being taken to some secret place, of being cuddled, of telling her the whole story ... about Mummy and Uncle Dickie, and how much she loved Daddy, and how he didn't write to her, so she must have done something wrong, something bad. And – no, she wouldn't say what she'd done; she'd say how sorry she felt for the poor little orphans in Dr Barnardo's Homes who had no parents at *all*, and so she was trying to cheer them up; and then in the vision Hermione was saying, 'Goodness Charmian, what a kind person you are!' All this sped through her mind in seconds, as Hermione's soft fair hair tickled the side of her neck. But Charmian said nothing. She had learned about silence.

'Well,' said Hermione, in a disappointingly senior way, 'you'd better hurry back to your form-room. But *walk*, don't run.'

'Yes, Hermione,' said Charmian. She dawdled back to Miss Monk's boring maths lesson.

Constance sat in class huddled inside herself, trying to blot out the hostility of the others, who knew, of course, that she had been summoned to see the Head this morning. Her finger was throbbing where a splinter had gone into it a week ago and the pain and her thoughts plunged her into sullen misery.

She had expected to be one of those who was called to the study. She knew they all wanted her to be guilty. She was the 'new girl', the outsider. It would suit them if she were the one.

Mrs Birmingham had cross-questioned her closely – not so much about herself; she was not apparently a prime suspect, not in the Head's eyes anyway – but about who might be doing the stealing.

'You're intelligent and observant. You would notice the girls in your class, how they behave, what they're like. You must have drawn your own conclusions by now about which of them is honest or dishonest. I need your help, Constance: tell me what you think.'

Constance had longed to succumb to this mixture of flattery and reassurance, and longed most of all to be rid of the burden which Charmian imposed. But if Charmian were accused, everyone would know that she had split on her friend, and that was even worse than stealing. She hesitated. Mrs Birmingham noticed the hesitation, and extended her hands, palms upwards, upon the desk. This was an old, unconscious gesture of hers. It symbolized openness, defenceless pleading. It nearly worked.

Constance had sighed deeply, unconscious of her sigh, and looked down at her throbbing finger. The flesh around the nail was red and shiny. With each pulse the bright needle of pain zig-zagged through her. She squeezed the fingertip tightly in her clenched fist, and the red part glowed yellow and poisonous. It hurt more, and she squeezed it again.

'I don't know anything about it, Mrs Birmingham,' she had answered, looking at her finger. There was a long silence. Finally she said, 'May I go now?'

'You may.'

'Constance King, will you repeat for the class the formula for quadratic equations?'

'I'm sorry, Miss Monk, I don't know it.'

'But I have just this very minute explained it. Where were you?'

'I'm sorry, I didn't hear.'

'You mean you weren't listening.'

No, I wasn't listening, thought Constance. I hate maths. I hate the Lower Fourth. Most of all I hate Charmian. I want to go home. I shall run away. And, as she hadn't got a home that she could visualize, she thought, I hope there's a letter from Mummy at Break.

Charmian entered the room, glanced decorously towards Miss Monk, and slipped into the next desk. After a moment or two she looked fiercely at Constance and gritted her teeth. Constance shook her head imperceptibly. Charmian's shoulders relaxed and she reached over and squeezed Constance's hand, making the finger throb.

'Well done, Gogs!' she whispered, and smiled in a way that anyone else would have interpreted as sympathy, but Constance knew was pure triumph.

As the end of the week approached, the school was gripped by a single over-riding purpose. Saturday was Speech Day, when form-rooms were decked out with needlework and pottery, exercise books and text books, arranged so that the best were nearest the front, while pages marked 'Untidy work, Rachel: you must take more trouble' or 'You haven't understood, Charmian: please see me!' were hidden away at the bottom of the pile.

The school, of course, had no secrets from parents.

Up in the studio the best pictures were displayed on wooden battens along the walls or tacked on to easels with drawing-pins. Every girl's portfolio was there to be opened; some were simply more accessible than others. Fathers would walk round in navy blazers and striped or regimental ties, hands behind their backs, peering uncertainly at the drawings or paintings, stuck for words.

'Which one's yours, darling?' mothers would ask; and then, '*Lovely*, my pet! Oh, I *do* like it! Are you allowed to bring it home?' If the picture did come home at the end of term, rolled up and a little crumpled, the grey sugar paper already shabby, it would be folded and put away in a 'treasures drawer', and often not looked at again until years later. After the death of the parent, a dutiful daughter, now middle-aged, clearing through 'their old junk', would suddenly stop, rock back on her heels, and stare at this same drawing. Then the recollection of the high studio with its skylight and chalky easels, stained jam jars, splayed paintbrushes, and of their aprons splashed with bright poster paints, would flood through her with an emotion more acute than any evoked by her parent's recent death.

The amphitheatre was a natural dip in the ground behind the swimming-pool, surrounded by pergolas that had once been draped with Edwardian roses but were now sadly neglected because the gardener had no time, with just the one boy to help him, and the games field to roll and mow. Here, in the evenings, rehearsals for *1066 and All That* went on until the dormitory bell rang and the jaunty singing of 'Oh, we don't want to lose you, But we think you ought to go . . .' had to stop. In the long, light evenings of high summer it seemed as if their voices floated for miles across the green and leafy Sussex hills, vibrant as the sunsets, mellowing towards the finale.

Ginny Valentine, bright-eyed and endlessly enthusiastic, sewed and altered costumes every evening when rehearsals were over, and badgered other members of the staff to do the same. In her study, Mrs Birmingham sat writing her speech for the parents and school, searching for words that would reassure the parents without being dishonest about the state of affairs within the school. Usually the plump cadences would have rolled off her nib. 'And in this coming year, as every year, we shall strive to carry on that Christian tradition which is perhaps the school's proudest, and at the same time its humblest, boast . . .' How could she say that, when each girl and every member of staff knew that someone was stealing and at least one other person was lying? She could not set the girls an example of duplicity; yet parents – and in particular the bishop, who was to be this year's special guest and give out the prizes – needed to be told that the school was a character-building Christian community.

She had invented a prize for Sheila Dunsford-Smith – Best Garden, not that their square, unimaginative little patch really deserved it – in the hope that this would persuade the Major to bring his daughter back to the school. The child had said no farewells, and Mrs Birmingham knew from her own experience that a proper leave-taking was essential.

She remembered the disbelief with which she had greeted the news, brought by the village postman bearing a telegram. First Alistair. Dead. Then, two years later, Hugo. Dead. She could not reconcile her last image of them – in uniform, but so ebulliently, solidly alive – with the realization that now they were dead. Blown up, shot to pieces, left to die of thirst in some shell-hole: the details, however often she had tried to imagine them, were almost beside the point. It had taken years to accept that she would not see them again, not even when the war was over and life had supposedly returned to normal, except that her brothers were still dead.

Mrs Birmingham knew that Sheila needed the rituals of saying good-bye, exchanging home addresses, promising to write, to visit, to keep in touch. Even if she did none of these things, she ought to round off her time at the school. She hoped the child would come, and that she herself could find a moment amid the bustle and demands of Speech Day for a quiet word with her about the death of her mother.

On Saturday morning the girls dressed with unusual care, wearing everything clean, from white knicker linings and white ankle socks to freshly laundered dresses. Charmian, who usually spent hours doing her parting and combing through her bunches, dressed hastily and sped downstairs, leaving behind her the trail of a half-heard explanation.

She walked sedately past the staff-room in case anybody was in early, but once beyond the Covered Way she flew up the drive towards Pets. She was late; the postman must already be on his way down the drive. Concealed behind a bale of straw for the rabbit hutches she had kept her hoard of stolen things. All that was there now was the postcard album, Peach's string of seed-pearls and her titchy little silver cross and chain. Charmian grabbed the brown paper and string which she'd hidden a couple of nights ago. Using one of the pens (she gave it a good shake, and then unscrewed it and squeezed the rubber bulb, for the ink had dried up) she hastily inscribed in capital letters on the brown paper the address of Dr Barnardo's Homes; no return address. Impatiently, clumsily, she wrapped everything up and knotted the string round the parcel. Then she waited at the edge of the drive, praying that she wasn't too late to intercept the postman. He had already delivered the school's post and was wheeling his bicycle back up the hill. When he saw her, he stopped.

'Morning, Miss,' he said. 'Haven't seen you these last few weeks. Doing good works again, eh? Good lassie. Not such a tidy parcel this time. Think it'll hold together?'

'I don't see why not,' said Charmian breathlessly. 'Here's half-a-crown. Will that be enough? I've got to rush. It's our Speech Day today.'

'Half-a-crown's plenty, Miss, don't you worry. I'll give you the change next time I see you. Off you go now.'

Silly old fool, thought Charmian, as she bounced light-heartedly down the hill, and then, Phew! What a relief. She went into her class-room and fiddled with a few books before emerging to join the breakfast queue forming in the Covered Way. Nobody had noticed her. They were all too preoccupied with Speech Day, jabbering away about their mothers and fathers. Constance had noticed, though, and caught her eye, but Constance didn't matter.

The morning was taken up with final adjustments to the class-rooms and setting the chairs out in rows on the lawn in front of the portable dais that had been brought down from the gym. The prize books were piled on the table and covered with a cloth. Each had a slip of paper inside bearing the girl's name and what the prize was given for, written by Mrs Birmingham in her clear, round hand. Pasted on the flyleaf was a book-plate with the school crest and motto. Under another cloth, like a Communion set, was a row of silver-plated cups. All these the bishop would bestow in due course.

Lunch was early, and almost before it was over, parents started to arrive. They were directed by beautifully mannered prefects to seats in front of the dais. Sheila was sitting beside her father, stoical and out of place. Charmian saw her and, slipping along the line of parents with a murmured, 'Scusie . . . Scusie,' she put her arm round her and said, 'Sheil! How wizard to see you, what a surprise! Nobody said you were coming. Gosh, I like your dress!'

'Your mother was kind enough to send us a very nice letter,' said Sheila's father. He looked equally ill-at-ease. 'I have written to thank her, but if she is here today perhaps you would introduce me?'

'Of course,' said Charmian, thinking, No fear. She sidled back along the row of parents' knees again and made her way to sit beside Constance.

Finally the staff processed in, followed last of all by the Head and her Deputy escorting the bishop between them like a giant performing seal. He grinned wetly at the expectant rows and, after a complicit glance at Mrs Birmingham, who nodded, he said 'Shall we begin with a prayer? Almighty God . . .'

Heads were bowed and Speech Day began.

When the prizes had been distributed and the bishop, the Head, and the Head Girl had made speeches and given thanks, people went to change into their costumes and be made up for the play. They emerged unnaturally garish, smooth cheeks encircled with rouge, eyes emphasized with blue shadow and crudely outlined in black. Girls playing men's parts had moustaches drawn in over complexions darkened with Leichner stage make-up. They looked like marionettes and their behaviour had the same disjointed quality. They moved self-consciously among the parents, who were being served tea on the lawn in a parody of an Edwardian house-party. Some mothers sat on jackets on the grass, relaxed, absorbed in their children, bright-eyed with pleasure. Some stood in stiff, formal groups, making polite conversation with other parents.

Constance avoided the welcoming smile of Mrs Simpson, which was contradicted by a scowl from Mick and Flick, and piled her plate with mushy triangular sandwiches and lumps of school cake. She walked a little distance away and sat by herself on the edge of the lawn, barely visible behind a rhododendron bush whose brilliant flowers and stamens littered the grass. She minded very much that her parents were not there to admire all her exercise books, which were displayed in the forefront of the Lower Fourth's work. Auntie Marjorie had arranged to come, but had cancelled at the last moment. 'HARRY'S DOWN WITH MEASLES DARLING WHAT A BORE FOR YOU SO SORRY CAN'T COME BIG HUG MARJIE,' the telegram had said. It sounded so like her aunt's breathless, eager voice that Constance felt sharply homesick and conscious that she had been separated from her family for ten weeks, which was too long.

It was not the moment to be a tree, so she tried once more to summon up a happy time from her past that she had stored to use later, when she really needed it. She remembered squatting on her haunches beside a rock pool at Eastbourne, staring into a net held in the water and filled with tiny transparent shrimps with black eyes like those of the glass animals in the dormitory. She would tip them out of the net into her bucket of water to watch them dart about. Quick and miniature under her moonlike gaze, the shrimps zig-zagged to and fro, flicking in the bucket like fireflies. Grains of grey sand drifted down to the bottom. She found a ribbon of damp seaweed and some shells and dropped those in too, while her toes sank deeper into the wet sand at the edge of the pool, creating a mysterious drier, paler patch that followed the shape of her feet. Beside her, Daddy and Uncle Neil had been building an elaborate sand-castle, with a tunnel spiralling through the middle and emerging on the outside, so that you could start a ping-pong ball rolling and it would vanish inside the castle and then reappear, having gathered speed, on the outside, to plop into the moat of salt water. Her mother had been sitting on a towel nearby, with her socks and sandals off and her feet stretched out, very white and bony, half watching them and saying from time to time, 'Connie, darling, don't get cold. Let me put your cardigan on...' But Constance knew she didn't really mean it and then...

'Thank goodness I've found you!' said Sheila's voice. 'I've been looking for you everywhere. I've got to talk to you.'

Sheila was wearing a grey checked dress with a white collar, very much like the school summer dresses, with long white socks and black patent button-up shoes. Constance guessed that she had been bought lots of new clothes. She looked thinner, but her face was the same round, spotty face, and her hair was still greasy. Sheila's eyes were comically wide open as she gazed fiercely at Constance, who said, 'Are you OK? I didn't know you were coming.'

'Daddy said I had to because I'd won a prize. In the end it was for the garden and Charmian went and got it anyway. Gogs, listen, it's important and I haven't got long. You've got to tell on Charmie. I will, too, if you do. It's because secrets are wicked. They can kill people. She said something awful would happen and it did, but now it's happened and you'll be safe. I'm going to tell Old Ma B about her stealing and I'll say she's got you into it too and then it'll all come out.'

Constance stared at her for a moment, then shook her head.

'What's the matter, Gogsy? Why won't you? What's wrong? Go on.'

'I can't. She's really wicked, don't you know that? Charmie's the wickedest person I've ever met. She's all sweet and lovey-dovey on top, but underneath that she's awful. She scares me to smithereens. If she doesn't steal, she might do something worse.'

'Like what?' Sheila asked.

'I haven't the foggiest. How should I know? It's all right for you – you're out of it. I'm the one who'll get it.'

'No, you won't. Charmie will be expelled and that'll be that. Now that my mother's dead there's nothing more she can do. It's time she got into trouble, anyway. She always gets away with things, because she's pretty.'

'Boo!' said Charmian, jumping between them from behind the bush. She was grinning triumphantly.

'I knew I'd find you together. I just *knew* Sheil would want to come and be pathetic all over you. Cry baby bunting! You looked daft sitting there on your big fat BTM in the middle of the grown-ups. You're putrid and feeble. *Feeb*ile!'

'Well, you're much worse. I hope you heard what we were saying because it's true. You *are* wicked,' said Sheila with unexpected determination.

'Yes, I did, and a jolly rotten friend *you* are. But I heard

Gogsy sticking up for me. Good old Gogs. Come on, the play's probably started and I'm on in the second scene. 'Bye Sheila. Thanks very much I don't think!'

I didn't stick up for her at all, thought Constance, as she let herself be dragged away.

The play was over. The setting, in the sylvan glade of the amphitheatre, overhung by whispering silver birches, had been magical, but the performance was self-conscious. Several children, word-perfect until the day, had forgotten their lines. Only in the songs did their voices gather strength and confidence, pouring into the semi-circle of their audience. At the end they were rapturously applauded, since each mother had watched only her own child. Fathers found it hard to concentrate, and many dozed off in the warm afternoon. The cast called for three cheers for Miss Valentine, and one of the squits presented her with a bouquet of flowers. There were tears in her eyes as she accepted it, looked round at the children who were clapping her, started to speak, and then threw out her arms with an all-embracing, shaky smile. Everyone smiled.

'It was grand,' said the mothers afterwards, emotionally. 'Grand!'

By supper-time the last of the parents had gone. Some would return to take their daughters out for a picnic the following day, sitting around their cold food spread out on a tablecloth, awkward and uncomfortable on the bumpy ground. Mothers and daughters would unwrap sandwiches or cold meat pies and talk, a little out of touch, uneasily aware of the changes of the last few weeks, while fathers listened to the cricket on a portable wireless. At the end of the afternoon, with something like relief, parents and children would part. There were only exams still to come and then the school would wind down towards the long holidays.

At bedtime, up in the dormitory, one girl was unconsciously humming a tune from the play. Others picked up the song. 'We're going home ... we're going home ... We're on the road that leads to home,' they sang as they bounced on their beds.

'Thoroughly over-excited, all of you,' said Peach. 'No more bouncing. Singing's over. Lights out.'

She shut the door behind her, and as her shoes squeaked away down the corridor Charmie wheedled, 'Go on with the story, Gogsy. Good old Gogs, go on.'

'Yes, do,' said Anne. 'I want to know what happens to the horse.'

Constance remembered Anne and Fiona silhouetted against the pale midnight sky of high summer. I bet you do, she thought; ugh, you give me the creeps.

'No,' she said firmly. 'I'm tired and I'm going to sleep now and I don't care what you say so shut up.'

'Spoil-sport,' said Charmian, sulkily, but Constance knew she wouldn't insist. Got you under my thumb, she thought, because you're scared now, aren't you? Only trouble is, I'm scared, too.

'Good-*night*,' she said and rolled over, her face turned away from them all.

It was nearly midnight in the cottage. Sylvia had been drinking. As the evening darkened and the bottle emptied she had railed against the hypocrisy of Speech Day, the pantomime of text books laid out for parents; castigated the bishop; reviled the play; mocked Ginny Valentine. She was not mellowing or blurring into tiredness, nor becoming repetitive or mawkish. On the contrary, she was filled with clarity and an energy which drove her anger on, goading her brain to lash her tongue.

She is like an Amazon, Diana thought. She is a Valkyrie; she is wonderful when she's like this. Not self-pitying, as the uncles always were after their one bout of self-indulgence at Christmas, but high-coloured and flashing-eyed. She is everything I never dared to be; she is not in the slightest bit respectable or ladylike or proper, and she doesn't give a fig for convention. What would my mother make of Sylvia? Poor Mother, who has slipped through her days apologizing for living, trying only to be as inconspicuous as possible. Diana laughed.

The laugh brought Sylvia up with a jolt. Good God, does she have so little notion of who I am that she finds me *funny*?

Makes a change, anyway. I've seldom been thought a wit. Even as a girl I wasn't sociable. I grew up ugly and disagreeable, a loner and a swot. I knew I had to do well to get out, and that meant a good enough matriculation to get me to university. So I swotted, and was never asked to their tea-parties, or trips to the cinema.

I started early to crave the younger, pretty girls; always the same type as Hermione – fragile and airy, passing dreamily across my path and into my fantasies. But they laughed at me, heavy and awkward as I was, and turned away from my longing glances to whisper and giggle, not bothering to hide their contempt. I got out, though. I did manage that. Some of them are still there, crabbed Welsh housewives now, their beauty pinched and weather-beaten.

Then my father died during the war, not *in* the war, nothing as gallant and glorious as that. He was nearly fifty by then, still teaching in Gower, bitter and shrivelled into angry taciturnity. He developed varicose veins on his legs, walking and bicycling became difficult for him, and standing up for long, but it was an embolism that killed him.

I went to his funeral. I was nearly twenty and had already left home but I went back. I felt sorry for my mother. It was a shock to realize that she'd miss him. I didn't want her to have to see him buried alone, so I travelled back to Gower on one of the long, slow wartime trains, with endless changes at obscure stations, and got there the evening before the funeral.

If we were ever going to talk, it would have been then. She was raw and vulnerable. He had died from one moment to the next, without having been properly ill, and she wasn't prepared for it.

She gave me supper when I arrived, and then a cup of tea. We sat in the parlour together, conscious of his body lying upstairs. Probably she expected me to have a last look at him, but she didn't suggest it.

Before I could break the silence she looked up and said, 'He was a good man, your father. Never forget that, Sylvia, out there in your big world of clever people. A *good man*.'

Yes, I nodded, yes, a good man. She closed her eyes and the silence resumed.

Side by side we followed his coffin into the chapel. A lot of his pupils were there, and some parents, and stupid old Mrs Powell, snivelling. The minister orated about his achievements in the life of the community and then we processed out again and stuck him in the ground.

My mother shook hands numbly and sat, dignified and widow-like, over the Welsh tea laid on for the mourners. There was no sin-eater to consume his wickedness and send him safely to a better world. It was all so solemn that I was overcome by a desire to laugh. I left the room and they all snuffled sympathetically.

In the bathroom I looked at myself in the mirror as I grew red-faced, choking down my inappropriate glee. I lit a forbidden cigarette and smoked it to calm myself down. I struck several matches, one after the other, watching them flare and shrivel blackly and die. I was tempted to blow out the pilot light on the Ascot and, holding down the bi-metal strip, let the hot water run. If I then lit a match it would all go bang with a most satisfying whoosh. I looked at it for a long time, imagining the splash of light. There was a knock on the door, and Mrs Powell's ingratiating voice said, 'Sylvie, dear, are you all right? You lost your dada, is it? We all feel lost without him.'

Next morning I caught the train back again.

Diana sits grinning, waiting to be entertained again.

'Good old Monks, or shall I call you Monkey, ho ho ho! "Laugh, Kookaburra, laugh... Gay your life must be!" Share the joke, Monkey, come on, let's all laugh.'

'I was thinking how indescribably shocked my mother would be if she could see us now.'

'Well, poor old Mothah. A daughtah who's sharing her living quarters with a mad teacher, pissed as a newt as well. Drunk as a lord. Sober as a judge – no, wrong one – sloshed, Monkey, and stewed as a prune. Not like that pulpit-faced bunch this afternoon... Fat-arsed fathers and po-faced mamas, all with their hands up each others' skirts and down each other's trousers. God they make me sick, shick, thick. *And* their prissy, virginal, precioush little daughters!'

'Come upstairs, Sylvia,' said Diana, low-voiced and breathless. 'It's time we both got to bed. It's been a long day. I'm dead beat.'

'Oh, sensible, level-headed, sober as a monk you are! Righty-ho then, off to bed we go, ho ho, ho ho...' And singing like the Seven Dwarfs, Sylvia climbed the lino-covered steps towards their separate bedrooms.

'Did it go well?' asked Lionel Birmingham. 'Bishop do his stuff?'

'The bishop did his bit. Not fearfully inspiring, I'm afraid. Too much cosiness and not enough *gravitas*. It's a mistake to try and ingratiate yourself with children. Up there in his purple shirt and dog-collar: it's not his role to talk to them like an equal. Moral guidance, that's what they need. They don't expect a bishop to make them laugh. Girls are terribly susceptible, *en masse* like that. I told him they needed a bit of a pep talk and instead he waffled on about his schooldays. Great pity. Oh, well, never mind, listen to selfish old me grumbling. It went all right. The important thing is: what about *you*? How are you feeling? Did you manage to eat your supper? The strawberries were from the kitchen garden. I asked the under-gardener to pick them specially.'

Lionel tried to turn round and extract something from underneath his pillow, but he couldn't move his body far enough to reach his hand across, and after grunting heavily for a bit he sank back in exasperation and said, 'You get it. Can't reach. Fish about and you'll find it.'

The heavy smell of her clothes and her body loomed for a moment as Henrietta rummaged behind him.

'Oh, look!' she cried triumphantly. 'It's a letter from James!'

The thin blue airmail paper crackled in her fingers as she read it hastily.

' "... promotion promised for next year, provided all goes well ... new man out from England seems a good chap ...

brought Juniper to his cocktail party to meet the troops..."
Juniper? Who's Juniper? Lionel, do we know who this Juniper
is? We don't *know* anyone called Juniper. Not a very English
name. Oh, dear, I do hope James isn't being silly. He brought
her to the Chief's cocktail party ... well then, I suppose she
must have been suitable, though it's a curious name. Anyway,
then he says, where was I? Yes: "I shall be minding the desk
for Roger Ormiston while he's on home leave, and after that I
plan to come home myself for six weeks. Didn't mention it
before in case..." Lionel! Do you realize he'll be home in *less
than a month?*'

 *O God, I thank Thee for this Thy bounty, that my son will see his
father before he dies. Almighty God, Father of us all ... bring him
home safely through Thy boundless skies – and please,* she couldn't
help adding, *if she is to be important to him, let Juniper be a decent
girl, worthy of him, and English.*

Nine

It was now so close to the end of term that the Lower Fourths were making caterpillar calendars on which to count off the remaining days. First they would draw several overlapping small circles with a protractor, then a larger one at the end for the caterpillar's head, sometimes embellished with long-lashed eyes and antennae, and always with a joyous message like HOME! or LAST DAY OF TERM! Using scissors they would cut round these circles, each with its pin-prick centre, and finally colour them in with waxy Lakeland pencils. These creations were pinned to the inside of their desks and every morning one circle would be cut off and thrown away. This ritual was proof that the holidays were approaching as the curling caterpillars grew shorter every day.

The hot weather continued, light and heat hanging in the stifling air. The girls were sluggish, heavy-limbed, slow-moving, too hot to argue or revise. Several complained of aching limbs and headaches. The staff, immured in their cramped room during Break and after lunch, snapped at one another irritably and complained about their pupils. What was the point in setting and marking exams, when they would all be suitably married within ten years to dull, rich husbands, for no purpose but to create another generation of pampered drones?

At night in the dormitory the girls were listless, slow to undress and reluctant to lie under even a single sheet. The attic rooms were close and airless, although the windows were wide open and the curtains drawn back. Charmian was fretful, whining about a headache. She didn't feel well, her bones were all funny, it made her legs hurt.

'Mine too,' said Anne Hetherington. 'I wish Mummy was here. I wish this rotten term was over.'

'Come on, girls, none of that nonsense. I'm up to my eyebrows,' said Miss Peachey. 'Lights out. No talking. What *is* it, Charmian?'

'Peach, I don't feel well.' Charmian sighed.

'I've got too many on my hands in the sanatorium as it is,' said Miss Peachey. 'Don't you start. Too much sun, that's your trouble. Fair-skinned people should stay out of the sun. Look at you. Bright red! Now then, bedtime. Night-night all!'

They listened as her crêpe soles squelched away down the corridor. Then Fiona said, 'Tell us a story, Gogsy. Go on. Be a sport. Tell us the Thingummy and Thingummybob one. You know.'

Constance remembered the outline against the night sky, a pair of horses mating.

'I'm tired,' she muttered. 'Go to sleep. No.'

Charmian's voice came thinly from across the room. She lay in a graceless heap on her rumpled bed. 'Pleease, Gogsy,' she said. 'My head feels all funny. Tell us the story.'

'Shut up then and I will,' said Constance. 'I'll just finish off *Sohrab and Rustum* and then you lot leave me in peace, O K? Well, now, where ... oh, yes. So you remember, they had this tremendous battle, with everyone from the two armies watching, until even the horse let out a dreadful cry and the air was filled with thunder and lightning and the river rushed and the two of them battled to the death. Suddenly Sohrab's sword splintered into a thousand bits. Rustum saw his chance, and he lifted up his head and uttered his battle cry and gave a huge shout of "Rustum!" When Sohrab heard that he was so amazed – 'cos you remember, Rustum's the name of his long-lost father – that he dropped his shield and Rustum drove his spear at him and Sohrab fell to the ground.'

'Dead?' breathed Anne. 'You mean, he got killed? The son died?'

'*No!*' said Constance, her voice strong with anger. 'No, he didn't. He staggered to his feet and grabbed Rustum's sword and thrust it deep into his side, thinking, there you are then.

That's for what my father did! And he stood over Rustum, who lay dying on the sand. "My father abandoned me all those years ago and I've been searching for him ever since, but I can't find him, so you can die instead!" And so then, finally, with his dying breath, Rustum told him that *he*'d had a son once, and had put a mark on his arm so he would know him again. And Sohrab showed him the mark – like a vaccination, sort of – on his arm, and at last the two of them knew they were father and son. Rustum wanted to embrace him and get his forgiveness for having left him, but Sohrab wouldn't, because he thought it served him right for having gone away and left him on his own. That was his punishment. So he pulled out the sword, and his father's blood gushed out on to the sand, and he died. And Sohrab was the winner. And,' she added, 'that meant he got the horse.'

'Good,' said Fiona. 'I'm glad it was the old man that died. It's a wizard story, Gogsy. Jolly well done.'

'OK, so now everyone's got to go to sleep. 'Night,' said Constance.

She rolled over with her back to the others and lay curled up under the sheet. As she drifted towards sleep she had a vision of her parents and herself, joined by a cord, a long, plaited cord in three colours, one for each of them, pulsing like the blood in her finger, like an umbilical cord. It was stretched tight because her parents were so distant, and she feared in her half-sleep that it might break. If I have children, she thought, I'll *never* leave them.

Sitting in a biology revision class, Constance nursed her throbbing finger. Poison had swollen the top digit to three times its normal size and the skin was shiny from the pressure inside. With each beat of her heart a needle stabbed her. She breathed heavily, held her breath, then expelled it in a sigh, sometimes a groan. The others turned to frown at her, but she could not respond to anything but the rhythm of her own pain.

Sylvia Parry heard the sighs, clenched her fists and turned her back to the class, drawing diagrams on the blackboard so as not to see Constance's bowed head, her evident lack of interest in the lesson. The sighs went on. Miss Parry felt her anger like a rising tide. Behind her back, every minute or so, she could heard another dramatic groan. The girl was merely drawing attention to herself. If she ignored it, the groaning would stop. No one spoke, no intelligent questions were asked. Suddenly, like a tidal wave breaking across the shore, she reacted.

'For God's sake, Constance King, will you *stop* that interminable sighing! I am trying to *teach*. Now be QUIET.'

'I'm sorry, Miss Parry. It's my finger. It really hurts.'

'Poor little Baba, den. Does ums finger hurt?' she sneered, while the class quaked, avoiding her eye. 'Jesus Christ, why am I stuck with this bunch of half-witted infants? Get *out* of my lesson. Out! Away! Be off! Get lost!'

'Shall I stand outside or . . . ?'

'Go and see Matron, anybody, I don't care where you go, as long as the rest of us can get on with some *work*. OUT! Now!'

Constance left the room thankfully. Miss Peachey wasn't anywhere to be found, but on the topmost dormitory corridor she bumped into the medical sister, formidable, straight-backed Miss Girdlestone. She was hurrying past clutching an armful of pillows, followed by Anne, who looked feverish, with glittering eyes.

'Miss Girdlestone . . .' Constance began.

'Can't you see I'm busy? What do you want?'

'I'm sorry – it's my finger again. It honestly hurts like billy-o. Can you . . . ?'

'For heaven's sake, Constance! It's only a whitlow. Haven't you ever had a whitlow before? It'll go away in a day or two. I've got much more important things to worry about. Why aren't you in your form-room?'

'Miss Parry sent me out . . .'

'Well, go and sit in the Reading Corner. Anywhere. Just leave me in peace.'

The hall was quiet, dark and cool. At her back, the tall trees were motionless in the still air. Listlessly Constance turned the pages of *Punch* and *The Children's Newspaper*. She put them back on the oak table and enfolded her throbbing finger again. So much pain enclosed in such a small area. She could hear the blood surging through her ears. She moaned to herself, rocking gently.

The door of the study opened and the school doctor ushered Mrs Birmingham ahead of him. The Head was saying, 'I shall require a second opinion of course, doctor. It may be nothing more than heat stroke. If you will speak to your Mr MacIntyre in the paediatric department and let him know that I shall be telephoning, I will try and reach him after lunch.'

'Keep our fingers crossed,' said the doctor, and Mrs Birmingham said, 'I shall pray.'

At that moment she caught sight of Constance.

'Constance King, why aren't you in a lesson?'

'Miss Parry sent me out,' said Constance and stood up, suddenly audacious. She knew they would be shocked. She walked over to the doctor and thrust her hand at him.

'I was sent out of Miss Parry's class for moaning, but my bad finger hurt so much that I couldn't concentrate. Look!'

Her finger was the size and colour of a rotten plum. Her hand shook as she held it towards him.

'Good gracious, child!' said the doctor. 'That ought to be seen to. Have you told Matron?'

'Yes,' said Constance, 'and she sent me away. She said she had more important things to do.'

'It needs lancing,' said the doctor. 'It ought to be done at once. Mrs Birmingham ... I had better take this girl up to the sick-room and deal with this. I'll find my own way out.'

Mrs Birmingham's blue eyes, enclosed in fine wrinkles, smiled down at Constance with momentary tenderness.

'Poor old sausage,' she said. 'It does look nasty. Never mind. Doctor Duncan'll soon have you right as rain. Good thing you happened to be here.' She turned and walked back into the study.

The doctor escorted Constance up the main staircase, the one the girls weren't supposed to use, and straight into the sick-room. He sat her down, washed his hands, reached for an

166

enamel kidney-shaped bowl and balanced Constance's wrist over it, her palm upwards.

'You'll be surprised,' he said. 'This won't hurt a bit. Promise.'

Constance watched in fascination as he sliced through the ball of her middle finger with a fine sharp instrument. Immediately the flesh sprang apart and a thick torrent of yellow pus veined with bright red blood oozed out. He squeezed the two sides of the cut together and patted her shoulder.

'Brave girl!' he said. 'Top marks. Now then, strictly speaking I ought to put a couple of stitches in this, but let's try a butterfly plaster and hope for the best.'

He criss-crossed a plaster over the flabby white incision and wound a gauze bandage several times round that, till the finger looked as swollen as before.

'Now, it doesn't hurt any more, does it?'

'No,' said Constance, grateful and astonished. 'For the first time in days and days it doesn't hurt any more.'

'I'll see you again tomorrow, have a look at how it's getting on. Run away now. What lesson was it?'

'Biology.'

'Ah, biology . . . queen of the sciences. Tells us how we're made. Ever thought of being a doctor? No? You've got a good steady hand. That's one thing you need. Away with you now! I'll talk to Sister.'

Bloody woman, thought Dr Duncan. Deserves to be sacked. And I personally will see to it. That poor kid would have been reason enough on her own, but to ignore the symptoms of a major epidemic, in a place like this, was criminal. And unless I'm very much mistaken, what we've got here is polio.

'*Polio?*' said Mrs Birmingham. 'Are you absolutely certain it's polio?'

'Polio, yes, I'm afraid so,' said Mr MacIntyre. 'Five definites and two possibles.'

In the drawing-room Mr MacIntyre and Dr Duncan sat facing the Head and her Deputy. Sister Girdlestone and Miss Peachey sat rigidly side-by-side on another sofa. Sunlight streamed across the carpet, illuminating the faded colours of the Turkish rug in front of the empty fireplace. A slight breeze had started up, fluttering the edges of the curtains and blowing summer into their nostrils; a smell of cut grass mingling with the cloying scent from the bowl of roses on the table. The heat outside was unrelenting; today was the hottest yet, with the mercury rising towards the nineties. On the long slope of lawn beyond the windows the gardener was bent across the roller, mopping his brow. The topmost branches of the cedar moved sluggishly.

The specialist had finished speaking. Mrs Birmingham met his gaze.

'What must I do?' she asked.

'One, inform the parents of the sick girls who'll need to be taken into hospital. Parents may want to have them nearer to home. It's up to you to decide whether to close the school, but in my view, there's not much point at this stage. The incubation period is normally two to four weeks. The girls have all been exposed to it by now. It's too late to shut the stable door.'

'Do I tell the girls?'

'The rumours must be all over the school already. Once they see the ambulance arriving, they're not going to believe in the heat-stroke theory any longer. But you know more than I do about how they'll react. Adolescent girls are prone to communal hysteria, and soon you won't be able to tell the real cases from the self-deluders.'

O God, prayed Mrs Birmingham, still holding his eyes steadily, *O God, shed Thy comfort upon these Thy sick children. Grant that they may recover, and not be paralysed for life. And grant to me, O Lord, in this heavy time, the humility to know what is best for me to do. Forgive us all our sins, for the sake of Thy Son. Amen.*

'Can you explain to me exactly what polio *is*?' said the Head, in a firm voice. She glanced across at her Deputy and gave her a faint, encouraging smile. Peggy, she knew, would be devastated, though her face was impassive. They both looked at the two matrons, but their heads were bowed. The four women listened to the specialist in silence.

'Poliomyelitis, or infantile paralysis, is, as the name suggests, more common in children than adults, though it can be contracted at any age. It is a virus that attacks the central nervous system and can, in some 50 per cent of cases, result in partial or complete paralysis. Very, very rarely indeed it is fatal. It is most commonly spread by contaminated food or water. It starts with the kind of fever, headache, sore throat and aching limbs that in a hot spell like this can be mistaken for heat stroke. Those affected just want to stay in bed, lying down. They are weak and usually motionless. This stage is followed by increasing muscular pain, a very stiff neck and complete, prostrating weakness. The onset of paralysis may occur at this stage. If it does not, there is an excellent chance of full recovery. If it does, however, there is very little that we can do about it. Good nursing and total bed-rest go without saying.'

As he spoke, his voice as precise as though he were describing a species of mosquito from the Nile delta, Henrietta Birmingham suddenly saw a clear image of herself at sixteen. Those long summer days behind drawn curtains, beside her brother's sick-bed. The atmosphere of pain and weakness invaded her consciousness like a scent. She narrowed to become the slender girl she had been then, passive and silent through hours of vigil, galvanized into hearing by James's brusque, coarse, visceral memories. Her arms lost their creased texture, her hands their lumpy veins, as she saw her young arms stretch over the coverlet to lay the back of her hand coolly against a throbbing artery in his neck. Since then she had dreaded illness more than anything – much more than death. Yet she had married a hypochondriac who now lay dying. But Lionel was old. It was sickness in the young that plunged her into despair. Her adored brother Jamie, his leg monstrous and putrescent; that poor child's finger had looked just the same.

'Now, we have here five unmistakable cases, and another two which may or may not develop into the full-fledged illness. I have made arrangements for all seven to be admitted to St Patrick's immediately. All other children, and for that matter, members of staff, should be watched carefully for any of the symptoms I have described.'

169

'Have we been remiss? Could it have been prevented?' Mrs Birmingham asked.

'I don't think so. My guess would be that it was picked up outside the school and brought in, possibly by a member of staff, or by a girl who hasn't yet contracted the illness herself. When was the last time the girls went home?'

'Half-term. Four weeks ago.'

'That would be about right. One of them may have carried it back to the school.'

'And school hygiene?' asked Miss Roberts.

'Any institution where people eat communally is at risk, and unless you were forewarned, there's very little you could have done to prevent it. Could have been the swimming-pool, the changing-rooms, the bathrooms, the lavatories ... anywhere.'

Miss Girdlestone sat white and silent. The specialist glanced around at them all.

'Perhaps an experienced nurse might have identified the symptoms sooner. I can't say. What is important now is to take every complaint seriously. Better to go easy on a malingerer than to be too hard on a sufferer. Mrs Birmingham, you will have a great deal to do, and so indeed have I ...'

He and Dr Duncan stood up and, automatically courteous, the Head rose too. She escorted them to the door, murmured her thanks, and only turned back into the drawing-room when the front door had closed behind the two men.

'You should go back to the sanatorium, Miss Girdlestone, Miss Peachey ... This is a bad time for us all, and for you especially,' she said. When they had gone she looked at Miss Roberts, her face under the tidily waved hairstyle blanched with shock.

'Peggy,' she said. 'Oh, Peggy ...'

The dining-room at supper was a hive of rumour. Constance found herself the focus of interest, for it was known that she'd seen the doctor.

'What did he *say*, Gogsy? He must have said something,' Madeleine asked with unusual friendliness.

'He just lanced my finger. We talked about that.'

'You are *hopeless*. Didn't you ask him why he was here?'

'No.'

'You're an utter and total clot. Oh well, who cares . . . I bet it's just boring old sunstroke anyway.'

'I think it's scarlet fever. My cousin had it, and . . .' said Madeleine, and the speculation moved on.

At the top of their table, Miss Parry sat in heavy silence. The bandage on Constance's finger showed that something had been wrong. She ought to have investigated, ought not to have lost her temper. To calm herself, she glanced across at Hermione. Her colour was high, and the fine curls around her face danced as she turned aside. It was impossible to hear what she was saying. If I had looked like that, Sylvia thought, my life would have been different. Beauty has the world at its feet. *I* am at her feet. Someone will notice; I must stop staring. She looked away, and caught Miss Monk's comforting smile. She turned away from that too.

'Eat up, everyone,' she ordered. 'Let's have less chatter.'

As the girls filed out of the dining-room, the staff made their way through the hall to the drawing-room for an emergency meeting. Sister and Miss Peachey had hinted that the news was grave, but would not be drawn further.

The circle of books on the polished mahogany table had been moved aside to make room for a dozen cups of coffee, and each member of staff took one before sitting down. When they were all settled and attentive, Mrs Birmingham began to speak.

The specialist had confirmed an outbreak of infantile paralysis in the school; they were all now at risk. Miss Parry imagined a malevolent virus, swooping like an angry wasp over the heads of the tables at dinner, then dive-bombing a random victim. Miss Monk pictured the odds: 100–1 against? 200–1? Or perhaps much lower: 8–3 or 33–1, like a horse race. Miss Valentine had a vision of the angel of death hovering over the school, huge and black-winged like a bat, covering its victims with an unseen shadow. Miss Roberts was haunted by a medieval fantasy of the grim reaper, a skeleton with a scythe like those pictured in stiff Italian frescos, while the populace scurried vainly for shelter. Seven down – well, certainly five – how many more to go?

Mrs Birmingham tried to keep her mind fixed on a merciful God. At the end of the meeting, heedless of their embarrassment, she suggested that they should all pray. Lumbering out of her wing-chair, she turned and knelt on the carpet. Reluctantly, self-consciously, the staff rose to their feet, tinkling the coffee-cups in their saucers on the floor, and knelt too, burying their elbows in the deep cushions of the sofas and chairs.

'Our Father . . .'

Agog with suspense, the girls waited to be told the news. Why had the doctor visited twice in one day? Why had ambulances taken seven girls from the sanatorium? And where to? Charmian's head drooped, her fair hair sticky at the nape of her neck. Miss Peachey had asked her that morning in the dormitory whether she felt unwell, but she had only muttered, 'I'm a bit hot. I wish it would rain.'

'You're sure you're all right, dear?' Matron had said. 'Come and see me after lunch if you don't feel better.'

That morning in Prayers they sang 'O God our help in ages past' and prayed for the sick. Mrs Birmingham told them to sit, and the common-room rustled and swayed as a hundred girls settled on to crossed legs, elbows folded over their knees, chins jutting towards her. For a few moments she let the school listen to its own heartbeat. From the dais she surveyed them all. Thirds at the front, playful and distractible as kittens, with pert faces, wide eyes and twinkling legs. Illness, like theft, would seem impossibly remote to them. Such great events happened to other people. Behind them were the pubescent Fourths, lumpy and spotty, too fat or too thin, absorbed in their own internal clocks, agitated by hormones and secrets. At the back sat the Fifth-formers, young women in all respects but still disguised as children in their school uniform, impatient to get away and sample the adult world, not to waste this blossoming on their own sex. Some of these, she thought, will be crippled; their straight limbs will twist and stiffen; one or two may die. Then she stopped herself. I'm being presumptuous. We must all die. It is in God's hands. All I have to do is to speak now, telling them the truth but without alarming them unnecessarily.

As she explained what had happened the girls were silent, awed by the presence of a real crisis overshadowing what suddenly seemed the petty, footling business of the thefts.

'Finally,' she said, 'I want to make it quite clear to every one of you that this is no time for hysterics. I don't want anyone drawing attention to herself with imaginary symptoms. The sanatorium is already rushed off its feet. One silly, self-important girl *pretending* she is ill could prevent a real case from being attended to. I want you all to get on quietly with your lessons. End of term exams will go ahead as usual. There are over a hundred girls in the school, of whom seven are in hospital. There is no reason to suppose any more will be taken ill. The specialist hopes there will be no more cases, and so do we all. Your parents will be informed by letter today. Meanwhile I want you all to behave like responsible people and get on with normal school life. Is that quite clear?'

'Yes, Mrs Birmingham,' the school answered, docile and sibilant.

They stood up as the Head and her Deputy rose and watched them process with slow, heavy steps towards the door.

In the study the two women looked at one another.

'You were wonderful, Henrietta. Calm, firm, reassuring. I half-expected them to panic ... burst out crying ... you never know. You held them all in check. Oh, my dear, well done.'

'I had a sleepless night,' said the Head. 'I hope I've done the right thing. It would have been simple to send them all home but that would be shrugging off our responsibilities, surely?'

'You did the right thing. Now, we have a hundred letters to write. We can't possibly do them individually. You make a fair draft and I'll run them off on the duplicator.'

The morning's post lay in the centre of Mrs Birmingham's desk.

'Better deal with these first, to clear my desk ...' she said, and began to slit open the dozen envelopes with a silver paper-knife.

After a few moments' silence she drew a sharp breath, then passed a letter across to Miss Roberts.

'As though we hadn't got enough on our plate! Read *this*.'

The letter was on the headed paper of Dr Barnardo's Homes.

Dear Madam,

I write with much pleasure to thank an anonymous donor from your school for a series of generous gifts which have arrived for our homes over the last few weeks. One of your pupils has kindly sent us a number of items for our children, among them a couple of beautiful fountain-pens, some coloured pencils, a scrap-book doubtless prepared by herself with postcards of our Royal Family, and *most* generously, two small necklaces and a valuable silver photograph frame. This last item we plan to sell at a forthcoming raffle, at which I expect it to raise at least £10 for the homes. I am particularly touched that the child in question clearly required no thanks, for she did not even include a note giving her name. Indeed, I would not be writing to you now, were it not that the latest gift was wrapped in brown paper bearing, on the inside, the address of your school and the name Miss Charmian Reynolds. I assume, therefore, that we have young Charmian to thank. Before I write to her personally, perhaps you would verify that she is indeed the donor. I congratulate you on running a school which is obviously so keenly aware of its civic duties towards those less privileged.

Peggy Roberts looked up.

'Charmian Reynolds! Is *she* the thief? It could have been anybody's sheet of brown paper she picked up.'

'I know,' said the Head. 'But somehow I fear it *is* Charmian. I foolishly allowed myself to be side-tracked by her over that sorry business of her parents' divorce. I would never have expected a child of her age to be so devious. Well, I shall have to deal with this straight away. Dear heavens, what a time...'

Five minutes later Charmian was in the study, very small in

the upright chair, all her bravado gone as she faced the Head across her desk.

'I have received a letter this morning, Charmian, from Dr Barnardo's Homes,' began Mrs Birmingham. There was no need to continue. Charmian glanced up, then dropped her eyes and her shoulders shook. She said nothing.

'I suggest you tell me about it,' said the Head. 'Why did you steal other people's things, and send them away under the guise of charity?'

'I don't know,' muttered Charmian.

'You knew that what you were doing was wrong. You have caused a very great deal of trouble for everyone. The whole school has been punished because of you. No sweets, no puddings at lunch, and perhaps worst of all, a horrid atmosphere of suspicion. Everyone has suffered. You must have realized that?'

'Yes.' She stared white-faced into her lap, hands knotted into triangular fists to stop them trembling. I want my mummy, she thought. I want to go away from here. I don't feel well.

'Look at me, Charmian,' said the Head. 'Are you all right?'

Charmian remembered what had been said in Prayers that morning about the danger of pretending to be ill. The sun always upset her, and it had been baking for almost three weeks now. She was in enough trouble already.

'I'm OK,' she said. 'I mean, I'm fine, thank you very much.'

'Are you sure? You needn't be afraid to tell me.'

'It's been awfully hot,' muttered Charmian.

'Yes. Well, we are all suffering from that. Can you explain to me now why you took other people's things, and why you posted them off to Dr Barnardo's Homes?' And how you managed it, she added to herself.

'I suppose I just wanted to cheer up the poor children without any mothers or fathers. I don't know. I shouldn't have done it. I'm sorry.' She looked at the Head. One more try, she thought wearily. 'I'm really awfully sorry. I sort of didn't think I'd, you know, get away with it.'

'You haven't got away with it, Charmian. You know, of course, that I shall have to tell your parents. I realize that this sad business has been very upsetting for you. Was that perhaps why you did this wicked thing?'

'I don't care,' Charmian muttered. 'I'm going to live with Mummy and Uncle Dickie and he's very nice to me and gives me money and things. Mummy says I'll soon call him Daddy.'

'Is that what you *want*?'

'Are you going to have to write to my real Daddy as well?'

'Yes, I am afraid I am. I dare say he'll be very disappointed in you. Charmian, *why* did you do it? You're a popular girl, you have friends. You don't do too badly in your lessons. Why did you steal, and why did you lie to me?'

Charmian clutched her fists together, a hard square of fingers. I will not cry, she thought. She'll only despise me if I cry. My head hurts so, I can't think . . .

'I can't think,' she said aloud.

The Head glanced upwards in exasperation, and straightened her back. Her tone was brisk.

'Very well, Charmian. I have tried to understand, but you show no sign of remorse. From now until the end of the week you are to be silent each day until after luncheon. You may not speak a word to anybody unless it's absolutely imperative. You will take your meals at a separate table. And you will go to bed at the same time as the Lower Third. Now, since you may not speak, will you please take a note to your form captain, asking her to come and see me directly after Break. I myself will write to the director of Dr Barnardo's. I don't propose to ask him for the things back, since I imagine they will already have been distributed among the children. The exceptions are Miss Peachey's jewellery and the silver frame. Those must be returned. I suggest you had better make a donation of £10 to the charity.'

'Ten pounds! It's a terrific lot of money.'

'It is indeed. You should have thought about that before you took them. Now you may go. I hope you will pray to God to forgive you.'

After lunch Sylvia and Diana carried the kitchen tables and two chairs out to the small back lawn and were sitting in the shade of the trees. Sylvia was finishing the term's examination papers before having them run off on the ancient school machine that produced damp pages of smudged purple type. Diana, bent over a pad of Basildon Bond, was not really writing a letter. She was absorbed in fantasy. Sylvia would contract polio. It would cripple her down one side – the right side – so that she couldn't continue teaching. The school would allow them both to stay in the cottage. Sylvia, mellowed by her illness, would be nursed devotedly. She, Diana, would do everything for her. Together they would offer a living example of the love that was possible between two women. Above her head, a bird sang in the clear blue sky. She sighed.

'Fuck it, Monk, can't you stop that bloody sighing?' said Sylvia.

'I'm sorry . . . I didn't realize.'

'What's the matter? Don't tell me *you're* going to come down with it now?'

'I suppose one of us might – the staff – then what?'

'Then you'll be a bloody cripple, pensioned off and living with your mother. How would that suit you? At least one would get away from these blasted girls. God, how I loathe teaching.'

And what else could I do with my life? Sylvia thought, clear-sighted and bitter. Born into the wrong sort of body, to the wrong parents, from the wrong class, I'm not brilliant, or rich or pretty. No hope for me of escaping a lifetime of futility. I'm thirty-five. Another forty years to go. Jesus, what a prospect. What a life.

From a distant window came the sound of someone's wireless playing '*Oh mein Papa*'.

'Cheer up,' said Diana. 'It'll be a beautiful evening. Let's sneak off for a walk. You're not on supper duty are you? No, nor me. We can talk about plans for the holidays.'

'Oh, goody-goody-gumdrops,' mocked Sylvia. But she didn't disagree.

Constance had started her period that morning and so she was off swimming. The rest of the Lower Fourth, in Jantzen swim-suits, were shrieking in the pool, hurling curves of transparent spray against the shining sky. She walked past and went on up to the pets' shed. It was stuffy inside, the air foetid, the animals panting in the heat. She drew back the bolt of Flopsy's cage, reached in and picked him up. His food bowl was empty; he hadn't even got any water. She looked around and saw that none of the pets had water. She went out with Flopsy in her arms to look for the gardener, but he wasn't on the games field or in the kitchen garden or the potting-shed, so she leant her back against a tree and let Flopsy nibble the grass at her feet. Her mother had written that morning giving the departure time of the flight for Kenya. 'Auntie Marjie will meet you at Waterloo and take you to the airport. You'll be luckier than us, darling. You're flying BOAC, because the office pays. It's a long journey and you'll have two re-fuelling stops, but by Friday the twenty-fifth we'll be together again!'

How can I talk them into letting me leave? She felt like that Greek king her father had once read her a story about, who had to push a huge stone uphill, and it kept rolling back down again. As soon as she felt she had made some impression on them ('Don't think Daddy and I aren't worried that you're so unhappy, darling, we talk about it a lot . . .'), the stone would begin to roll down again ('We both wish we could do something to make you see sense . . .') and soon it was back at the bottom of the hill ('You must trust in our better judgement, Connie dear. Things will cheer up for you very soon, we both feel sure.')

The rabbit had stopped nibbling and lay panting in the heat, its flanks heaving, back legs outstretched behind its pointed tail. It was the gardener's job to give the animals water, so, cradling the rabbit in her arms, Constance set off again to look for him. He was sitting in the shade of the sports pavilion, the rake propped up beside him. Constance summoned her courage and went up to him.

'I'm frightfully sorry to bother you and all that,' she said, 'but none of the pets have got any water.'

'Quite slipped my mind in this heat,' he said. His sparse hair was stuck to his skull and he smelt sweaty. Beads of perspiration stood out on his forehead.

'Give us a hand up, there's a good lassie,' he said. Constance didn't like the thought of clasping his hand, its creases and finger-nails dark with earth, but she put the rabbit down for a moment and helped him up politely.

'Would you like me to give them their water?' she asked.

'That'd be right good of you,' he said. 'Don't know why it slipped my mind. Must be the weather. Take one of them watering cans from the potting-shed, twist off the rose or you'll be spraying it all over them – not that I'd mind a bit of a spray, myself – and then you can fill it up from the rain barrel. Not the tap. They like rain water.'

'You look dreadfully hot, if you don't mind my saying so,' Constance told him shyly.

'It's shocking, this weather. My legs have gone all to jelly.'

'You'd better look out, or you'll get polio.'

'What's that? Polio?'

'The Head told us all in Prayers. Five people have got it already, and two possibles.'

'Nobody said nothing to me.'

'Well, I don't suppose you've got it. Anyway, I'd better go and give the pets their water. Look at him. Poor old Flopsy's dying of thirst.'

'Good of you, Missy,' he said again. 'Run along, then. And if you happen to see that lazy lad of mine, send him here and tell him I said to get a move on!'

The pets' shed was dark and filled with rustling sounds. Some of the animals stood up eagerly on their hind legs, their front feet pressed against the wire, as Constance walked in holding the handle of the watering can with both hands. One by one she drew back the bolts of the tiered cages and filled the dusty water bowls. She felt tender and responsible as she watched the guinea-pigs, rabbits and hamsters emerge from their nests in the straw. She was concentrating so hard that she didn't hear anyone enter, and Charmian's voice made her jump.

'She knows. She found out,' said Charmian flatly.

'Who?' Constance asked.

'Old Ma B,' said Charmian. 'She called me in after Prayers and gave me a terrific telling-off. I couldn't care less, anyway.

She gave me a note to give to Mick. The whole form'll be told. There's going to be a form meeting this afternoon. Didn't you know? Miss Valentine'll take it and everyone's got to go. I don't care. I'll *make* Mummy take me away. I hate this measly, smelly old school.'

'Charmie! Why didn't you tell me before?'

'I couldn't. I'm not allowed to talk till after lunch for a week. Plus I've got to go to bed at the same time as the squits. So what? Fat lot I care.'

'How did Old Ma B find out?'

''Cos the silly ass at Dr Barnardo's wrote her a letter. How on *earth* he knew it was me... Anyway it couldn't matter less. I just want to get away. I feel rotten.'

'You ought to tell Matron,' said Constance. Charmian looked unnaturally bright-eyed and her cheeks were hot with colour. 'If you don't feel well you ought to tell Peach.'

'I did, last night, and she wouldn't take any notice.'

'Just like with me and my finger,' said Constance. Charmian showed a spark of interest.

'Let me see. Oh, go on, show me, be a sport.'

'The doctor said I mustn't. He did a new bandage today and said I mustn't undo it or it'd get infected. It looks really disgusting.'

Their heads bent over Constance's finger as she unpicked the knot in the end of the bandage. In the light from the doorway the exposed finger was a pulpy mass. The edges of the wound looked white and dead.

'Ugh!' said Charmian, turning away. 'It's all squelchy and horrible.'

'I told you,' said Constance.

In the far distance the flat, rhythmical tolling of the bell signalled the end of games.

'Quick! I haven't finished watering the pets,' said Constance. 'Come on, you can help me.'

'Why on earth are you doing it? That's the gardener's job.'

'I know, but he said he was feeling groggy or something.'

'He's probably got polio,' said Charmian. 'He can do his own watering. As long as Flopsy's got some. Oh, come on,

Gogs, I don't want to go by myself. Everyone's going to be foul. Anyhow, I'm not going to come back next term. Sucks to them.'

I shall run away, thought Constance. I've got to start planning. I'm so miserable.

Chairs scraped over the dusty parquet floor as the Lower Fourth rose to their feet. Miss Valentine entered the room.

'Sit down everyone. Geography revision will start in about ten minutes' time, but first I have something very serious to say to you all. Michaela, will you come up to the front please? Stand here. And Charmian Reynolds, can I have you on the other side of the desk, please? Facing the class. Thank you. Now, as your form mistress, I have decided to talk to you myself, before Mrs Birmingham addresses the whole school in Prayers tomorrow. I expect you can guess what it's about. Yes, Rachel? The stealing.'

Charmian stood limply, avoiding their eyes, while Miss Valentine spelt out what had happened. She caught disjointed phrases ... 'Thanks to the courtesy and vigilance of the director...' and 'This sad train of events has brought shame upon me, as your form mistress, upon Michaela, as your form captain, and most of all, of course...' but she felt neither defiance nor regret; just a great weakness. Her head was heavy and her legs hardly had the strength to hold her up. She bent first one knee and then the other, shifting her weight. The culmination of her private drama was infinitely remote and unimportant. She looked towards the window, but the sunlight speckling the grass hurt her eyes.

'Finally,' – the voice seemed to come from a distant room – 'I want Charmian Reynolds to tell us *why* she stole other people's property, so that we can try to understand and forgive. Charmian? *Charmian!*'

Charmian moved a couple of paces towards the desk, leaned one hand heavily upon it, and looked at Miss Valentine. Then her legs gave way beneath her and, like a statue falling, she sank to the floor in a shimmering cloud of dust.

*

The common that evening held the suspended heat of the day. The bracken was dry and crackled underfoot. Larks still sang overhead in the deep blue sky that immediately preceded dusk. A tussock of moss was warm to the touch as Sylvia and Diana, their faces and bare arms reddened by the sun, sank into its springy green cushion.

'You look awfully, you know, *flushed*,' said Diana. 'You're not feeling ill? Did we go too fast or anything? You should have said.'

'I'm not that feeble!' said Sylvia in exasperation. 'For that matter, you're bright red yourself. Positively ruddy. *Not* wildly becoming, I have to say.'

'No. Well, never mind. Hasn't it been a day for dramas? First Charmian's unmasked – '

'What did I tell you? Didn't I say it was her all along?'

'I remember. That day in the staff-room. How did you know?'

'Sly little bitch. Always thought so. Sucks up to the staff, gets round everyone, manipulates the girls, forever dashing about sweet as pie. Obvious.'

'It wasn't obvious to anyone else. You know she's been taken away in an ambulance with suspected polio.'

'Polio my foot! That'll turn out to be another piece of manipulation, just you wait and see.'

'Ginny was shattered by what happened. The child crashed to the floor in a dead faint, apparently. She can't have faked that.'

'Maybe not. But it was fury at being found out that made her faint. That child's not ill, she's pretending.'

Diana lay back with her hands behind her head and gazed up at the clear, cloudless sky. She closed her eyes. After a few moments she opened them again. Sylvia's breathing had quickened and her face was tense and alert.

'What is it?'

'Shut up! There's someone over there in the trees. Shush, keep quiet and listen!'

Diana held her breath and after a moment she too heard a distant murmuring of voices, a stifled laugh and a little shriek.

A man and a girl, by the sound of it. The two women strained to hear. Diana felt embarrassed.

'Oughtn't we to go?' she said.

'Don't be such a fool,' hissed Sylvia. Her colour was even higher, her face sharp with anticipation. Well I'm damned, she thought, bucolic coupling! They have to do it somewhere, I suppose. A girl's high, nervous gasp came from the middle of the coppice. She sounded very young. Lucky sod, thought Sylvia. Suddenly the shrieks and giggles turned to screams of real panic, and footsteps crashed through the trees. The two women sat up as, seconds later, the dishevelled figure of Hermione Malling-Smith burst into the open, followed by the stumbling, hopping gardener's boy tucking his shirt into his belt with one hand and groping at his fly buttons with the other.

'Here! Whatsamatter? Come back! I ain't finished...' His indignant yells faded abruptly as he caught sight of Sylvia and Diana.

'Blimey,' he muttered, suddenly childish, as Sylvia stood up. Her eyes were starting from their sockets and she was shaking with rage. 'It's the bleeding fiery furnace we've got 'ere.'

Hermione stumbled towards them, tripping clumsily over the uneven ground.

'Help!' she cried. 'That filthy, horrible boy tried to...' But her voice too trailed away as she took in the extent of Miss Parry's fury. She stopped a few feet away.

'How DARE you?' screamed Sylvia. 'Dirty-minded, lecherous, mucky little tart! Disgusting, depraved, squalid slut. Bitch! Cunt!' She yelled the word over and over again, shaking her head wildly from side to side. 'Cunt cunt cunt cuntcuntCUNT!'

Diana, open-mouthed with horror, took a step towards her but Sylvia rushed forward and struck Hermione hard across the cheek.

'There! That's what you deserve! Dirty ... little ... CUNT.'

Hermione stood as though paralysed, her hair a wild halo around her face, her arms fallen to her sides. The top button of her dress was undone, and her belt hung loose. Behind her, the gardener's boy turned and lumbered away, one hand still clutching his trousers.

'It wasn't my fault,' Hermione said. 'I couldn't stop him...'

At the sound of her voice Sylvia lurched forward and hit her a second time. The girl crumpled and lay in the heather, gasping and panting. Already the colour was deepening on her cheek where Sylvia's hand had struck it. Sylvia was about to rush at her again, but Diana held her from behind, pinioning her arms with desperate strength, feeling the stocky body twist and turn in a struggle to loosen her grip. Sylvia's feet lashed out wildly, trying to knock her off balance.

'Go *away*, Hermione!' Diana gasped. 'Quick! Run away. He's gone. You're all right. *Go!*'

The girl scrambled to her feet, glanced at the two women swaying and panting, and ran towards the road.

'Bitch!' called Sylvia after her. 'Cunt! Bitch... Let me *go*!'

'There, there,' said Diana. 'Yes, yes, I know. Calm down, it's all right now. All over. There. Good. Yes. There.'

Gradually Sylvia ceased to resist and became still. Her breath dragged up from her lungs in huge, drowning gasps. Diana turned her round and enfolded the heaving body in her arms. The sunset flared and swept across the sky, running and merging like a glorious watercolour, paintbrush streaks of crimson and orange slashed above the horizon, the sun a reverberating copper disc.

'I love her,' Sylvia said at last. 'That vile, filthy boy... I would have been so gentle, Monkey, I would have done it so tenderly, oh, Monkey, you've no idea: so infinitely tenderly.'

'Yes, yes, I know. 'Course you would. Poor love.'

Diana stroked Sylvia's wiry hair and sun-tanned shoulder, the acrid smell of sweat in her nostrils.

'You never said you knew. Poor old Monkey...'

Diana inhaled deeply. The tears trickled down her hot face, drying into shining streaks like the tracks left by a snail.

Ten

In Break next day, the morning that end-of-term exams began, Constance received a rare letter from her father. Her hands trembled as she took it away to open it in secret. Perhaps her pleading had persuaded them to change their minds and she needn't run away after all. She went into the communal lavatories and, choosing the end one that had a window, she slid the bolt into its socket and sat down. Someone else was noisily at work in an adjacent cubicle. It sounded horrible, like the plop plop of a horse. She held her nose with one hand and with the other smoothed out the blue airletter on her lap and began to read.

Dear Constance,

I hope you are reading this with your full attention because I want you to concentrate hard on what I'm going to say.

Ever since you started at Raeburn your mother and I have received weekly letters filled with nothing but complaints. We have tried to be sympathetic, and I know Mummy has written you lots of nice, cheerful letters, although she's been very busy getting us straight and meeting new people. So I have decided to write to you myself.

The crackling of Bronco interrupted her reading. The chain flushed and she heard a door bang as the unseen girl ran off.

We went to a lot of trouble to find a really good school for you. [No, you didn't, Constance thought. You picked the very first one you looked at.] We are both saddened to find you so ungrateful and uncooperative. It's time to buck up, pull yourself together and make a go of it. We don't want to have to put up with you being black-doggish all through the holidays. You will have exams coming up soon, and we expect top marks. You've been blessed with a good brain, and we know you can do well if you put your back into it. Make up your mind *now* that there'll be no more defeatism and self-pity . . .

It went on like that for several more lines, but Constance only skimmed the rest. She screwed the letter into a ball, threw it into the lavatory and pulled the chain. Then she sat down again with her head in her hands. She wanted to feel tears welling up, but she was quite dry-eyed. She fidgeted with the knot on her bandaged finger and unwound the gauze. The wound had closed up and was beginning to heal. With her finger-nail, she picked at the scab delicately and persistently. It hurt, and her eyes began to smart. She went on till the scab had come loose, then tore it off in a fine line of pain. She squeezed at the fingertip and a ribbon of blood oozed out. At last tears prickled and she felt moisture gather in the corners of her eyes, but although she blinked several times she still could not cry.

Now I shall *definitely* run away, she thought. Then they'll have to take notice. I'll start planning today.

The bell rang for the end of Break.

Miss Parry was invigilating a depleted Lower Fourth as they laboured over the maths exam. Half-a-dozen girls had been sent home early at their parents' request, and Anne and Charmian were still in the isolation ward at St Patrick's. The remaining sixteen sat with bent heads, pen-nibs squeaking across the squared paper.

Constance hadn't written anything. She was staring blindly out of the window. I'll go to Auntie Marjie, she thought; Norfolk can't be all that far. I'll get a train to London and then catch another train from there. The practical difficulties overwhelmed her. How would she pay for her railway tickets? How would she get to the station, let alone slip away from school unobserved? She stared at the patterns of shadow thrown by the cedar across the grass: a deep, dancing pool of shifting greens. I could get up early one morning, stop a car and ask for a lift to the village; then if I went to a shop I might be able to sell my watch...

'Constance King! Either get on with your work or leave the room. Which is it to be?'

'Sorry, Miss Parry. I was thinking...'

I ought to go to the Head, Sylvia thought, and tell her what we saw. Perfectly natural, after all – two members of staff take an evening walk across the heath, nothing wrong with that, and happen to be there in time to avert a rape. I might even get some credit for it. *I love her*! I love her, want her, dream about coaxing her, patiently, as she discovers her own amazing pleasure. How gently my butterfly fingers would stray across her breasts, brushing her nipples as if by accident, waiting until she drew breath sharply, then again ... guiding her towards the moment of her first climax. She is ready for it, waiting for me; otherwise how could that lout have persuaded her to come with him? Clumsy oaf. Coarse, red-faced, thick-witted peasant. *He* has touched her, and I, oh, I have not.

A hand went up.

'Miss Parry, please, sorry but I've done so many crossings out, can I have some more paper...?'

'Thick-witted child! And if I say no?'

'But we're allowed to ask for...'

'You are allowed, Rachel, whatever *I* decide you may have. Is that clear?'

'Yes, Miss Parry.'

At least it had broken the train of thought. Constance's too. She heaved a sigh and began to study the exam paper.

Isolated in a small room beside the sick-room, Hermione woke in mid-morning from a deep sleep. She got out of bed, but found she could hardly keep her balance, staggered, and clung to the iron bedstead. She had a headache and her face hurt, especially her mouth. She looked down at her legs, which were streaked with iodine. Sitting on the bed, her back to the door, she pulled down the front of her nightie. Her chest was marked with fine parallel scratches. She shuddered and got back into bed, trembling. Shivers ran up her body and her arms and legs shook. Her breathing was fast. I was nearly raped, she thought, the secret, thrilling, adult word becoming real for the first time. William Truett nearly raped me. She clenched her fists to try and still her arms. Oh God, she thought, is that what it's like? Is that what men want? No wonder girls are supposed to stay virgin till their wedding night. Nobody would get married if they knew. It's horrible. He was so strong. And he smelt disgusting and common. I must have a wash. What on earth do I look like? What if he's marked my *face*? I must see.

There was no mirror in the next-door bathroom, but Hermione felt her face gingerly and knew that it was swollen. She found some TCP in a cupboard, and diluted it in a glass of water. It wasn't strong enough, so she put the bottle to her lips and drew a long, stinging gulp. She rinsed her mouth and gargled vigorously, spitting the pale liquid into the basin. She locked the door and ran a bath.

Lying in the tepid water, she examined her scratches and bruises. William had fought quite savagely to pinion her and keep her quiet. She looked at her flat body and pointed breasts and at the memory of his rough, pawing hands she began to breathe fast and her heart raced. She drew long, deep breaths and closed her eyes, floating passively in the water until she became calm again.

The door handle turned.

'Hermione? Is that you?' asked Miss Girdlestone.

'I'm in the bath.'

'Well hurry up, will you? Nobody said you could have a bath. The doctor will be here in about ten minutes. He's going to want to examine you.' There was a silence.

'Are you all right?' Still silence.

Ten minutes later the doctor was standing beside her bed.

'My dear young lady,' he said. 'I hear you've had a very nasty experience, and I'm afraid the next few minutes may not be very pleasant either. But it has to be done. Will you try and relax, don't resist, and please believe that I have to do this? It'll be over very quickly, I promise, but I need to have a dekko.'

His cold hands drew back the sheet and he pulled up her nightie, exposing her body to his gaze and that of Miss Girdle-stone. She tried to relax, but was very aware of him man-ipulating her legs apart and probing gently. She shut her eyes.

'She's OK,' she heard him say. 'No permanent harm done. Keep an eye on those scratches. It could be nasty if they turned septic. The main thing she needs is lots of rest. Give her a dose of this now, and another sleeping-pill last thing at night. Young girls are very resilient. In a week or two she'll hardly remember what happened.'

'Poor child,' Mrs Birmingham's voice said from by the door. 'Poor Hermione. She may not forget quite that easily.'

Hermione's scratches had been painted with iodine again, the doctor had gone, and she lay in bed flicking idly through one of the sick-room's collection of old magazines. The door opened and the Head came in, sat on a chair beside the bed and folded her hands in her lap.

'Feeling a bit better now?' she asked.

'Yes, thank you.'

'Good. I expect you will be relieved to know that William Truett has gone. He has been dismissed. He will never come near the school again. You, of course, will not be punished. Now, dear, do you want to tell me about what happened yesterday evening, up on the heath?'

Hermione blushed. She couldn't tell the Headmistress – nor anyone, for that matter – about that. She shrank from the thought of his hot pushing hands, his breath whistling in her ear, the weight of his sweaty body as he tried to straddle her and hold her down. And after that Miss Parry, her rage, the force with which she'd slapped her, the struggle as Miss Monk had tried to hold her back.

'I can't,' she said.

'Listen to me, Hermione. I'm afraid young men can some-times be carried away by their feelings towards girls, especially if they happen to be rather lovely. It's why we – your parents, and I – have to try so hard to protect you. But you're *all*

189

right apart from a few nasty scratches. You *are* still a virgin, Hermione. It's important for you to know that. You may be quite, quite sure. You have nothing to hide from your future husband. Don't be embarrassed, my dear. It is right that you should know, and that I should tell you. Finally, I am dreadfully sorry that this horrible thing should have happened to you. But it will not ruin your life, however distressed you may be feeling now. And it certainly hasn't spoiled your pretty face.'

Hermione blushed, more to be caught out in vanity than because of the Head's calm words. She didn't care in the least what her future husband would think. She doubted if there would *be* a future husband, after this.

'I'm dreadfully sleepy,' she said.

The Head rose cumbersomely to her feet.

'Of course you are. Sleep's the very thing you need. Now, I shall go and telephone your parents – oh yes, my dear, I am afraid they have to be told – and we'll see what they want to do next. I'll come and see you again later. And I shall remember you in my prayers.'

'There have been no new cases for a week, Mrs Malling-Smith. We believe the outbreak is now contained . . . The polio is not, however, my main reason for telephoning you. I tried to make contact with you yesterday evening . . . The theatre. Yes, I see. Well now, I am afraid something rather unpleasant occurred yesterday. Yes, it involved your daughter.' In measured tones, she described the attack. 'Yes, of course you may remove Hermione before term ends. The choice must be yours . . . May I finish explaining? Then you will be in a better position to decide. She has, of course, been seen by the school doctor. On health grounds, as I have said, I do not think it necessary to send her home. Hermione is, of course, rather shocked, but she is in good hands, and at the moment she is sleeping peacefully . . . I understand. For the time being. Of course you must talk to your husband. Very well.'

The study door opened, and Peggy Roberts came in. Henrietta raised her eyebrows to indicate exasperation, and ended her conversation with slightly more emphasis.

'Of course, Mrs Malling-Smith. Yes, *I'll* tell her. Not at all. And once again, please accept my profound apologies for what has happened. Good-bye.'

She looked at her Deputy and her shoulders slumped. 'Hysterical mothers are the final straw. Hermione Malling-Smith has quite enough on her plate without having to listen to a melodramatic outburst from her distracted mother. However, I can hardly prevent them from speaking on the telephone. Unfortunately it seems far more likely that she will get into her car the moment she puts the receiver down and remove the child forthwith. But enough of that. How was the hospital today?'

'Very distressing, I am afraid.'

'Shall we go into the drawing-room? Will you ring for some tea?'

Mrs Birmingham walked heavily through the connecting door into the next room, sank heavily into her armchair and sighed. *Be with me, O Lord, in this tribulation. Make me strong. Give to these Thy sick children comfort and hope. Lay Thy blessing upon Hermione and, O Lord, give it also to me!*

All my life, she reflected, it has fallen to *me* to be strong. When I first knew that I was expecting James, I told Lionel and he said, 'Hetty, my dear, I don't know if I'm cut out for fatherhood. It's all right for you, but . . .' and I had to reassure *him*. I tried to suggest he might earn some money, since Papa's allowance would no longer be sufficient. That's when he said he wasn't born to be a bank clerk. The humiliation of trailing round my family, my pregnancy increasingly obvious, asking them to find him work that wouldn't offend his pride. 'He'd like to be in *charge*,' I used to say; and I could read their thoughts. They had never suspected him of possessing qualities of leadership, or much intelligence, for that matter. He didn't even go to the right tailor. And then James was born, their first grandson, their only grandson, and somehow a position was found for Lionel, a nanny for James, and for a few years we were content – until the war came. And I had to be strong yet again . . .'

'Henrietta? Your tea.'

'Peggy ... tell me about the hospital. How are they all? Is there any improvement?'

'It's not easy to tell with those children. They lie there, very still, not daring to move. They look so pale and frightened. It is hard to be cheerful and encouraging.'

'What chance of ...?' asked Henrietta.

'Too early to say. Little Katherine Wilson seems most at risk. One daren't think about it.'

'And Charmian?'

'She didn't say a word. The nurse tells me that she keeps asking when her mother is coming. Her father's been, I'm glad to say, but her mother ... I don't know, Henrietta. I don't pretend to understand these women.'

A sudden knock startled them both.

'Come in!' called Mrs Birmingham.

Miss Parry's wiry head looked round the door.

'Please come in. Sit down. I was going to ask you to see me. I understand that you and Miss Monk were able to intervene yesterday evening? It was most fortunate for Hermione Malling-Smith that you happened to be there.'

In the pause they all heard Mrs Birmingham's wireless; although it was turned right down, a Chopin *Étude* was faintly audible. The clear, plangent notes fell like grains of sand into the silence.

'I came to tell you,' said Miss Parry steadily, as though she had rehearsed in advance what to say, 'that Miss Monk and I were walking on the heath when we came upon Hermione Malling-Smith just in time to prevent her from being assaulted. We heard her cries for help. Who knows what might have happened otherwise? The boy is strong, and seemed determined to ... Well, fortunately we were in time. When he saw us he ran away. Hermione, I am sure, was not to blame.'

'Hermione had presumably made some sort of assignation with the under-gardener, for she had no business being on the heath, alone, at that hour. To that extent she *was* to blame. However,' said the Head, 'she has in my view been punished quite enough, and I do not propose to discipline her further.'

'What will happen to her?' asked Miss Parry. The question

192

was her only reason for coming to see the Head.

'For the time being she is resting in the sick-room. It is up to her parents what they decide. I spoke to her mother earlier. They may wish to remove her immediately, since it is almost the end of term. I have not yet discussed with them the question of whether she will return.'

Sylvia Parry fixed her intent gaze upon Mrs Birmingham for what seemed like minutes. Chopin sweetened the tension. Eventually she drew a deep breath.

'I have a great many papers to mark.'

'I am grateful to you for giving me your own account of what took place,' said Mrs Birmingham coolly. 'Unless you have anything further to add, you may go, Miss Parry.'

When the afternoon exam was over, Constance knew she had done well. It was English, her best subject, and she'd answered the questions with ease, writing until the last moment. She didn't join the others clustering round to commiserate with one another, but headed up towards the pets' shed. Flopsy would be thirsty after another hot day.

She found that once again, none of the animals had been fed or watered. As she trudged to the rain-water barrel and back, filling their bowls first with water and then with oats from the sack in the corner of the shed, she tried to sort out her plans for running away. It all seemed terribly difficult. First she would have to make her way to the station in the village – a good twenty minutes' drive in the school coach, so that meant, what? Ten miles? How long would it take her to walk ten miles? Perhaps she could borrow someone's bicycle. But she daren't confide her plans, so that meant taking it without the owner's permission, which was dishonest. She couldn't do that. Well then, she'd have to get up very early one morning, slip out of school unseen, and walk. Maybe she'd meet someone who could give her a lift. But how would she pay for her train ticket? They were only allowed ten shillings pocket money a term, and that was kept in a locked petty-cash box in the staff-room. It was all much too complicated. She'd never manage it.

Having finished her task, Constance took Flopsy out of his

cage and sat cuddling him on a bale of straw in a dark corner of the shed. Oh, how I wish I were grown-up! she thought. Grown-ups can do whatever they like. They don't have to ask permission, nobody criticizes them or orders them about. They're free. I feel like poor old Flopsy, stuck in a cage; and I want to get out. But *they* make it impossible.

She heard the bell ringing for supper, and bent to kiss Flopsy's twitching nose before putting him back in his cage. It's disgraceful that nobody's feeding the pets, she said to herself as she ran down the drive towards the Covered Way. The gardener's boy ought to be doing it, or Waterman himself. As she was passing the cottages she encountered Miss Parry.

'Excuse me,' she began politely, 'but do you by any chance know where I would find the gardener's boy? He hasn't . . .'

A deep red washed across Miss Parry's set face and she rounded on Constance.

'The gardener's boy?' she said. 'And what, may I ask, would *you* be wanting with the gardener's boy? Another loathsome little assignation, I suppose. Nasty, dirty, over-sexed little girl. Well let me tell you the gardener's boy has been dismissed. Pronto. Out. That'll be a *big* disappointment for you, I suppose.' She thrust her face close to Constance's and sneered at her, breathing hard.

Constance looked wildly around for escape, but all the girls were lining up in the Covered Way. Miss Parry yanked her by the shoulder, shaking with rage.

'*Will* you pay attention when a member of staff is speaking to you? Take an order mark for rudeness. And let me tell you, you little slut, that the gardener's boy is down at the police station, which, if you're not very careful, is where you'll find yourself too. Now skedaddle! Out of my sight! GO!'

In another moment she might have hit Constance, who turned and ran down the path and into the Covered Way. She didn't join the queue for her table, but made for the lavatories. She slammed and locked a door behind her, then sat down to let her panting subside.

Indignant despite her terror, she thought, Right, that's it! That settles it! I'm *definitely* going, after that! How dare she call

194

me a slut and a nasty, dirty, over-sexed little girl? Oh, it's all so unfair and I'm so *unhappy*.

As she began to calm down her mind was churning with plans. Saturday morning: that would be the best time to go. They got up half an hour later at weekends, at twenty-past-seven instead of ten-to. If I slipped away at six, I might even catch the first train in the morning, certainly the second. I'd be in London by ten, surely; then all I'd have to do is find out which platform the Norfolk train went from. To think, by lunchtime on Saturday I could be there! Aunt Marjie may be cross at first, but when I explain how miserable I've been, and how Mummy and Daddy just wouldn't take any notice, and specially if I tell her what Batey Parry said just now, she's bound to sympathize. Then she can phone them and say I'm safe with her, and *she'll* persuade them I was right to run away . . . Constance felt light-hearted by the time she joined the supper queue.

Rachel was standing in front of her. She turned round and beckoned Constance closer.

'Have you heard?' she whispered excitedly.

'No. Heard what?'

'About Hermy-One. She's got polio!'

'She hasn't. How do you know?'

' 'Cos Jennifer found out that Mick saw the doctor being taken up to the sick-room by Miss Girdlestone in Break. So then Mick crept up to the aunt next door and hid, 'cos you know she's got this terrific pash on Hermy-One. Well, anyway, after he'd gone, she didn't dare go in, though she wanted to, but she could hear Hermione. Apparently she was all crying and awful. *Poor* Hermy-One!'

I almost wish I could get it, thought Constance. Then I'd be out of all this. Before she could answer, the final gong went, and they trooped into the dining-room.

That evening in the dormitory the girls were subdued. Miss Peachey had refused to give any gory details at bedtime, merely assuring them that Hermione was all right and had not developed polio.

' 'Course she's got polio!' said Mick. 'She was crying her

eyes out. I *heard* her. Peach might have told us whether she's going to hospital or what.'

'Fat chance,' said Rachel. 'She's been sworn to secrecy, you bet. Mean pigs. It might be me next. Any of us.'

'But it isn't you. It's Hermy-One,' said Mick, close to tears.

'Come on, everybody,' said Deborah. 'What shall we do to cheer ourselves up?'

'I know,' said Fiona. 'Let's play Spotlight on Beauty!'

'Don't be daft – there's not enough of us. With Sheila gone and Charmie gone, there's no point.'

'Why don't we get Swallows to join us, then?'

'We're not allowed,' said Rachel.

'Don't be so wet. It's nearly end of term: who cares? Come on, who's going to ask them?'

'I will,' said Constance.

The others sat up excitedly. 'Good for you, Gogs! But go *quietly*. On tiptoe. Don't let Peach catch you.'

Constance got out of bed, stuck her feet into her slippers, and tiptoed along the top corridor. She knocked on Swallows' door and slipped inside. There were only four of them, and three were sitting on Flick's bed, comforting her as she wept dramatically.

Constance remembered that Hermione had been Flick's 'pash', too.

'Come on, cheer up,' she said. 'We're going to play Spotlight on Beauty only there's not enough of us left so you've got to join in. Peach isn't around so it'll be OK so long as you don't make a row.'

Ungainly with caution they went along the corridor stifling their giggles. The girls in Starlings were already brushing their hair and pinching their cheeks. The four from Swallows arranged themselves on the two empty beds and borrowed brushes and mirrors. Everyone concentrated on their faces, frowning as they nipped the heads off spots, then licking fingertips and smoothing their eyebrows into perfect arcs.

'Don't anyone take off marks for my nightie being torn.'

'That's your hard cheese!'

'Well, then, I'll put on a clean one.'

'Swizz. If you do everyone can.'

'Meanie.'

'Shut up, Rachel,' said Mick. 'This is to cheer me and Flick up and you're spoiling it. Ready everyone? Who's going to go first?'

'You do, and then we'll go round in order.'

Fiona reached into her bedside cupboard for a torch. She crossed over to Mick's bed and crouching beside it, angled the beam of light on to her face. Mick assumed a theatrical pose, thrusting her shoulders back to exaggerate her little breasts, her chin jutting up to lengthen her neck, her gaze fixed upon the far corner of the ceiling. She held this position motionless for a minute, while the others studied her critically.

'Everyone ready?' said Fiona, and switched the torch beam off.

Mick's shoulders collapsed and she smirked.

'How was I?'

'You looked just like Mummy,' said Flick. 'Honestly, you were wizard. Well *done*.'

'Shall we do the marks now, or afterwards?'

'Afterwards is more fair. Has everyone got pencils?'

Two people had pencils in their diaries, so it was agreed that they should both keep the scores and tot them up at the end.

One by one the Lower Fourth struck poses from *Picturegoer*, held their breath for as long as possible, then expelled it and slumped their shoulders, suddenly foolish.

'Can I do it with my glasses off?' asked Constance. They discussed this and agreed that it was allowed. Constance folded them carefully and placed them on her bedside table. She knew she wasn't pretty enough for a film-star pose. Instead she crossed her legs, arranged the folds of her nightdress gracefully over her knees, and sat with bowed head and splayed palms as though she were holding a book. Fiona shone the light on to her face.

'Take your Kirbigrip out, Gogsy, let your hair loose!' she said.

Constance removed the grip and her hair fell in a shining fringe across her forehead.

'Now we can't see your face!'

'Who cares?' said Constance. 'This is how I want to be.'

They studied her intently, then crossed the room to whisper their marks. I know I won't win, thought Constance. I know I'll never be pretty. But I'm cleverer than any of them. And I'm going to run away.

'Jolly good, Conce,' said Rachel. 'Honestly, you look terrifically nice without your specs.'

They had almost gone right round the room when they caught the squeak of Miss Peachey's shoes approaching.

'Quick! Hide!' said Mick, and the four Swallows squashed themselves under the empty beds, the long sides of the counterpanes making them invisible.

'I heard a lot of rustling and talking,' said Miss Peachey. 'Come along now: what's going on?'

'Nothing, Peach, honestly,' said Mick, looking wide-eyed and startled. The others lay unnaturally still in their beds.

'You've been having a talcum powder fight, haven't you? The dormitory reeks of it!'

'Honestly and truly we haven't,' they said.

'I've got enough trouble on my hands without you lot playing me up. Now go to sleep. If I have to come in again, it'll be order marks all round.'

After she had gone they abandoned the game. The two sets of marks proved to be entirely different and no winner was declared. Swallows withdrew to their own dormitory. The wood-pigeons cooed and a distant dog barked monotonously, over and over again, and then started to howl: a hopeless, despairing howl that expected no answer, for it knew, finally, that the good, kind master would never come.

Eleven

'We shall leave here at the end of the first week in August,' James's letter concluded, 'so we will arrive after the school has broken up, which will make things easier for you. And me!' he added. 'Juniper is very excited about coming to England. It's her first visit – she's always lived in HK, though her brother is at Harrow. I plan to take her up to Scotland and also show her something of London, but all that can be arranged once I've seen you and Father.'

Lionel lay back in bed, asleep or dozing, his breakfast tray untouched on the table beside him. In the light that poured through the bedroom window Henrietta saw him for a moment as if with James's eyes, and realized how shockingly he had changed. He looked worse than old; lying there with his veined hands crossed on the linen sheet, he looked dead.

'Lionel!' she cried in alarm. 'Are you all right?'

As he opened his eyes and looked at her she said, 'You haven't touched your breakfast.'

He struggled to sit, and she had to prop him up on pillows like a sick child. Only he didn't feel like a child, for all his frailty. His body was slack, his limbs so wasted she felt the bones might snap in her grasp.

'Oh, Lionel, I'm so worried about James. He's bringing this girl with him, Juniper, whoever she is. He says she's never been to England before. He's going to take her up to Scotland and show her Raeburn; that sounds very significant. Whoever can she *be*? He never mentions her surname anywhere. Look. You read his letter. But first drink your tea, dear.'

As she drove the Humber Hawk down the drive, Henrietta realized that her husband might not even live long enough to see his son again. He scarcely ate anything and seldom moved from his bed. He was immobilized by the magnet of death. She could smell it in the air of his bedroom, however often she threw open the windows: the bluish, metallic odour of decay. I shall have to wear black, she thought, and then I shall be like my mother, forever in mourning, for Alistair and Hugo, for Jamie, and then for Papa. She must have been younger than I am now when Alistair died. Let me think: in 1916 she would have been in her early forties. Yet I never saw her wear anything but black for the next thirty years. She mourned like a true Victorian, with crêpe and jet and black gloves, even though she was still a comparatively young woman. Was it real grief, I wonder, or merely observance? How unjust I am! Of course it was grief.

Stopping the car on the circle of gravel outside the school's front entrance she closed her eyes and prayed. *May the souls of my parents rest in peace; also keep in Thy remembrance my three brothers, James, Alistair and Hugo, who are no more, with none but me left on earth to remember them. And of Thy infinite mercy, O Lord, let my son see his father once more before he dies. For the sake of Thy beloved Son. Amen.*

I must talk to the doctor, she thought. Lionel's right: I've been so preoccupied with the sick children that I have neglected him. I ought to see the gardener as well, find out if he can manage on his own until the end of term. Well, I dare say Peggy can talk to him. And then there's Sylvia Parry. Ought I to give her notice? I must talk to Peggy. And I have to telephone Mrs Malling-Smith and let her know how Hermione's getting on. I must try and persuade Mrs Reynolds to go and see Charmian in hospital. For that matter, I must go and visit the children myself. I have so much to do, and all the while my husband lies sick unto death and I cannot attend to him.

In morning Prayers, after they had sung 'Praise my soul the King of Heaven' and their soft young voices had followed her through the staccato phrases of the Lord's Prayer, the Head told the girls to sit. They subsided on to crossed legs like a wave, billowing and flickering as they arranged their skirts modestly over their knees and pushed the hair off their foreheads. When everyone was silent and still and she had their full attention, she began to speak.

'First of all, I know you are anxious for news of the girls in St Patrick's. Miss Roberts visited them yesterday, and she will tell you about them herself.'

The Deputy Head, who rarely spoke in Prayers, rose awkwardly to her feet and said a few stilted words. Doing so well ... being so brave ... unfortunately no visits from friends possible yet ... all sent cheerful messages: chins up, and so on. Then the Head resumed.

'They are looked after devotedly by dedicated doctors and nurses, and everything possible is being done for them. Next, I want to quash the rumours about a new case once and for all. Hermione Malling-Smith has *not* developed polio. Is that quite clear? Good. Sadly, however, I have to tell you that I learned only just now that our gardener, Mr Waterman, *has* been taken ill. As we wait for the diagnosis to be confirmed one way or the other we will hold him in our prayers, as we do all those who are sick. His helper, the under-gardener, will not be returning to work in the school grounds.

'And now finally for some better news ... at any rate for some of you. Here are the first examination results. Upper Fourth, History...'

I don't care, Constance said to herself; it doesn't make any difference what I get. Miss Parry was the last straw. I dreamed about her last night. She'll haunt me unless I get away. It's no good my telling Mummy and Daddy what she said because they'd never believe me. They always think grown-ups are in the right. How am I going to get the money for my train fares? What if I were to sell my watch? When Daddy gave it to me at Christmas Mummy whispered that he had paid five guineas for it, which is an awful lot.

Suppose I go to a jeweller's and get three pounds, might even be more, then that'd be more than enough and... Her thoughts were interrupted by the sound of her name.

'First, Constance King with 86 per cent. Second...'

'What was that?' she whispered to her neighbour.

'English, you clot. You came top.'

After lunch, while the girls lay resting on their beds, Sylvia and Diana sat opposite one another marking examination papers. Their red pens slashed through the pages, tick, tick, cross, an exclamation mark in the margin, and at the end, a scribbled figure.

'Your coffee'll get cold,' said Diana after a while.

'Blast the coffee. I'm hot enough as it is. And blast this weather. I wish it would rain.'

'It's bound to soon. Does your head ache?'

'Head, feet, back – everything bloody aches. This place gets me down.'

'Have you heard any ... news?'

'How could I? You can hardly expect me to go to the sick-room and inquire after her?'

'I thought perhaps ... Would you like me to?'

'Use your loaf, Diana. *No.* She hasn't got polio. The fact is, she's a hysterical, frustrated little virgin. Shut up about it, will you?'

They worked on in silence after that.

In the study, Henrietta Birmingham picked up the telephone and dialled. She sat tensely as it rang ten times, eleven ... and was answered.

'Dr Duncan? I hope I haven't disturbed you? It's Mrs Birmingham speaking ... No, it isn't about the girls, although of course they are always on my mind. I am worried about my husband. I think his condition has worsened in the two weeks since you last visited him ... The pain-killers seem fairly effective. Even so, I feel he should now be under constant medical supervision. I am afraid ... Dr Duncan, I think my husband is dying ... That would be most kind. At about four o'clock? I will be at the Lodge myself. I am most anxious that he should not be alarmed unnecessarily. I believe he has no idea how ill he is. Perhaps you could find some excuse for visiting? Thank you, doctor. Good-bye.'

The pool sparkled with crisp, cold sheets of water. Lithe young bodies sliced into its turquoise depths, angled like scissors through cellophane. Mrs Whitby was taking the Lower

Fourth for a diving lesson. One after another they balanced on the frayed rush-matting of the diving-board, toes curled over the end, then breathed in, swung their arms wide like dragon-flies, bounced once or twice to gain momentum and flew spread-eagled through the sunny air before plunging into the water.

'Good!' called Mrs Whitby. 'Next.'

Constance walked along the board. Without her glasses everything was blurred. Sunlight flickered on the surface of the water.

'Ready? Now, arms wide, don't look down, two nice high jumps and ... go!'

For a split second her back arched, her arms formed a wide crescent, her toes pointed and she sped towards the sun. Then she closed her arms in a long straight line and entered the water with scarcely a splash. She felt her tummy graze the bottom of the pool and held her line until she broke the surface smiling in triumph.

'Good, Constance! Very well done! That was a beauty.'

She gripped the rail beside the steps and climbed out, thinking, I did it! I did a swallow! Already the next body was cleaving the air as she sat down on the warm stones of the wall. The sensation of flight still vibrated through her body. I *did* it!

The changing-rooms were full of shivering girls, their teeth chattering after cold showers as they towelled themselves dry. Lank swim-suits dripped from the clothes line, deflated swimming-caps hung suspended by rubber straps. The slim, long-legged girls paraded themselves, flinging their towels on to the hooks and then reaching upwards to retrieve their clothes, talking over their shoulders as though unconscious of their nakedness. Others, ungainly and thick-bodied with rolls of flesh around their hips and heavy arms mottled with cold, clung for as long as possible to the protection of their damp towels, sheltering inside them as they tried awkwardly to fasten their bras and climb into their underpants.

'You were brilliant, Gogs! You were best out of everyone,' said Rachel. 'I did a frightful belly-flop. Look!' and she drew her towel aside to show the dark-red mark where she had hit the water hard and flat.

'Poor you, jolly bad luck,' said Constance; but her mind was on the time. She had to feed the animals, for with neither of the gardeners around, who would do it?

'Hey, Rachel, hurry up and get dressed and come up to Pets with me. Nobody's giving them any food or water and they must be dying of thirst.'

Her feet were clammy and she had to drag her socks on, noticing the pale grey ovals left on the white cotton by the fan-shaped pattern cut out of the front of her sandals. She fumbled with the buckles, scrubbed at her damp hair, dragged a comb through it, and together they ran up the drive, swerving to make way for Old Ma B's car.

The last period of the day was revision. Constance held a ruler against the line of irregular French verbs in her exercise book, muttering them under her breath and then revealing whether she'd got them right. But it was hard to concentrate, when her mind was preoccupied with the practical problems of getting to King's Lynn.

Did she really want to run away? The swimming had been so much fun, and people were starting to be nicer to her. We do the thinking for you, Daddy always said; and perhaps he was right. She was top of the form in two out of her first three exams – not maths, of course, but then she hadn't finished the paper.

No. It was too late to have second thoughts. She was committed now. Stick to your guns, Daddy always said; make your mind up to do something and then see it through. But he also said, if a thing's worth doing, it's worth doing well. She had done well – in exams, at any rate – but she still wasn't happy, surely? The idea of selling the watch frightened her most. Everything would be easy once she'd managed that, but her parents would be furious when they found out she'd sold her precious watch, on top of losing her pen. Best not to think about it. Back to the verbs: *aller ... allant ... allé; asseoir ... asseyant ... assis; avoir ... ayant ... eu; boire ... boyant ... bu* – no! *buvant.* The revision period was ending, everyone's concentration dissolving into raucous shouts.

'Quiz!' someone shouted, holding aloft a French text book, but there were no shouts of 'Ego!'

As Constance entered the Covered Way, head down and deep in thought, she nearly bumped into Miss Valentine.

'Hold on!' she said. 'Hold on, look where you're going. Don't frown like that – the wind might change and then you'll get stuck. Mrs Whitby told me after games today that you showed real promise as a diver. Good girl. And your examination results have been very good so far.' Then she looked more closely into Constance's face. 'My dear, are you all right? You *do* look anxious. Are you quite sure you feel well?'

'I'm fine,' muttered Constance, and knew she had been given a chance and that she had thrown it away.

The following afternoon was cloudless and scorching, like all the days before it. Mrs Birmingham was alone in the study. A plate with two sugar-dusted Nice biscuits stood on the desk and beside it a cup of tea. They were untouched. The school was very quiet. Most of the girls were sitting exams. For once, there was no sound from the swimming-pool.

Dr Duncan had been breezy and casual. 'Just come to give you the once-over,' he'd said to Lionel. 'Standard procedure. Can't have you catching polio as well!'

Had Lionel believed him? His eyes, dull and heavy, had looked at her without fear or questions.

'I'll be with you in half a tick, Mrs Birmingham. This won't take long,' and she had left the room. Ten minutes later he had joined her downstairs.

'Heart's weak; his lungs are very congested; and the kidneys are dicky, too. He's got no strength to fight. His circulation's sluggish because of all the time he spends in bed. He ought to move about, even for ten minutes twice a day. There's a risk of thrombosis otherwise. If you can't get him on to his feet, then I should take him into St Patrick's, have him under observation.'

'He'd hate it,' she had said. 'If he must, I suppose, but ... will it make any difference?'

Dr Duncan had looked at her in silence.

'No,' he said eventually.

'Then he will stay here. Term ends soon. Meanwhile, I'll employ a nurse. Our son will be here in two or three weeks' time. Can he, do you think ... will he last that long?'

'Impossible to say. Given something like that to look forward to, yes, perhaps. Here' – he tore a prescription off the pad – 'get him these. They'll deal with the pain in his kidneys. No chance of persuading him not to smoke, I suppose?'

Henrietta smiled. 'I'm afraid not. I've been trying for years,' she said.

An hour later, from the junior common-room below the study window the sound of 'Stranger in Paradise' drifted up to her. 'All lost in a wonderland/ Of all that I've hungered for,' the deep voice crooned. Strings swooped in tremulous unison. Henrietta gazed blankly ahead at the door of the study. Finally she reached into the drawer of her desk for a pad of airmail paper, unscrewed her pen and wrote:

My darling boy,

Thank you for your letter and the good news of your impending arrival. I have missed you very much. The sooner you can be here the better. Is there any chance of moving your flight forward by a week? Because, James, I have to tell you the truth: your father is much worse. He is very ill indeed. The doctor came to see him again this afternoon, at my request, and warned me he might not last the month. You must see him soon. Mercifully, Father does not know how ill he is. We have had a heat-wave for several weeks now, and he attributes his lassitude and lack of appetite to the effects of that. His breathing is dreadfully hard, and he coughs painfully. I am sorry, my darling, to bring such fearful news, but I thought it best to prepare you.

We shall look forward to meeting this young woman, Juniper (what is her surname, by the way? I don't think you've mentioned it, or perhaps I have forgotten), but in the circumstances it might be better if you could make your first visit to us alone. Please tell her she is welcome after that. I am sure she will understand.

James, dear Jamie, I feel it is all in the hands of God now. This has been a very trying term, but I won't burden you with any more of my worries. I look forward to seeing you more than I can say.

She lifted her tea-cup and drank without noticing that the tea had gone cold. She heard the heavy wooden front door creak open – Peggy must be back – and at the same moment there was a timid knock at the study door.

'Who is it?' she called, irritable at the interruption.

Constance King entered.

'Not now, dear,' said Mrs Birmingham. 'Not unless it's something really important. I'm busy just now. Come back after Prayers tomorrow.'

Constance stood back to allow Miss Roberts to enter, then closed the door silently behind her and walked away.

'Peggy, tell me, what news?'

'Good news. Katherine Wilson is going to be *all right*.'

'Thank the Lord for that. So the doctor thinks they're through the worst?'

'The worst is over. Except that poor Waterman is very ill. He, I fear, may be the one to be paralysed.'

'We can look after him. We will. He can live in the cottage, he and his wife and that howling dog of theirs. Poor Waterman. But, oh Peggy, thank heaven the girls are going to be all right!'

In the midst of life we are in death. But at least the young will live. Nothing is worse than the death of a fine, vigorous young body.

It was late in the evening. Henrietta had gone home, but had not yet been able to face Lionel. She sat downstairs in the Lodge's darkened drawing-room, holding a photograph of her brother Jamie taken just before he had left for the front. The photograph in its silver frame had stood on her piano for so long that it had become invisible. It must be years since she had looked at it. She switched on the standard-lamp beside her chair and scrutinized his square young face, still very much the face of a boy. How her James resembled him! She had never seen it so clearly before. She bent the prongs at the back of the frame to take it out and look at it more closely. Behind it was another picture, long-forgotten: Jamie and Roly, spanking smart in their brand-new uniforms, posed side-by-side.

Roly! Her hands trembled with shock. She had never expected to look at his face again. He had been a good-looking young man, arrogant, certainly, but with reason. The crisp black hair curled over his forehead despite the military hair-cut and his dark eyes looked back at her across a gap of nearly four decades. She had never learned what became of him. After the visit to Raeburn House and the episode on the hillside, he had refused all other invitations. Jamie was hurt and couldn't understand why his best friend did not come to see him. Henrietta had pretended to be equally puzzled.

A letter had arrived for her, just one, some weeks after that visit. It was a formal note of apology, so elaborately and archaically worded that she could not be sure he wasn't laughing at her. A phrase swam up from her memory: 'Should you need my assistance, be it financial or practical, allow me to assure you that I shall be at your service.' No, she had not needed his assistance. How old would he be now? ... The same age as brother Jamie, two years older than she was – he would only be in his mid-fifties. Fifteen years younger than Lionel. There was every reason to suppose he was still alive.

On impulse she took down *Debrett* from the bookshelf. 'Graham, Roland Alastair,' she read, 'see 6 Baron Mountfordham. She turned over the heavy pages. 'B. 22 Sept 1898. Educ.' – yes, yes, she knew all that. Her eyes swept on. 'Marr. 1933, Alice Warren-Eagleton ... 2s. 1d. Suc. on death of er. bro. Hugh, 5 Baron, 1944. Marr. diss. 1947. Heir, s. James ...' So, she thought: married late, and it didn't survive the war. He hadn't married again. Son: James. Well, that was something. 'Clubs: Athenaeum, Brooks's. Address:' She slammed the heavy book shut. She didn't want to know his address.

Ironic, to realize only now how suitable he would have been! No wonder her mother had been so gracious. Just the right age, a young hero and, unlike so many heroes, a survivor. She sighed at the belated discovery that her mother had been match-making; that their solitary walks across the moors had probably been taken with her parents' knowledge and connivance. She looked at the photograph again. There was bitterness, even sadism in the drooping lips, as she had discovered for herself, and that roving eye would not have rested on her alone for very long. No, she realized, the man of her life lay upstairs.

For a time she had thought her brother would be the man of her life and had sworn naïvely to dedicate herself to his care. When he began to venture downstairs, he had leant on her shoulder for support, cursing as he manipulated the crutches and swung his ungainly artificial leg. She had learned to drive, so as to take him out in their parents' car, to visit the friends of their childhood. She needed their support. They had been welcomed at first but Jamie was so bitter, and swore so vilely, that soon most people's tolerance vanished. They would have cosseted a returning hero, maimed for his country; but this sour-faced young cripple reproached them all, a living reminder that most of them preferred to push away. Those whose sons or brothers had been killed thought him lucky to be alive. Jamie would have preferred to be dead.

Gradually, he had spent more and more time brooding at Raeburn, resenting his solitude and inactivity, angry that his best friend stayed away, and still haunted by exploding nightmares. He took to sitting up late with his father over bottles of port and brandy. He became a drunkard; his formerly handsome face blurred and coarsened. His coming-of-age was a humiliation.

Henrietta, meanwhile, entering her twenties, became increasingly conscious of how few young men crossed her path. She wanted to marry; she was, after all, the only one left who was likely to continue the ancestral line. Jamie raged about the young girls he met, calling them brazen hussies or else witless infants. He never seemed to consider that she might want a husband; he took it for granted that she would nurse him for the rest of his life. No wonder he had hated and despised Lionel.

When she returned from Egypt, no longer the Hon. Henrietta Campbell-Leith but Mrs Birmingham, it was to the news that Jamie had shot himself. Late one night, after drinking heavily as usual, he had gone to the gun-room, leaned his crutches against the wall, carefully selected the .455 Webley revolver, his old army pistol, and put it to his forehead. No, they said, he had left no message.

At first she had thought she would be crushed by guilt. 'I shouldn't have left him!' she had wept.

But her Scottish nanny had been brisk. 'Nonsense, my lassie, don't let me hear ye talk like that again! You have your own life to lead, just as he had his. Ye've a husband to think of. Now, will you act like a wife and no' like a bairn!'

Her mother had been straight-backed, monumental. 'I grieved for James long, long ago,' she said. 'The war killed him, just as certainly as it did Alistair and Hugo. Control yourself, Henrietta. We must carry on.'

She had been left with Lionel. He is, she thought again, he is indeed the man of my life. For nearly a quarter of a century we shared the same bed. We marry for better reasons than we know, and without him I would have been less of a person. I have never given him credit for enabling me to be myself. And what did I enable him to be? He is the man of my life, and now he is dying.

She slid *Debrett* back into its place beside *Who's Who* and re-assembled the photograph frame before replacing it on the piano. Then she climbed the stairs, calling as she did so, 'Darling? My darling, I'm back!'

Once again she entered to find him apparently asleep. She sat on the chair beside the bed and gazed at his shrivelled, putty-coloured face. His eyelids were wrinkled like string, the eyebrows sprouting with incongruous vigour. His sparse hair was white. Around his nose and mouth were deeply engraved lines, caused, she was sure, by the sixty cigarettes a day he had smoked ever since she had known him. The deep suction as he pulled the smoke down into his lungs was now etched permanently on his face. The flesh had sunk around his temples, eyes and cheeks so that his prominent nose jutted out, making him look harsh and beaky.

He had never been a handsome man. She had never found him physically attractive, although shyly and in secret she had imagined the joys of the marriage bed. Had he been skilled, had he been patient and conspiratorial, coaxing her towards their joint and private pleasure, it might have been different. But he had not; and so they had never properly known each other.

It was not only that. He had never been an active man. She loved walking, but it had always been a struggle to persuade him to come with her. Yet this body had fathered her son, these gnarled hands had held hers, had kneaded and needed her. How many years ago had that been? As young James grew from babyhood into boyhood and then adolescence, she had recoiled from the thought of her son − lying awake with a book, perhaps − overhearing his father's panting struggle. All sexual congress between them had ceased ten years ago, perhaps more. For her, it had been a relief. Had it been a deprivation for Lionel? She never knew. She had never asked. Have I failed him, she thought; did I deny his manhood? For if he is the man of my life then I am the woman of his. She recalled a Victorian saying that her mother had quoted, enigmatically, the night before her wedding. 'Never forget that your husband is also a man.' She had forgotten, and now he was a man no longer.

She closed her eyes and shivered with remorse. Her parents' prurience, or Roly's impatient, callous initiation, or − why blame other people? − the distaste she had come to feel for her husband's hot, sour-smelling body had precluded any pleasure in their marriage bed. Well, soon she would sleep alone for the rest of her life.

His breathing rose and fell with agonizingly long gaps between one wheezing intake and the next. She took his wrist: it was cold and the pulse was faint, fluttering irregularly, pausing between beats.

I have been a passionless wife, and now it is too late. He would be embarrassed if I tried to explain − and, besides, after a lifetime of sexual modesty how would I bring myself to frame the words?

Lionel's hand jerked convulsively, he drew a couple of quick breaths and opened his eyes.

'Don't worry, old girl,' he said. 'It said in James's letter, her brother's at Harrow.'

He smiled, and his eyes closed again. She took both his hands between her cupped fingers and sat holding his life within her grasp.

Twelve

Friday was the last day of exams. It was followed by ten carefree carnival days before the school broke up. Teachers turned a blind eye; lessons were cursory; matrons pretended not to know about the midnight feasts that were being organized. End-of-term parcels arrived containing tinned cream to pour over tinned peaches and fruit cocktail; chunky squares of concentrated jelly in acid colours; packets of shortbread and chocolate biscuits; home-made cakes. These were hidden in bedside lockers, together with sardines, spam and packets of crisps. Someone's alarm clock would go off at midnight and sleepy girls forced themselves awake, spread out their hoard on each other's beds, shushed and giggled, and gorged straight from the tins. They drank Ribena and orange juice out of tooth mugs, and – if someone's mother had been a really good sport – cider from a bottle passed round between the beds.

'Mm, yummy!' everyone said, and, 'Greedy guzzler!' They fell asleep with tight, gurgling bellies, the sweet taste of jelly turning sour in their mouths.

In the evenings, down in the junior common-room, records in square brown paper sleeves were scattered across the floor and the wind-up gramophones blared noisily. 'How much is that doggie in the window?' and 'It's cherry pink and apple blossom white/ When your true lover comes your way...' The juniors sang irreverent songs celebrating their coming freedom. 'No more Latin, no more French/ No more sitting on the hard school bench!' The tables were turned, and now it was the staff who had to submit to the discipline of marking exam papers and doing school reports, working out class positions and percentage marks, while the girls lolled outdoors, exposing their already sun-tanned limbs to yet more sun, shading their faces under battered straw hats, comparing sock-marks and watch-marks, beaded with the lustre of heat and indolence.

The temperature had risen buoyantly all through the term. The thermometer outside the changing-rooms shimmered in the heat. In the final days of term it finally reached ninety-five degrees, and stayed there as though becalmed, vibrating like a mirage.

Heat blanketed the school. During exams the girls had had to sit still, in forced silence, concentrating. Now, as marked papers were handed round, they fidgeted, uncrossing their legs stickily to wipe off sweat that had trickled between their thighs and made rivulets along their brown legs. Some of the girls smelt of perspiration, especially the seniors, and many revealed wet crescents when they lifted their arms. Everyone's cotton frocks were creased and clammy, sticking between their shoulder-blades and at the backs of their legs. The school was torpid. Everyone breathed slowly, heavily, fanning themselves with hats or exercise books. The temperature was unrelenting, inescapable. Only the swimming-pool, and cold showers afterwards, gave relief from the humid, clinging heat.

In the slanting light of evening, when the sun seemed suspended, never to set, they played Kick the Can. By now, twelve weeks after term had started, all the obvious hiding-places were known. The game was more difficult and the players more skilful. Their brown, outflung arms, rocking skirts and twinkling white feet darted like fireflies over the dry grass as the catcher counted down the numbers in metronomic rhythm.

At night everyone slept under a single crumpled sheet. Waking up sometimes, restless, in the small hours, only then was it possible to recall how it felt to be cool. Next morning the skies would be clear and blue and cloudless again.

The fear of polio had receded. Familiarity made people indifferent to those who still lay, pale and bored, in St Patrick's Hospital. The Head and her Deputy continued to visit on alternate days; and the gardener's wife had been summoned, comforted, and assured that she and her husband would be looked after for the rest of their lives in the cottage. Mrs

Birmingham fell unconsciously into the practised tones her mother had used in speaking to the servants. 'You'll be able to sit him in his chair out on the lawn, Mrs Waterman, and he can watch all the hustle and bustle of school life. He will still be an important member of the Raeburn family. And I'm sure we can find some work for you in the kitchen, so put your mind at rest.'

This arrangement led to an awkward meeting with Miss Parry and Miss Monk. They sat tensely, not side-by-side, waiting to hear why they had been summoned. Was there some new development involving Hermione? She had been sent home early, that much they knew, but not whether she had added anything to Sylvia's clipped account of the evening on the heath.

'I have asked you both to see me so that I may explain the new arrangements for next term,' the Head began. 'As you know already, our head-gardener, poor Mr Waterman, has been severely affected by polio. The doctor says he will almost certainly be in a wheel-chair for the rest of his life. Naturally, it is my responsibility to take care of him and his wife. I have therefore offered them a lifetime tenancy of the cottage. This means that next term you will be found accommodation along with Miss Valentine and Miss Pope in the flat above the garage. I expect you know it. There are four single bedrooms and a shared bathroom and small sitting-room. It is, I'm afraid, a little more cramped and less private than you have become accustomed to, but no doubt you will welcome the additional company.'

She paused, daring Sylvia to speak. Sylvia stared impassively back.

'You may, of course, if you prefer, look for accommodation in the village. I believe some local people let rooms. Perhaps you will let me know before term ends what you decide. As for Hermione, she has been very shaken by what happened, as is only natural. Yesterday she was collected by her parents, who will let me know their decision regarding her future here.'

Sylvia was containing her rage, though the purplish islands of colour on her neck betrayed it. Diana drew a deep breath and spoke in a tense, high voice. 'I would like your assurance, Headmistress, that this change of accommodation is not in any way a punishment. I think you may not appreciate how lucky it was that we happened to be there. Hermione had already been assaulted, and would undoubtedly have been violated if we had not intervened.'

'Yes, Miss Monk, I am indeed aware of that. I do not quite follow your reasoning. Why should you regard being moved as any sort of *punishment*?'

A dangerous silence fell. The three women looked at one another, wary and poised in the charged atmosphere. Sylvia thought, good God, she's going to make the supreme sacrifice. She's going to own up like a loyal little friend protecting her accomplice. I can't let that happen.

'Of course we are not being punished,' she said icily. 'We are, however, being inconvenienced. I personally shall be considering whether to offer my resignation. And now, if you will excuse me, I still have a number of reports to write.'

How painful, O Lord, are the workings of the human heart, thought Henrietta, slumping briefly in her great wing-chair as she gazed at the door that closed abruptly behind them. *Shed Thy light upon these two misguided women, that they may see the infinite blessings Thou dost offer to all who follow Thee.*

The rooks croaked harshly in the woods and from below her window came the sound of giggling. 'Education! Education!' someone sang, and other voices took it up: 'You are nothing but vexation!/Stupid pupil, harassed teacher/Each is an unhappy creature...'

Out of the mouths of babes and sucklings, thought Henrietta Birmingham. She worried briefly about whether she would have to give William Truett a reference. 'Capable gardener – not to be trusted with young girls.' She could hardly say that. Perhaps (she smiled wryly to herself) it was the fate of young girls to meet untrustworthy men.

Sylvia and Diana walked to the cottage in silence. Diana was afraid – of Sylvia, of losing her, of her own cowardice, of the uncertain future. She could not resign from yet another school.

She didn't want to leave Raeburn. She had been happy, and not just because of her love for Sylvia. Her mother and uncles depended on her. She dare not risk the loyal grand gesture. But Sylvia would regard it as a betrayal if she stayed.

Sylvia fiddled impatiently with the key and flung the door open. A hot, stale, womanly smell cluttered the still rooms. Armchairs sagged; exam papers were scattered untidily over the table. The rooms were bare of any ornament, except for Sylvia's overflowing ashtrays. The lino-covered floors needed sweeping. How drab it is, thought Diana, yet surely I have been happy here?

'Shall I make some coffee?' she asked.

'Don't be so bloody ingratiating!' sneered Sylvia. 'Coffee! What the hell use is coffee at a time like this? I need a *drink*.'

'I don't think we've got anything,' Diana said.

'There's a bottle in my locker. Next to the bed. I suggest you go and fetch it.'

Two hours later the gin bottle was almost empty. Sylvia sprawled across a chair, one arm hanging down; ash had fallen from her drooping cigarette on to the floor. Diana, exhausted by tension and alcohol, watched her through half-closed eyes. The sun was setting and the room had got darker, but neither stood up to put the light on.

Finally Sylvia said, ''S all right, Monkey. I understand. I understand. Your family. Your *people*,' she added, mockingly.

'They do depend on me . . .'

'I damage everything I touch,' Sylvia began. 'Don't deny it, Monks, I'm being serious. And honest, for a change. No, I won't go and see a trick-cyclist to please Old Ma B, to make me safe. What could anyone do for me? I'm rotten, Monkey, rotten. I am. A bad apple. I'll go away. Time to start again somewhere else. All I can do is keep moving on. Another school, another Hermione, maybe even another Monkey. Holidays, back home to Mother. Nowhere else to go. She's senile nowadays, or she pretends to be, so as not to have to talk to me. Deaf as well. She hobbles along to chapel on Sundays, with me the dutiful daughter supporting her, and we pray to God the Father. Heavenly Father. Eternal Father, strong to save.'

She laughed. '"Ephemeral father, weak to destroy, if only I had been a boy!" Good, eh? Come on, Monkey, you've got to laugh.'

Diana, sitting rigidly in her chair, eyes fixed on Sylvia, suddenly pitched forward, hands clasped over her head, and buried her face in her lap. She rocked to and fro, choking spasmodically as though about to be sick. Sylvia made no move. She was used to pain.

Starlings rose and fell like a ship with the breathing of sleeping children. In the light midsummer sky the moon hung white, marbled with grey, above the slate-blue trees. Constance had set her alarm clock for five-thirty and put it under her pillow, but she could not sleep. What if it didn't go off, or if she woke one of the others? She could see the face of the man in the moon. Was it night in Africa too? She tried to work out the time difference. It was about three hours later there. Say, four o'clock in the morning. Her parents and Stella would be asleep, probably. The dawn would be breaking. It would be evening by the time Auntie Marjie rang them. They'd have to take her away.

I'm not happy here, she thought. I never could be. I haven't got any friends. The swimming is fun, OK, I like that. But there won't be any swimming next term. Hockey. I can't play hockey. It'd be easier without Charmie, and she's not coming back. Sheila might, I suppose. I *do* want to leave. Her eyes drooped, and she struggled to keep them open. She got up and walked to the window.

The horizontal branches of the cedar made a strong, jagged shape against the sky. The lawn fell away beneath the window towards the rhododendrons. The school cruised over the rolling landscape. It felt familiar and solid and safe. I *do* want to leave! said Constance to herself. She went over to her bed and took the clock from beneath her pillow. It was hard to read the time, so she put on her glasses and held it up towards the window. One-thirty. Should I turn it off, in case it wakes people? She deliberated, her finger poised above the serrated round knob on top. No. Let it ring. She climbed back into bed and slept.

In the pearly morning light the clock rang, waking Constance and no one else. She gathered up her vest and knickers, socks and sandals, and, clutching them inside her dressing-gown, tiptoed to the bathroom. School uniform had been a problem – all the local people knew the Raeburn uniform, and she would have been stopped at the station – so she had decided to wear her flowered cotton dressing-gown. With the belt round her waist it could pass for a summer frock.

She washed her hands and face, cleaned her teeth, stuffed her nightie inside the sponge-bag and hung it back on its hook. Then, with fast-beating heart, she tiptoed down the back stairs. The school was silent. As Constance walked through the Covered Way for the last time, past the notice-board with the deportment ladder, meals rota and parcels list, she heard a door shutting somewhere behind her. The Scandies must be getting up.

The great double door at the end of the Covered Way was locked. Constance rattled it, but it wouldn't open. Ignoring her momentary surge of relief, she thought again, I want to run away! The changing-room door was locked too, and the windows were shut. She went into the lavatories, and found the window of the end one open. Heaving herself up from the lavatory seat on to the windowsill, she climbed awkwardly through, jumped down and stood outside in the warm morning air.

I've got to say goodbye to Flopsy, she thought. That's not procrastinating. ('*Pro*', for; '*cras*', tomorrow; '*tenere*', to hold: holding off until tomorrow, Miss Monk had explained in Latin, and Constance remembered her delight as she suddenly realized how language was made and why Latin mattered). She put the memory aside and stepped into the dark, rich-smelling shed. The sleeping animals quivered and sat up, ears pricked. Constance walked over to Flopsy's cage in the corner. She slid her hand inside it to where he cowered against the back, and stroked his fur, running her fingertips gently along his flattened ears.

'Bye-bye, Flopsy,' she said. 'Be a good bunny. I do love you.'

As she turned away she worried about who would give him his oats and water. She should have left a note for Rachel or someone. Too late now. On an impulse she turned back, took him out of his cage and set him down gently on the grass under the apple trees.

'There you go, Flopsy,' she told him. 'Eat up. You're free.'

She climbed through the rough grass behind the shed towards a gap in the high hedge that led down on to the road. Birds were singing in the treetops and the clear, still morning heralded another flawless day.

Walking along the road that she had travelled so often in the school coach, going to and from church in best straw hats and Sunday dresses – the sprigged Liberty print ones worn for Speech Day and church only – she looked at the flowers in the hedgerows, remembering a biology lesson with Miss Parry. She had led them along this same road and made them write down the names in their exercise books, under the heading Common English Wild Flowers. People had straggled and gossiped, dawdling behind and not paying attention. But Constance, a town girl, had been fascinated, and had written down all the names. Now she recognized them, and took pleasure in being able to identify them. Miss Parry was right. It *did* make a difference if you knew what they were called.

There were tiny wild pansies, purple and violet, and golden birdsfoot trefoil and sky-blue periwinkles and veined harebells; foxgloves, and crimson poppies that crumpled and faded the moment you picked them. Fragile things like dandelions, for telling the time, old man's beard; and, poking through the exuberant greenery, the spidery heads of cow parsley. There were stinging nettles just the height of your legs, and plantains or dock to soothe the itching. Much more dangerous, Miss Parry had warned them ('Are you concentrating, there at the back? This is important so *listen*!') were the poisonous, shiny berries of deadly nightshade. Most dramatic of all were thrusting spikes crowned with brilliant red and yellow berries that were called wild arum, and which country people nicknamed lords and ladies. It had been fun, that lesson, observing something she'd never looked at properly before.

I could pick some flowers for Auntie Marjie, she thought, and suddenly it seemed a brilliant idea. She bent down to snap off a thick, engorged stem of wild arum, and then, across the other side of the road, just before it curved round a corner, she caught sight of another. Smiling to herself at the thought of her aunt exclaiming with pleasure as she arranged Constance's beautiful bunch of flowers in the vase that stood on her drawing-room windowsill, she headed diagonally into the road. She didn't even hear the car as it turned the corner sharply, braked, swerved, and just failed to avoid her. She heard its tyres slither as they slewed across the road. She felt gravel pressing sharply against the skin of her cheek and her crumpled right arm, and grinding into the leg which was hooked underneath her. Faintly, as though in a trance – not an unpleasant trance – she heard a woman begin to scream. The screams rose like the cries of a bird into the blue, blue sky over her head, and Constance felt vaguely that she ought to get up and see what was wrong, yet somehow she was quite disinclined to move.

'Well you *are* in a pickle,' said Mrs Birmingham.

Constance opened her eyes. Her head felt heavy and her face hurt.

'It's nearly dark,' she said.

'Yes. It's after ten o'clock. I was on my way up the drive, but I thought I'd pop in once more to see if you were awake.'

'Have I been asleep all day?'

'They brought you in – oh, it must have been before eight o'clock this morning. Sister gave you a mild sleeping draught and put you to bed up here, so you wouldn't be disturbed. The doctor came: you remember that, don't you? How do you feel? Can you move your legs?'

The day swam hazily back into focus, assembling itself from a welter of images, some of them dream, some harshly real. Constance recalled lying on the stony surface of the lane, hearing Miss Peachey's voice in the distance, and someone screaming. She'd been touched and prodded, and then Miss Peachey and some stranger had picked her up and laid her across the back seat of a car. And then what? The doctor had been. She had a vague memory of him feeling her limbs and rearranging her more comfortably in bed. He'd taken away her pillows. She'd been given something to drink. Then the dreams – climbing and diving and flying, weightless and disembodied, flying to Africa, but not in an aeroplane: she'd been flying in the sky, arms outstretched, soaring . . .

'Mrs Birmingham – oh, please, have you told Mummy and Daddy?'

'I put in a trunk call to your parents this morning, yes. Naturally they were very upset. Never mind all that now – we'll discuss it tomorrow. Tell me dear, how are you feeling?'

'My head's all sort of stiff. And my arm aches like billy-o.'

Constance lifted her arm from under the sheet and looked at it aghast. It was covered with deep scratches, which had been painted with yellow stuff.

'Oh!' she said. 'Oh, no! I remember . . . I got knocked down, didn't I? When I was trying to . . . Oh, gosh. Oh, I am sorry, honestly I am. Oh, goodness.'

'You've had a lucky escape. The important thing is that you're safe now, and no bones broken, the doctor says. Wiggle your toes for me. There, you see? *Very* lucky.'

'What did they say when you spoke to them?'

'Your parents both send you their love. Now, Constance, I don't want you to talk any longer. You must get a good night's rest, and I'll come and see you again in the morning. Sister's going to bring you a little snack – you haven't eaten all day – and before you go to sleep I want you to say a prayer to thank God for having watched over you and kept you safe.'

Mrs Birmingham took Constance's arm and laid it under the sheet, then brushed the hair back from her hot forehead, bent down and kissed her. Constance shut her eyes. No one had given her a kiss since she said good-bye to her mother at the end of Parents' Weekend. She felt tearful and shaky.

'Sister will bring you something to make you sleep. Night-night, dear. God bless.'

Moments later, Sister Girdlestone entered, her face grim with disapproval. She placed a tray of bread and butter and a glass of milk on the bedside table. In a tiny white box with pleated edges lay two pills.

'Now do I have to watch you or can you be trusted to take those?'

Constance sat up gingerly, took the glass and the pills and swallowed them in one gulp.

'You are a very wicked girl, Constance King, and I hope you're thoroughly ashamed of yourself. If Miss Peachey hadn't been passing on her way in, what on earth might have happened? You in your dressing-gown – unconscious – nobody would have known *who* you were! And what about the poor woman who ran you over? Have you stopped to think about how she must feel?'

Constance stared into Sister Girdlestone's pinched face and said nothing.

'No shame. No remorse. I wash my hands of you.'

Constance went on staring, until Sister dropped her eyes and walked out of the room.

An hour later Constance was drowsy but still awake. She swung her legs stiffly out of bed and hobbled next door to spend an urgent penny. Back in the sick-room, she walked across to the window and drew aside the flimsy curtain, but she couldn't see the moon. The sick-room was on the wrong side of the house, two floors above the Covered Way. She looked along the drive, and could see lights on in the cottage where Batey Parry lived. It's all her fault, she thought fiercely; if it hadn't been for her saying those foul, unfair things to me, I might not have gone. She decided me. Nobody calls me a slut, and a dirty little girl. 'Sticks and stones may break my bones but words will never hurt me.' Well that's wrong, anyway. The stones didn't break my bones. Her legs, swathed in bandages, were beginning to tremble and her head was swimming. I must go to sleep, thought Constance; those pills are working.

Next morning Miss Girdlestone brought her breakfast in silence. Constance looked at the tray of congealing porridge and cold toast and left it untouched.

'Can I have my sponge-bag?' she asked.

'It's in the bathroom, next door. Wash your hands and face and give your teeth a good clean. Doctor'll be back to see you this morning so make yourself presentable.'

The doctor had unwound her bandages and applied clean dressings – 'I know you're a brave girl, ducky, but I'd rather you didn't have a squint just yet. Better to lie back and keep your eyes shut. All right? Jolly good show.' Then she had heard the school coaches rev up and take everyone to church. Later she heard them come back, and the laughter and chatter of the girls as they scrambled out. She wanted to lean out of the sick-room window and wave but she didn't dare.

The door opened and the Head came in. She was wearing a long flowered two-piece and white peep-toe shoes, and she looked as stately and imposing as old Queen Mary. Constance felt nervous. The Head sat on a chair beside the bed and folded her hands in her lap.

'Feeling better this morning?' she asked.

'Yes, thank you.'

'Good. I remembered you in my prayers in church.'

Constance didn't know how to respond to that, so she muttered 'Thank you.'

'My dear, now that you have had a good night's sleep, and a bit of time to think about what happened yesterday, I wonder if you can explain to me what you were doing in the lane, in your dressing-gown, at that hour of the morning? It is, to say the least of it, an unusual time to go and pick flowers...' She smiled, to show that it was meant as a joke.

For the first time, Constance realized that the Head didn't know that she had been trying to run away. Suddenly she didn't want to tell her. It had been a crazy plan, it couldn't possibly have succeeded. Yet what other excuse had she to offer? She looked down and fiddled with the sheet. She was no good at telling lies, and anyway she couldn't make one up on the spur of the moment.

'I was going to run away. I planned to get a train to London and then go to my aunt's. She lives at King's Lynn. I was on my way to the station to catch a train.'

She stopped and looked at Mrs Birmingham.

'*Why* were you going to run away – especially now, when it's practically the end of term?'

'I kept writing to Mummy and Daddy and saying I wasn't happy but they never took any notice, so I thought if I ran away that would convince them.'

'But Constance, why didn't you talk to someone about it? A friend ... you've got friends. Your form mistress. You could have come and talked to me.'

'I know. Actually I did try, once. But you were busy,' said Constance.

'Why were you so unhappy?'

'I don't know.' It was true. She couldn't remember. Her present pain and misery and confusion were much worse than anything she had suffered during the term.

'Well, I am afraid you have succeeded in your intention, although not quite in the way you had planned. I told you that I had spoken to your parents yesterday. First I talked to your mother, and after that your father rang me from his office. They are both understandably very shocked and very angry. Not only with you. *I* have failed in my duty to care for you, failed in my responsibility for your well-being. They have informed me that you will not be returning to Raeburn.'

'What?' cried Constance.

'You will leave at the end of term. You will travel to Kenya and your parents will decide what is to become of you. Your father informs me that his decision is final.'

'Oh, no! No, I don't *want* to leave! I want to stay! Please let me stay. Talk to him for me, please – persuade him.'

The Head smiled at her unexpectedly, and laid a hand over hers. 'Constance, Constance. First you want to leave, and now you want to stay. What are we to make of you? You'll be home in a few days' time. Talk to your parents. They know what's best.'

'They never *listen* to me! Sorry to be rude, but they don't.'

'Well, I'm listening to you now. And what I hear is a very muddled little girl. Now, although it was wrong of you to try and run away, you didn't deserve what happened. Are you feeling any better today?'

'It still hurts a fair bit.'

'Yes, well, I expect it will do for a few days. But it might have been a great deal worse.'

'Can I ask you one more thing?'

'What is it?'

'Is Flopsy all right? My rabbit – I let him go because nobody'd been feeding them.'

'I'll find out for you. And now, Constance, since you weren't able to go to church this morning, and you need the love of God particularly at this time, I want you to close your eyes and fold your hands and say a prayer with me. *Dear God, the Father of us all . . .*'

When Mrs Birmingham had gone, Constance lay back in bed with a great sigh. She thought about Raeburn, and the hundreds of details that had arranged themselves into the pattern of her daily life. The clang of the rising bell in the mornings. The squeak and drumming of sandalled feet hurrying downstairs to line up in the Covered Way for the breakfast gong. Bed-making, with her nightie neatly folded under the pillow and the counterpane smoothed over. Lining up again for Break, wondering if there'd be a letter. Sitting in the Reading Corner, looking through *Punch* or *The Pony Club Magazine* or *The Field* – those remote worlds lived in by other people, so different from her own.

She thought of Rest, when everyone lay on their beds after lunch 'to digest' and after that, the hurry and excitement as you changed into games things and took your tennis racquet, heavy inside its wooden press, up to the courts for a practice, or the drowsy peace of playing cricket and being a fielder. She thought how funny it always looked, as girls in bathing-suits zig-zagged delicately over the gravel on their way up to the swimming-pool. Diving – the proud bliss of that swallow dive, as her body did exactly what it was meant to do, quite independently of her mind. The sun beating down on the games field during house-matches, when you cheered and made daisy-chains: sticking a fingernail into one stalk and pushing the next one through, like threading a needle, until finally you had a wilting string of pink and white daisies to drape round your neck. Shouting encouragement to the school team: 'Two, four, six, eight, who do we appreciate? RAEBURN!'

And then the evenings – the beautiful, light-hearted evenings, grubbing in the earth round Charmie's roses while, just within earshot, people shrieked with excitement playing Kick the Can. The soft fur of Flopsy and his tremulous affection as she cuddled him and stroked his twitching nose. Cosy evenings sitting hunched up on the floor of the library reading while next door the common-room was noisy with gramophones and shouts of laughter or protest. Bath-night, twice a week: four baths in one bathroom, each with a shining, soapy figure giggling and splashing water over those who passed by. And finally bedtime, and the way they'd all listened as she told them the story of Sohrab and Rustum. She'd changed the ending, but no one had noticed. And at the end of every day, the wood-pigeons cooing, always cooing in the high trees beyond the dormitory.

It had all been strung together in a familiar routine, and one she had learned to take pleasure in. You'll find your niche, Daddy had told her, and it was true after all. Charmie wouldn't be there next term to bully her, but Sheila might – and who would be friends with poor Sheila except her? I don't want to leave, thought Constance in despair; *I don't want to leave!*

Thirteen

A week later, the Head sat alone in her silent study. The school had broken up. Trunks had been hauled down from the dormitories and piled by the front and back entrances. Carter Paterson's vans had collected them and driven off. Excited girls, in a cacophony of tears and laughter and cries of 'Hope you have good hols! Will you write? Promise you won't forget?' had been taken away by their parents, or driven in the school coach to the local station and put on the train up to London.

There had been a final staff meeting. Miss Parry had regretted to announce that she would not be back next term; she had found an excellent post at a school in Wales, where she would be nearer her ailing mother. Mrs Birmingham, knowing that she was lying, had said nothing.

Reports had been completed and sent out. 'Constance has the potential to be a real asset to the school,' Mrs Birmingham had written. 'She has an excellent, inquiring mind and a remarkable feel for poetry. We should be very sorry not to see her again.' She hoped her plea would be heard, but suspected that it would not. Mr King's outrage had made itself plain down several thousand miles of telephone line.

Hermione was another whom she would probably not see again. Her parents had been tight-lipped when they came to collect her, though the upper-class conventions of bland courtesy had held while Hermione was in their midst. Then, just as they were leaving, Mr Malling-Smith, a heavy, choleric figure, had turned back.

'Perhaps I might have a final word?' he had asked. She had taken him into the study and closed the door.

'What am I to say to her future husband?' he had expostu-
lated. 'That my daughter is *damaged goods?*'

'Hermione,' she had answered him evenly, 'is not, as you
put it, "damaged goods". She was the unfortunate victim of
an attack, from which she was rescued in good time. She is still
virgo intacta, Mr Malling-Smith.'

When will fathers stop thinking they own their daughters?
she thought wearily. When will men stop demanding virginity –
and taking it, wherever they find it?

Some of the teachers had lingered for a day or two, finishing
reports or sorting out next year's timetables and ordering text
books, but now only Miss Parry remained. In an awkward,
belated gesture of sympathy and (she admitted to herself)
curiosity, Henrietta had invited her to dine at the Lodge that
evening, but Sylvia had replied brusquely,

'I am driving to Wales this afternoon. It will not be possible.'

The kitchen staff had gone, the Scandies home to Sweden,
the cook back to her house in the village. Yesterday, after
finishing the accounts and writing out individual bills to be
enclosed with each girl's school report, Peggy too had left for
the holidays. Every year she and a woman friend spent a month
in Italy visiting the voluptuous masterpieces of another time,
another world. The two tall, dry spinsters would go from
museum to church to gallery, guidebooks in hand, noting the
details of painterly technique and quoting Berenson to one
another, while before their eyes sumptuous amber flesh spilled
across the canvases and marble statues intertwined, striving,
striving for union.

The great house lay still, bathed in the morning glow of a
brilliant July. The roller stood abandoned under the cedar tree.
I have to engage a gardener, thought Mrs Birmingham, and
someone to help him. I have to advertise for another biology
teacher. I have two sets of prospective parents coming this
afternoon and, please God, let them decide to send their daughters here. After what happened to Hermione and Constance
King, and with the polio epidemic as well, it isn't going to be
easy. Word gets around.

Finally, she allowed herself to think about Lionel, shrinking daily towards his death under the impassive eyes of the nurse. *Almighty God*, she prayed, *I have sinned. I have failed my husband and failed the girls who were placed in my charge. I am not worthy of Thy love. Yet I pray Thee, of Thy all-forgiving goodness, let my husband live until his son comes home. Do not let me be alone when he dies, I beseech Thee. Amen.*

On her desk a bowl of roses flared crimson, orange and yellow, as lush as a funeral bouquet. I am afraid, she thought; I am afraid of death and loneliness and failure. I have to be strong, but I feel helpless.

The great iron ring on the front door rattled, and she heard the rustle of post falling into the wire basket inside. Henrietta Birmingham stood up, leaning one hand on the desk to help her get to her feet, and fetched the morning's mail. She picked out the jagged red and blue edging of an aerogram and, reaching for her father's crested silver paperknife, she slit open her son Jamie's letter first. Her heartbeat quickened and she muttered under her breath, *please God, please God*, not knowing what it was she asked for.

Darling Mater,
    Your news came as a great shock. I had no idea that Father was so gravely ill. I have managed to arrange for my leave to start a week early, and Juniper and I will be flying by BOAC from Hong Kong into London Airport, arriving at 11.15 on the morning of Friday, August 1st.

Tomorrow! Jamie would be here tomorrow! Her eyes skimmed the paragraphs. There it was, right at the end. The words leapt off the page. 'Her surname, by the way, is Fung. Juniper Fung. It's a beautiful name, I think. Much nicer, poor her, than Juniper Birmingham.'

Late that same night, Henrietta, having dismissed the nurse, sat alone beside her husband's bed. The night-light on the bedside table cast deep, contoured shadows across the dry furrows on one side of his face, and the shadows quivered and slid each time he drew a long, subterranean breath. Two cups of untouched tea had grown a stagnant, greyish skin. The clock ticked very loudly. It was almost midnight. Exhausted by prayers so fervent that she had fallen into a trance-like state, disembodied, communing directly with her God, Henrietta dozed.

Half a mile away, in the cottage at the end of the drive, Sylvia Parry paced up and down the cramped lounge. She had drunk a bottle of sherry, finished the gin which she had found hidden behind the bread-bin in the larder, and now she was on the last of the cider. She swung the bottle up and down, waving her arms as though conducting. 'Dance for your Daddy-o,' she sang; and then, 'Cry, baby bunting/Your Daddy's gone a-hunting.' Noticing that drops of cider were flying out of the bottle and blotching the letter she had been trying to write, she put the bottle to her mouth and drained it. Then she stood still, rocking slightly on her feet.

Now what? she said to herself. Now what?

A cigarette packet lay on the table, but the matchbox was empty. How did that happen? she thought. Careless. Didn't notice. She picked up the matchbox and shook it. Definitely empty.

'Blast!' she shouted. 'Blast and fucking damnation! No fucking booze and no fucking matches either!' She went into the kitchen, and there (good old Diana) was a household box of Bryant & May placed neatly on the shelf beside the gas cooker. Time for a fag. Here's another nail in your coffin. She lit up, inhaled deeply, and walked purposefully back to the lounge.

'Dear old Monkey,' the letter began. She took a red biro and wrote with firm strokes on a fresh sheet of paper: 'Dear Diana, I am writing to wish you well in the future and thank you for your patience and understanding...'

'N O!' she shouted, smashing the cigarette into the wet ring in a saucer.

'No, damnation, no, no, no, *no*!'

She stood up, trembling, and her head and shoulders slumped. 'No...' she whimpered. 'Oh, no, please, no, not again...' She rolled her head from side to side, hearing the tense bones in her neck crack.

What's the matter? she asked herself soothingly. Go on, you can tell me. Tell me your secrets, Sylvie duck. Safe with me. The wheedling voice inside her head fluted its goblin questions. Is it Hermione, then? Pretty, *pretty* Hermione? But you can't have her, my lovey, can you now?

'Shut up!' she shouted aloud. 'Shut bloody *up!*'

Her legs buckled, and she collapsed awkwardly into one of the sagging armchairs. SAFETY MATCHES, said the box on the table next to her. With an effort, for it slipped off the first time, she balanced her foot across one knee and tried to strike a match against the sole of her shoe. There was a rasping sound, but no spark. She tried again, pressing harder. Still nothing. She threw the matches across the room, then lumbered to her feet and retrieved them. She lit another cigarette and leaned against the mantelpiece, flicking ash into the curving reflector of the dusty, one-bar electric fire.

Filled with inchoate energy and no way to discharge it, she leant forward and slammed her forehead against the wall several times, harder and harder, until it hurt so much that she was forced to stop. She kicked the edge of the lino where it curled against the tiles of the fireplace, then bent down and began to pull off threads of matting where it had frayed along the edge. Stroking her throbbing forehead, she talked to herself, mumbling harshly. 'Alone again; on my tod, now and for ever, for ever and ever, Amen. Should have gone to supper with Old Ma B. Never seen inside the Lodge. Crumbling to dust, I expect. Like that husband of hers. Who needs husbands? Who needs fucking *anyone*? I need fucking, that's for sure.'

Need to spend a penny. The bladder is a muscular sac which, at its fullest capacity, holds over a pint of liquid. Bottle of sherry, three-quarters; plus maybe a quarter bottle of gin, makes one pint, plus another half pint of cider. Time to piss, Sylvia. Got to go upstairs to the bog.

She had to hold on to the rickety banister as she lumbered up the stairs. Sitting on the warm wooden seat of the lavatory, she released a hissing stream of urine. The bathroom was garishly lit by one unshaded bulb. On the shelf above the basin was another box of matches, in case the pilot light on the Ascot went out. She stared at them, then lowered her head to look at her feet planted on the checked linoleum floor. There were pools of rust around the claw feet of the bath. She looked back at the matches. 'Bloody awful life,' she said, speaking clearly and emphatically. It was quite dark outside. The owl hooted, and in the distance a dog barked. 'Bloody. Awful. Life.' She began to chant it, running the words together: 'Bloodyawfulife, I've gottabloodyawfulife, hate my bloodyawfulife.'

Sylvia rose to her feet. She pulled her knickers up, and smoothed the good Liberty skirt down over her hips. She walked across to the Ascot and blew out the pilot light. She turned the hot tap full on so that water gushed into the bath, and, using the handle of her toothbrush, held down the bi-metal strip. She could hear the steady, soft roar of gas below the rush of running water. She began counting out loud, slowly, distinctly, not hurrying, even though after a while the nauseating smell of gas made her feel wobbly. When she had reached fifty she said, 'Hermione. Good-bye, my love. And bye-bye Monkey.'

She struck a match. With a thunderous crack, the gas ignited. A tongue of fire shot out and the room exploded with golden light.

Twenty minutes later, woken by the frantic barking and whining of her dog, the gardener's wife drew back the curtains of her bedroom window and leaned out to shout it down. Far away, over the other side of the fields, she could see bright sparks of flame spitting and whizzing into the night. She ran downstairs to the telephone. 'Fire,' she gasped, before she had even dialled. 'Fire. Fire. Fire.'

The bedroom in the Lodge reverberated with the dry sound of two people breathing. Henrietta, fully dressed, slept at last. Her white head had fallen forward on to her chest, her shoulders were slack, her hands lay one across the other in her lap, palms upward. Beside her, Lionel's wheezing punctuated her quicker, shallower breaths.

In the drawing-room, the telephone began to ring.